EXCLUSIVE DEBUT EDITION

Thanks for being a trusted reader and purchasing this Exclusive Debut Edition.

You hold one of only 100 copies of this edition in print.

Printed with linen cover stock in Kansas City, USA, in July of 2026.

This is a pre-publication copy and is still going through final proof edits and design elements.

Final publisher editions will be released for worldwide distribution.

he LIVED
not like
them

I told my first lie
when I realized they would
never UNDERSTAND me for
who I was

The MOUNTAINS were
an old song
that he
knew well

He wasn't going to tell
a single person where he went
when he left the CITY
That was his place
and they didn't need
to know

In search
of the last
SOLITUDE

He was in PAIN because she did not
understand him
and he felt lost because
nobody ever would

This looked
like a good spot
for a GUNFIGHT
As good as any

I wonder if
the RIVER still
remembers

YOUNG
but FREE

a novel

Daniel J. Rice

Riverfeet Press
Livingston, MT/Bemidji, MN/Abingdon, VA
www.riverfeetpress.com

Young but Free: the novel
Exclusive Debut Edition
Daniel J. Rice
Fiction: High School/Mountains/Fly Fishing/Wildlife/Coming of Age

ISBN-13: 979-8992007725

This title is available at a special discount to booksellers and libraries. Send inquiries to: riverfeetpress@gmail.com

Cover design by Creative Pear Graphic Design
Author photo by John LaTourelle
Mayfly and Stonefly illustrations by Timothy Goodwin
Lion Eyes illustration by Carly Rice

Riverfeet Press is independently owned and operated.

For my brother.

"People were nature too and it was schizophrenic to try to separate them from what we ordinarily thought of as nature."

—Jim Harrison

YOUNG
but FREE

a novel

Daniel J. Rice

None of this is true.

All of this is real.

APRIL 1999

SUN	MON	TUE	WED	THU	FRI	SAT
				~~1~~	~~2~~	~~3~~
~~4~~	~~5~~	~~6~~	~~7~~	~~8~~	~~9~~	~~10~~
~~11~~	~~12~~	~~13~~	~~14~~	~~15~~	~~16~~	~~17~~
~~18~~	~~19~~	20	21	22	23	24
25	26	27	28	29	30	

Eddie rolled over to grab the half-joint, and put the resiny end into his lips. He tufted the pillow behind his head, and grabbed the lighter off the nightstand. He lit the flame and inhaled deeply with closed eyes. Fuck, he thought, it's a school day. He pulled another cloud of smoke deep, and then opened his eyes. The sun was cutting angles around the window curtain, enough to illuminate his bedroom. He blew the smoke out through his nose and watched it separate towards the ceiling.

He sat up and extinguished the joint, then slid it into the top drawer with the rest of his roaches. The canister of Lysol was tucked between his mattress and box spring, so he pulled it out and gave the air a quick shot. Then he heard the clattering of dishes in the kitchen upstairs, and knew his mom was busy preparing breakfast for his half-brother. Eddie had started to dislike that scene, watching his mom as a *mom* again, and listening to his baby brother fussing all the time. It was better to stay downstairs as long as possible, and not have to deal with the noise of her questions and the crying baby.

He also preferred to wait and not leave his bedroom until he knew his step-dad was gone. Cole had married his mom a couple years ago, and because he never had any children, he wanted to start right away. Cole wasn't such a bad guy, he worked at some desk job downtown, always left in a suit and tie, but Eddie didn't know what he did, or why the tie was necessary. He didn't really care either, he was too damn busy with his own life.

Eddie retrieved his cargo pants and a blue silk button-up shirt from the closet, and snuck into the bathroom upstairs to get ready. The floor was littered with baby toys and the garbage full of dirty diapers. He picked up the toys and piled them neatly in a corner, and then removed the garbage bag and tied it tight. After the shower he got dressed and lathered his hands with mousse which he massaged through his short hair, parted down the middle. Preparing his hair typically took longer than the shower. Not because he was a pretty boy, but because he learned that by looking clean and maintained, he could get away with more trouble. He dropped some Visine into his eyes and then took out the trash.

"How's little Carl doing this morning," he said as he entered the kitchen. Carl would turn one soon, and Eddie thought it was about time he started shedding that baby fat and stopped crying so much. Then he looked at Carl who had apple sauce all over his face and chest. He thought that Carl should also stop using his mouth only for making a mess. Then he considered his mouth would always make a mess, at least, that seemed true for most people.

"He loves this organic apple sauce," replied his mom. "It's so much healthier too, you'd be surprised how much garbage they put in regular old apple sauce these days." She looked over at Eddie who didn't appear to be paying attention. "You're running a bit late today, are you gonna make it to school on time?"

"Don't worry so much mom. First class is boring anyway."

"Is that why you're failing?"

"Who said I was failing?" Eddie rummaged through the cupboards, grabbed a granola bar, and started towards the door. The last thing he needed right now was a lecture.

"I got a call from your English teacher. What was his name?"

"Bonnell." Eddie was pulling on his shoes with a granola bar in his mouth.

"Right. He said you're not doing so good. I thought you liked books. Or at least you used to." She wiped apple sauce from Carl's chin.

"Books are okay. I've got to run mom."

"Just slow down Eddie. This is important."

"I'm going to be late."

"He wants us to go in for a conference. I scheduled one for tonight at five-thirty after Cole gets home so he can watch Carl. It's important you come with me. This is your final semester of high school, and you can't fail any classes."

"I'm supposed to work at five."

"Can't you tell them you'll be late?"

"Okay, fine," replied Eddie as he walked out the door.

Eddie drove a 1998 Land Rover Discovery that he paid cash for last summer. His mom was suspicious when he told her he earned enough money at his part time job to afford a car like this, but she was too busy with Carl to really put much more thought into it. Eddie loved this car. He gave it a custom paint job with two-tone black and green metallic paint and chrome runners. The stereo system was custom built with sixteen-inch subwoofers, sonic insulation throughout the trunk to enhance the bass, with touch screen controls. It was the envy of his friends, and he always cranked it as he drove through town.

Paused at a red light, he blasted the stereo louder. It was his favorite CD, *Scarface: My Homies*, "Can't understand my city's under siege..." was blaring out his windows. He noticed the eyes of drivers from all four corners of the intersection look his direction. He tucked his sunglasses over his eyes, and pretended not to notice everyone was watching. Light turned green and he rolled slowly through the intersection so that everyone would see him. Quarter mile down he crossed a bridge over the Lost Horse River, and he caught just enough of it from the corner of his eye to make him remember something. What he remembered wasn't too clear, but it gave him a momentary sense of peace, happiness, and belonging. Had something to do with the way the river was gleaming in the early light, but he didn't want to think about it any more than that.

He pulled into the high school parking lot and the kids standing by the front door all turned to look when they heard his stereo blasting. The building was old brick, full of old memories, old ghosts, and old dreams. The thousands upon thousands of youth who had been here before, who had lived in this city, who filled their heads with the same ideas, and each had ideas of their own. They were all known for a time and now forgotten. Their footsteps had been covered with new shoes, new paint, new dirt, and new time. Eddie didn't play any sports, or join any clubs, but he was still known. He filled a niche that earned admiration from his peers. He put the Rover in park and turned off the stereo. He kept a one-hitter in the ash tray and loaded it up. He was the only guy at school with access to such good weed. He held the smoke deep in his lungs and saw Darnell approaching.

Darnell walked with five other guys and he was in the lead. Always had a giant smile pasted upon his face. Cheek to cheek, giant white grin. This made Eddie smile as Darnell got nearer and instructed his crew to turn and walk away.

"What's up dog?" said Darnell as he slid into the passenger seat. The two slapped each other's right hands, and then held the other's index finger, turned their hands and curved up their middle fingers and thumbs. This was their secret handshake, and only a dozen others knew it. It was important for them to have secrets that distinguished them above the rest. There were strict requirements if you wanted to be part of the crew that knew this handshake. First, you had to be on good terms with the entire crew – and they weren't easy people to be on good terms with. Second, you had to have a reputation for being a bad ass – which typically meant you had no pause when it came to breaking the law. If you met the first two criteria, then the third step was to stand in a circle of six members of the crew and fight them with fists for three minutes. If you were still on your feet after three minutes, you had their trust. Three minutes of fighting was a long time. After you'd bloodied and bruised each other, you were now *boys*. The funny thing was, when somebody did something to lose this trust, it ended the same way – getting bloodied and bruised.

Eddie blew the smoke out slowly. "Shit. How about you?"

"The same. Fucking national holiday. Hand me that." Darnell pulled in a deep hit, held it a moment, and then puffed out rings of smoke. "My cousin's crew wants some of that good shit," he continued. "What are you working with?"

"Only the best. How much you want?"

"Still got that neon green sticky?"

"You know it."

"Shit. Better give me an ounce. I can move that dank fast."

"Sure you don't want more? The price gets better the more you buy."

"Just give me an ounce dog. I'm gonna smoke half of it and sell the rest."

"You got the cash?" Money was a circular thing, always changing hands, coming and going. This made Eddie's a circular economy. Just last night this money was in a cash register at the Broken Records paraphernalia shop where Darnell worked; he got paid in cash weekly because the owner liked to keep things off the books, and now it was going into the hands of a drug dealer who would likely hand it to his drug dealer who would inevitably purchase some paraphernalia from the very store it was used at last night.

"Why the fuck you ask me that?" Darnell pulled a thick wad of fives and tens from his pocket. "Two-fifty?"

"You know it's three hundred."

"I'm just messing with you dog. Always so damn serious."

Eddie reached into his backpack, removed a Ziploc bag and digital scale. He placed the scale on the center console and grabbed out a handful of puffy buds that smelled like pine trees and skunk. He could hit the weight perfectly every time without using a scale, but his customers always appreciated the confirmation. He was in the industry of customer service, and so always used a scale to keep his clients happy. "Know anyone who wants more? I'm trying to move some weight." He handed the ounce to Darnell.

"Might. My cousin slangs a bit. He's a gangster mother fucker, so you shouldn't go alone."

"Bet I've seen worse."

"Whatever you say dog."

"Tell him you got a connection for the good stuff. It costs a little more, but it will make him higher profit."

"Shit. May as well go see that fool. When you want to do this?"

"Right now."

"Cool. Fuck class today."

"Twist one up," said Eddie as he cranked up the volume and pulled out of the parking lot. The traffic moved slow in the city morning. They kept the windows up to keep the smoke inside. Outside the cityscape was high and buildings reached towards the clouds. These buildings were all young once as the people who built them. They were all old now and those people were gone. Eddie's sociology teacher told them this city was changing for the worse, that the denizens no longer cared about the future, but he didn't think too much about that. This was his home and he was known.

They turned down a street that took them away from the highrises. The bus stop benches were layered with graffiti. The small shops that used to be successful mom-and-pop businesses were now either armored with steel bars on the windows, or the windows had been boarded up and the walls painted with gang signs. There were men and women in dirty clothes waiting at the stop lights to wash your window for a dollar. There were others waiting who would rob you for less. This is what they called Bad Town. Eddie knew the danger of these streets, he knew it personally, but he didn't care. He was too young and too strong to believe himself anything other than immortal.

They pulled up to a dilapidated yellow house. "This is the spot," said Darnell. "You better let me go in there first, tell him what's up. Just wait here."

"Whatever you say."

Eddie watched him walk into the front door. He took out his one-hitter and pulled on it again. He looked back towards the house, the door trim falling off, the window that had a blanket duct taped over it, the flower pot hanging from the front porch that held a brown and crumbling plant. The rocking chair missing a leg and the broken porch light. He turned his head and looked down the street. The houses were stacked close together, close enough to reach out of a window and pass a joint to your neighbor, and they all looked equally uninviting. Even in this neighborhood, traffic filled the road. Farther on, past the houses, beyond the highrises, miles distant, etched above the horizon, he saw a mountain peak. He thought about how vast the prairie was between the city and the mountains. He had been there before, he knew of the quiet life, and he started to remember. He remembered a mountain stream and the sight of an angler wading gracefully through the turbulent water. This memory made him uncomfortable, as the past typically did, so he took another pull.

Darnell knocked on the window and told him to come in. Eddie followed him across the short yard, up the creaking porch, and they entered into a dimly lit and smoke-filled room with six young men sitting at a table. They all eyed Eddie as if he were an alien creature. He eyed them back and didn't flinch.

"This is my cousin, they call him Blunt," said Darnell, gesturing towards the heavy-set dude at the end of the table who was wearing a cocked hat and dark sunglasses. When he pulled down the sunglasses, Eddie could see a large scar running across his left eye, from the forehead above his eyebrow, down through his cheek. There were five other dudes sitting at the table, each one had their hats cocked and wore fat fake gold jewelry.

"Darnell says you got the good shit," said Blunt, peering over his sunglasses.

"He would know," replied Eddie.

"Well shit, let's see it."

"How much do you want?"

"Don't know. I'm gonna have to taste it first."

Eddie pulled the one-hitter out of his pocket. It still had a taste in it. He started to hand it to Blunt, who said, "No no, that won't do. Better make that shit a blunt."

Eddie laughed. "Why the fuck not. I'll be right back."

Eddie returned with his school bag and sat at the table. He reached in and removed a handful. "Better let me do that," said Blunt.

"Go for it."

"Damn this is some sticky shit. Where'd a young fool like you get it?"

"I'm resourceful."

"Shit, I bet." He finished wrapping the cigar paper around the green buds and put a flame to it. They passed it around and Eddie took a pull. The cigar wrap made it taste sweet like artificial caramel flavoring. He handed it to Darnell and then looked to Blunt.

"What do you think?" he asked.

"It's some good shit alright. How much you got?"

"I got enough."

"You're a cocky little shit, aren't you."

"I've been called worse."

"Shit, I bet. Yo Gunner, grab the cash," said Blunt, looking to one of the other guys at the table. He handed the money to Blunt who placed a small stack of bills on the table. "We work hard for our scratch in these parts. Shit don't come easy."

"I can hook you up any time you need," replied Eddie.

"Just last week some fools came right up in here and tried to jack us," continued Blunt. "Shit, Gunner over there pistol whipped one of them. We took everything they had and sent them back to the streets crying like bitches. You don't want to fuck with us."

"I just do business. If you've got money, I've got weed."

"That right? How much you got then?"

"Already told you, I got enough."

"I'll take it," said Blunt.

"Three hundred an ounce, or a grand for the quarter pound. If you do good business, after several transactions I can cut the prices."

"Fool, you weren't listening. I said I'll *take* it."

Eddie stood up with his bag and started backing towards the door. "What the fuck is this?" he looked at Darnell.

"Blunt, I told you this dude's cool. What are you doing?"

"You bring some punk in here I don't know, waving the good shit around. Think I won't jack him?"

"Fuck this," said Eddie, and he turned to the door. Before he reached the door he was rushed by two of the guys from the table. He felt an arm wrap around his neck and quickly kicked back and hit a kneecap. The other struck Eddie square in the cheek with a solid punch that sent him shuffling. By the time he caught his balance he was being tackled by the first. They pinned him on the ground and sent a couple blows to his chest.

"Bring me his bag," said Blunt. "Looky here, this is more than a quarter pound. How much more you got?" They stood Eddie up and pinned his arms.

"Fuck you. Let me go."

"This dude's got a temper. Where'd you find him Darnell?" Darnell looked to the floor and shoved his hands in his pockets. "Looks like he's wised up," said Blunt. "What about you?" he asked, looking at Eddie.

"Give me my shit and let me go." He broke his hands free and started to rush Blunt. He felt the fist hit his right eye, but that was all. Darkness.

. . .

When he woke up he was in the passenger seat of the Rover parked in an alley. He pulled down the visor and looked at his face. The cheek was already swollen and his eye was showing a bruise. He dug in his pocket for the one-hitter but it was gone. "Fuck," he said. This was going to hurt, but not until tomorrow. He was too pissed off to feel any pain. He looked under the seat for the rest of his stash, but it was gone. What a mistake they had made.

He drove several blocks to the phone booth, dropped in a quarter and paged Darnell, "420-211-187," which meant weed-robbery-murder. He waited several minutes, holding his transparent blue pager in his hand, waiting for it to vibrate, but he got no reply. He fired up the engine and cranked the music loud. He had paid two grand for everything they took, and planned to make five off it. That was everything he had. He wanted to go home and smoke his roaches, but his mom was there with Carl, and he couldn't deal with that now. School would be getting out soon, so he returned to the parking lot to wait.

Eddie sat in the Rover watching kids flow out the doors. What a boring life they lived, he thought, spending their day here in this prison. He'd been skipping most classes this semester, ever since he turned eighteen, and he was making a name for himself. He still showed up to enough classes to pass most of them, but people knew the majority of his time was spent on the streets.

Alex walked out of the front doors, and Eddie waved him over. "What's up man, how was class?" he asked as Alex popped in shotgun. Alex swung his right hand across, and Eddie grabbed it, confirmed with the secret handshake. Alex's hands were always damp. He always seemed nervous and disoriented. But they were boys, part of the same crew. The same crew as Darnell. Eddie turned his head and looked out the window. It was possible that Darnell had set him up, but he couldn't be sure.

"Ah, same old bull shit," replied Alex. "I turned in one of my new poems for a creative writing assignment. That teacher, you know, Bonnell? He's an idiot. Doesn't know good poetry unless it's written by some famous dead Frenchman." Alex wiped his arm across his nose, which left a long trail of snot on his sleeve.

"You'll have to let me read it later."

"I'll read it for you now. Already memorized the thing. It's short."

"Let me hear it then."

"Alright, this was about a vision I had. More like a daydream. I imagined myself being part of a real family, like you. I wondered what that would be like, if it's actually possible to love someone more than yourself. These words just came out while thinking about that. So here we go," he took a deep breath. "I hope I die sooner than my mother, father, sister and brother. I hope my friends outlive me, acquaintances, even enemies. I've grown too attached to understand life without these. Perhaps this explains my self-destructive tendencies."

"Damn dude, that's some deep shit. When did you write it?"

"Last night."

"Don't fucking lie to me."

"I'm not dude." Alex turned his head and looked out the window, then continued, "But the best part of the day was, right at the end of last class, I could hear your subwoofers in the classroom, just banging the windows. It really pissed off Bonnell. Did you get new speakers?"

"Nope, just a new amp."

"Well that shit sounds wicked, I'd kill to have a system like this." Alex pulled a handkerchief from his back pocket and blew his nose. "Did you skip all day?"

"Had some shit going on."

"What the fuck happened to your face?" He was wiping his nose while sucking snot in.

"It's nothing. At least not for me. How's those allergies?"

"Ah fuck man, it's relentless. I got so many damn allergies, I swear I'm allergic to oxygen and sunlight."

"Aren't we all."

Alex sneezed and tears dripped from his red eyes. "Shit, it's nothing like this. Trust me."

Eddie laughed, "Got any weed?"

"You're asking me for weed? That's a change. I'm dry though. It's a fucking holiday, thought you'd be loaded and ready. You get jacked or something?"

Eddie waved off the question and replied, "Damn, you know anyone who's got some?"

"I was supposed to smoke up with a few guys later."

"Alright, well beep me when that happens."

"Will do."

"And Alex. You're a damn fine poet. Don't let anyone say different."

Eddie cranked up the stereo again, and sat in his seat pounding on the steering wheel. His face was throbbing which only made him angrier. Then Scott jumped into the passenger seat and yelled, "Turn that down man."

"What's going on?" asked Eddie.

"I was going to ask you the same thing. You were supposed to be my partner in science lab today. I'd ask why you weren't there, but that face says a lot. Who'd you piss off this time?"

"Don't worry about it. How'd lab go?"

"Fuck, I don't know. We mixed some shit together that changed colors and created some steam. Would've been pretty cool if I was stoned."

"Speaking of which. Got any weed?"

"You sell that whole stash already? Or did you get jacked?"

"Dude, forget about it. Do you have any or not?"

"I got a little of what you sold me yesterday."

"Let's smoke."

"Alright, but pull out of here. I need to get away from this place."

Eddie put the Rover in gear, cranked up the stereo, and pulled into the line of cars waiting to get out of the parking lot. He started to think about Darnell, after all they had done together, he considered him a close friend. The type of friend he expected to have his back when shit went down. That proved false, and he figured Darnell was over at Blunt's place right now smoking his weed. Eddie could go over there, kick in the door … Then he noticed something out the window. "Who's that?" he asked Scott.

There was a young woman walking alone out the front door. Everyone else had already rushed out of the building and was either in their car or loaded on a bus. She walked out with an arm full of text books. She wore a long blue dress that reached her ankles. She had dark brown hair braided down her back and a narrow face. "Dude, who is that?" he gestured towards her.

"Her? Some new girl. She was in my Algebra class today. Think she's from the country or something. Seemed kinda weird."

"Really." Eddie watched her in the rearview as she passed behind them and continued walking out the parking lot. The line of cars started to move and Eddie turned out in her direction. He slowed down and pulled up alongside of her.

"What are you doing?" asked Scott.

"Just chill a sec," he turned down the music and opened his window. "Hey," he said to her, and she looked up. "You new here?"

"Yes."

"I thought so. What's your name?"

"Vanya."

"Vanya? Nice to meet you. I'm Eddie."

"What happened to your face?"

"Hazards of stardom," he gave her a smile. She smiled and looked away. "So, you must live close if you're walking home?" He was inching along at idle speed beside her.

"Not really. I just like to walk."

"Yeah? Well, we could give you a ride. You never know when a storm might come over the mountains."

"No thanks. I can walk. I like loud music less than I like storms."

"Well, nice to meet you then," replied Eddie. He cranked up the stereo and drove on.

"You're an idiot," said Scott.

"Who doesn't like the new girl?" he replied with a grin.

"Not that one. So, where we going?"

"Let's just drive man." Eddie drove through the stop lights, between the highrises, past the neighborhoods with their dilapidated houses. He drove until there was no more traffic, until there were no more buildings or houses. Most of the people he knew in the city rarely left the city. The thirty miles of prairie between the city and the mountains were mostly uninhabited, except for a few ranches. Up in the mountains was a wilderness, known only to a few recluses. Last autumn a dead body had been discovered by a fisherman, killed by a mountain lion, or at least that's what they suspected, since they never found the animal. It had been on the news for a week, and then the story dropped and was replaced by the local sports and celebrity gossip.

Scott rolled a joint on his lap as they drove out of the city, neither of them saying too much. The road was bending up and down over small hills, and weaving curves along the river. Scott rolled down his window and then dug in his bag. He now held a joint in one hand and a disposable camera in the other. He hung his head slightly out the window and yelled, "It's so fucking beautiful out here. Slow down Eddie so we can see it."

Eddie slowed their speed, "You act like you've never been here."

"It's been a long time. All I do is go to school, work, hockey and home. I forgot how beautiful it is out here."

"Yeah, it's something. Hand me that joint."

"Here, you hold this so I can take a picture." Scott held up his disposable camera and cranked the thumbwheel. "Three pictures left. Slow down more so I can make them good ones." He hung out the window, snapped three shots, cranking the thumbwheel between each one. "Those are going to be awesome, I can tell. I'll probably print them on eleven-by-seventeens, show it off you know. Or better yet, I'll make a shadowbox out of them, call it getting stoned in nature."

Eddie turned his head and sighed. As if this automobile, this steel and rubber and glass, were a part of the natural world. Perhaps, in a sense, it was, but it was not the nature Eddie remembered. What he remembered most about nature was the expansive silence. He remembered how even the softest sounds – the riffle in a river, the flapping of a wing, or the landing of a leaf – drew attention and admiration. He couldn't remember the last time he admired a sound inherent to the city. So he blasted his radio.

Eddie tried to distract himself from what happened earlier today, and hoped the scenery would calm his mind. He looked out the window at the rolling hills and started to remember again. He remembered the ranch when he was young. It was tucked behind one of these rolling hills with a stream that flowed behind their house. Back then the city was a foreign place, a cruel place, and this was his home. He had been too young to control the changes that would come. Maybe nobody could control them. He inhaled deeply, and tried to feel the peace and simplicity again. But it was gone.

"This is fucking boring," said Scott. "I don't have any pictures left. What the hell are we doing?"

"Just driving man. What else is there to do?"

"Let's go hookup with Kathy. She's always hanging out with a couple hot chicks."

"Works for me." Eddie looked at the clock. "Shit."

"What's up?"

"It's five o'clock."

"So. What happens at five?"

"Nothing, but I'm supposed to be somewhere at five-thirty."

"Cancel. Trust me, we'll have more fun with Kathy."

"I can't. But I'll drop you off there and try to get back after."

"Whatever you say man. I can't promise there'll be any weed left."

Eddie did a u-turn in the road and pushed down hard on the pedal, putting the mountains farther behind them. When they got into the city, he turned on Maclean Boulevard which was trimmed with deciduous trees that had started to sprout new spring leaves. The neighborhood was nice, almost opulent, except for one house. Halfway down on the north side of the street was a large house with cedar trim that hadn't been stained in over a decade and was starting to rot. There were garbage bags piled on the side of the garage that had been torn into by raccoons and neighborhood cats, and a rusty 1987 Oldsmobile sedan in the driveway. Kathy lived here with her dad who was usually drunk, and either didn't know, or didn't care that she used the basement as a place for teens to drink cheap beer and get stoned. "Save me some weed," he said as Scott stepped out. Scott closed the door, stuck up his middle finger, and walked around the back of the house.

. . .

When Eddie parked at the school he pulled down the visor mirror and had a look. The eye was now dark and swollen practically shut. What a fucking day. He got out and walked inside.

"Eddie, what happened to you?" asked his mom as she reached her hands to his face.

He pushed her hands away. "It's nothing mom, don't worry about it."

"You're always so nonchalant about things. Why don't you talk to me?"

"It's alright, just a bruise."

"Is that why you missed my class today?" asked Mr. Bonnell, who was sitting at his desk with his legs crossed. Eddie always thought he looked pretentious, with his wide-frame glasses, thin little mustache, perfectly creased slacks, and polished shoes.

"Maybe," he replied, and sat down across the desk.

"Please, Samantha, can I call you Samantha? Have a seat."

"Yes, Samantha is fine."

"So, if you don't care to elaborate on the condition of your face, perhaps I will start. What are your thoughts on my class, Eddie?"

"My thoughts?" It was getting difficult to see out of his right eye. "It's alright, as far as classes go."

"That's not telling me anything. You'll have to do better."

"I think it's okay. I mean, you assign the same old books every English teacher in America assigns, and you expect the same answers every student gives. But it's okay."

"That's interesting. Have you read any of the books I've assigned?"

"I read them all before you assigned them."

"Is that so? Well, why haven't you turned in any of the assignments? If you've read all these books that should be easy for you."

"What's the point?"

"Eddie," said his mom, "be respectful. Mister Bonnell is trying to help."

"Eddie, you've passed all the tests, at least the ones you've shown up for, which leads me to believe you have read the books, and that alone is typically enough to earn a passing grade. Listen," he rubbed his thick eyebrows, "I wouldn't have called you and your mother in here if I didn't believe you had more potential. Believe me, I have students who are failing because they simply don't have any interest in literature, probably never will. That isn't you. However, if you want to pass my class, you will have to prove it."

"What can we do?" asked Samantha.

"I want your experience in my class to be about more than just reading the same old books. The purpose of these books is to help stimulate creative thinking and observation. If you can demonstrate to me that these are skills you have learned from your independent reading, I will pass you."

"How am I supposed to do that?"

"A big part of understanding literature is learning to see the details in the world around you, and applying that skill to your own life, your own perceptions. I have a unique assignment for you, and if you complete it satisfactorily, I will pass you."

"Does that mean I don't need to do any other assignments, or pass your tests?"

"I would of course prefer that you do, but this assignment will only be given to you, none of the other students will know about it. It is important for you to understand that I am not offering this as an easier way to a passing grade. In fact, I believe it will ultimately be more difficult. So, the choice is yours."

"What's the assignment?"

"You will record a journal. It can be written, or if you have a voice recorder, then verbal. But the final product will need to be typed for my review. What this means is at least once a week I will expect you to record your thoughts, not only about what's going on in your mind, but also about the world around you. It is due before the end of this semester, and will be graded based on the honesty of your observations."

"That sounds like some ridiculous psychology experiment."

"Eddie," said his mom, "be polite. He is making you a generous offer that I think you should consider."

"Eddie, being a senior in high school has never been easy for anyone. Everybody faces their own unique challenges, and I'm aware of some of the struggles your family has faced," Bonnell looked at Samantha and nodded. "This assignment will not be easy for you, but neither will your life be easy after high school. I encourage you to take your time and consider my offer. It won't be given again."

"Thank you Mister Bonnell," said his mom as she stood up. "I assure you Eddie will put his full attention on this project. He is a good kid. As you said, we've all faced our own challenges, and he's no exception."

"Yes Samantha, I understand. Eddie, the choice is yours."

"Can we go now?" asked Eddie.

"Actually, I was hoping I could speak to Eddie a moment in private," Bonnell said to Samantha.

"Certainly," she replied. "Eddie, behave yourself."

Mr. Bonnell folded his hands together and rested them on his desk. "Eddie, I'm going to give you a moment of honesty that not many people will give you the time for. I had your older brother in my class, and he was a good kid, a smart kid. What happened was terrible. You seem to be more affected by it than you let on. I understand, it's difficult for a young man to ask for help, or to express emotion. Some people will perceive that as a weakness, and nobody wants to be taken advantage of. I don't expect you to talk to me. I probably wouldn't have at your age. But, I want you to use this assignment as a chance to explore what is going on, to question your own thoughts and actions. It is truly a big world out there, much more than just this city. If you continue with what you're doing, you will be trapped, not only in this city, but in this lifestyle you are leading."

Eddie looked away briefly, and then returned his eyes to Bonnell. "It's really not that simple."

"I agree. Young men are serotinous. Do you know what that word means?"

"Something about pine trees needing fire to reproduce."

"Close enough. Like a pine cone that requires fire to release its seed, young men must walk through fire to be born. You must know of the danger and the pain, understand it personally, before you are prepared for this world. The fire you are walking through has the potential to burn away the waste, refine you into something better, stronger. Or it could consume you entirely."

"Where'd you read that?" asked Eddie.

Bonnell dropped his hands to his side and rolled back on the chair. "I could talk to you for hours about the trials of youth. Ultimately my words are only mine. You must learn your own."

"I already know my own words."

"I'm certain you do." Bonnell looked out the window towards mountains in the distance, and then returned his eyes to Eddie. "It is important that we express as much as we can in this short span of our lives, because that is the only chance we have of being remembered. But know this, your words will not guarantee you to be remembered favorably."

"Can I go now?"

"Of course. As always, the choice is yours. But Eddie, I do mean this choice is entirely yours. I'm not going to remind you, and I'm not going to contact your mom again. You either do it, or you don't."

Eddie rushed out the door and passed his mom who quickly followed. "Do you have time to talk before you go to work?" she asked.

"Not really. I'm already late."

"What time will you be home?"

"My shift goes until ten, but sometimes they keep me late."

"Alright. Let's talk tomorrow. Can you wake up early so we can talk before school?"

"Sure. Listen, thanks for coming, but Bonnell is whacked. His class is a joke and I could pass it without this ridiculous assignment."

"Eddie, why can't you see he's trying to help?"

"He's not trying to help. He's just doing his job. Asking me to record a journal. Where'd he get a crazy idea like that?"

"I think it would be good for you."

"I have to go. We'll talk tomorrow mom."

Eddie blasted his radio and rushed out of the parking lot. It was still early and there was plenty of time to get to Kathy's. The music wasn't loud enough to cover his thoughts. A journal, what the fuck was that? Last thing he needed now was another school assignment. He had to get a new stash. People depended on him for that, and it was his game. Tomorrow he would make a call. Everything would work out. Tonight he was going to get drunk and stoned and maybe fool around.

Kathy's street was quiet and well-lit by street lamps. He looked at his pager, hoping to have a message from Darnell, anything to give him a hint of if they had planned to jack him or it was random. Nothing. The only message was from Kathy's landline, it read: 6969. That was Scott sending him a code that there were two girls here. He got out of the Rover and walked around the house through the long grass that was still muddy from the snow that melted several weeks ago.

"Eddie Eddie, about time you made it," said Scott.

Eddie couldn't tell if Scott were more drunk or stoned, "Where's Kathy?" he asked.

"She ain't here man. But no sweat. Do you know these two?" He gestured to the girls sitting on the couch, and then whispered in Eddie's ear, "I'm making a move on Christine tonight, so you can go for Shelley."

"Why don't you introduce me," replied Eddie.

"I'm Christine," said a short blonde haired girl who held a can of cheap beer in one hand and a small bong in the other. "We had Geography together last semester. You probably don't remember, since you never came to class."

"Any weed in that thing?" he asked.

"A little bit." She stood up and handed it to him.

"Got a flame?" he asked, and she flicked her lighter over the bowl. Eddie covered the port and sucked in through the bubbles.

"Share that with me," said Christine, as she wrapped her hand around his. He blew the smoke through their hands into her mouth. After she exhaled, she placed her hand gently on his bruised eye.

Scott placed his arm around Christine and said, "She's the captain of our volleyball team. I just love the way you look in that uniform." He started to lean in towards her, but she backed away.

"Where's the beer?" asked Eddie.

"Upstairs in the fridge. Its Kathy's dads', but he won't even know. Drunkard," said Scott, still clinging to Christine with one hand.

Eddie went upstairs and returned with four beers, and then shotgunned the first two. "That was impressive," said Christine. They all sat on the couch. Shelley on the far end with her nose in a copy of *Seventeen* magazine. Scott sat close to Christine who had her shoulder turned away from him.

"Rough day?" she asked Eddie.

"Fuck it." He opened the third beer and handed Christine the other. She put her hand on his lap and cracked the can. "Let's get oblivious," he said.

APRIL 1999

SUN	MON	TUE	WED	THU	FRI	SAT
				~~1~~	~~2~~	~~3~~
~~4~~	~~5~~	~~6~~	~~7~~	~~8~~	~~9~~	~~10~~
~~11~~	~~12~~	~~13~~	~~14~~	~~15~~	~~16~~	~~17~~
~~18~~	~~19~~	~~20~~	21	22	23	24
25	26	27	28	29	30	

Eddie rolled over in bed and dug in the drawer for a roach. He pinched it tightly between his short fingernails and lit it. The resiny smoke filled his lungs and he closed his eyes. He didn't remember how the hell he got home last night. He didn't remember how late he stayed or what happened with Christine. Fuck, it was too early to get up. His mom wanted to talk, so he grabbed some clean clothes and headed for the shower.

The hot water permeated his skin but not enough to refresh his mind. When he stepped out of the shower, he took his time drying with a towel, eyes focused on the mirror, and then applied the mousse with extra care. He had to look exceptionally good today because he was feeling extra bad. He walked towards the kitchen and saw his mom and Cole sitting at the table sipping coffee. Carl must still be asleep, which meant there'd be no distraction. He'd have their full attention and they'd expect something from him. Damn, he had one hell of a hangover.

"How was work last night?" asked his mom.

"It was alright. I'm exhausted. Any coffee left?" He walked over to the counter and filled a cup.

"You look beat," said Cole. "Must've been some heavy packages?"

Eddie told them he had a job in the loading dock at UPS. Eddie had a client and he gave him a discount on the deal that he would cover for him if they ever called, and it was a place they would never just drop in to say hello. "Yep," he answered. He didn't like answering Cole's questions. The guy tried hard, and Eddie was glad his mom seemed happy, but he was too old to be given a new father figure.

"I didn't hear you come home last night," said his mom. "Did you go out after work?"

"They kept me late. I needed the hours." He had no idea what time he got home.

"I see. So did you have time to think about Mister Bonnell's offer?"

"I still think it's a joke mom. He's obviously just messing with me. I think he feels belittled that I've read all the books he's assigned. He doesn't know what else to do."

"Maybe you're the one who feels belittled," said Cole.

"Cole," said his mom, "please, we need to be reasonable with him."

"Being reasonable isn't going to work. Listen Eddie, I knew kids like you when I was in school. They had a rough time with things so they stopped caring about what was important. I see them now and they haven't changed. Always blaming others as an excuse for their problems. You only get a few chances in life, and the older you get the less frequently they come along. Your mom loves you and worked hard to raise you right. Don't throw that away just because you can't deal with your personal issues."

"What do you know about it?" replied Eddie. He began to stand up.

"Eddie," said his mom, "please sit down. Cole is just trying to help."

"So what do you think, if I make some voice journal everything's going to be alright? What a joke. That's not going to change anything."

"You're right," said Cole. "It's going to take a lot more work than that. But it's a good place to start. You've got less than one semester left of high school, then you're out in the real world. This is your only chance to do it right, and despite what you might think, there's no time to waste."

"Listen, Cole," began Eddie, "I appreciate your age and experience, but you don't need to get involved. I didn't ask for your advice, and advice is something that should only be given if it's been asked for, otherwise it sounds presumptuous."

"Is that so?" replied Cole as he pulled a sip from his coffee and looked Eddie directly in the eyes. "You've really got the wrong attitude about all of this. What would Steve think if he saw you this way?"

"Cole!" said his mom. They never talked about Eddie's brother, her oldest son. He was a specter who lived behind the scenes, and Eddie often lay in bed at night planning what he would say when Steve returned home. It wouldn't have to be much, a simple hello and the sight of his smile would be enough. It's been three years since he died and they still continued to celebrate his birthday every January.

Each year his mom would contact the man who owned the fly shop on the outskirts of town, he was a renowned fly tier, and she'd ask for one single custom fly. The instructions were simple, it had to be a stonefly nymph. The stonefly was Steve's favorite, she'd explain each year, because it got less notoriety than the mayfly or caddisfly. She would go on to explain that Steve liked things simply because they weren't popular. Every year when the custom fly arrived, all Eddie wanted was to see Steve again, sit on the shoreline and watch him drift a stonefly nymph through a pocket of water.

Cole supported their need to remember Steve, and for the past two years he built a wooden placard to which he mounted the custom flies. These were displayed now upon the mantel above the fireplace in their living room.

Eddie's mom walked over and put her hands on the mantle. With her back towards the room, she said, "I think he'd like this one the best. It looks the most like the ones he tied." She turned her head and smiled as a tear dripped down her face.

"He'd love all of them," said Eddie. He forced a smile, but his stomach felt hollow. He was envious of her tears. He didn't cry at the funeral, and he felt like this was cheating Steve. Steve deserved his tears. So he would often visit the grave alone, smoke a big fat blunt, and try to remember all the good times. This had the opposite effect on Eddie, and rather than breaking out in remorseful tears, he found himself laughing out loud, verbally reciting play-by-play the time he hooked his first trout, and Steve got so excited that he dove into a deep pool to net the fish. They had gone to the river directly after the first day of school that year, so Steve was wearing his newest clothes, which were now fully drenched and muddied. This had upset both their mom and dad so much that the punishment for Steve was three days without fishing. Steve had told Eddie it was worth it to net that fish, but Eddie knew those three days were not easy on him.

"I'm sorry Sam," continued Cole, "but Eddie needs perspective." He looked at Eddie, "I know this is difficult for you, and you may not care what I have to say, but I am here to help. Your mom already lost a son, and what you're doing isn't helping anything. You think we don't know about you skipping school? We know what the kids who skip school spend their days doing. We were young once too."

"Get off my case," said Eddie, and took a couple steps towards the door. He turned around and walked back to the table to kiss his mom on the forehead, then left the room. He hopped in the Rover and popped in his Juvenile CD, and the song *Spittin' Game* blasted out the speakers. It was still early and he knew it would wake up Carl and the rest of the neighborhood, but he didn't care. Fuck them. Fuck Cole. He was just showing off for his mom. That guy didn't know anything.

Eddie pulled up to the pay phone and paged Lynch, "121-504" which meant "Need to talk - Urgent." He aimed the Rover towards the Casino. The west side of town was Rez Land, but the city had grown to encompass it, surrounded tightly on all sides, with the only geographic boundaries being the massive casino on the south side, a world famous horse track on the west, a top three pro golf course on the east, and the rows of mansions with large manicured yards on the north.

Lynch's family ran the Casino, ran everything on the south side. They were the richest people Eddie knew. Lynch's sister Cassie was only nineteen but had her own mansion where she lived alone and was known for throwing large crazy parties. It was custom for fully automatic machine guns to get pulled out and fired at the sky. One time they aimed their guns at Cassie's 1962 Corvette and lit the thing up. She didn't care, thought it was funny. She owned seven more Corvettes in her giant car barn.

Eddie got a page from Lynch. "17-183," which meant "no–I'm busy."

Eddie pulled into the Quick-Go convenience store and used the pay phone to reply: "505" which meant "SOS."

Lynch had a mansion on the golf course, but Eddie knew he spent most nights in the suite above the casino. When he pulled up, the parking lot was full. This place was busy all day every day. These fuckers were loaded, only because everyone's pissing away their money on slots and poker. Eddie wondered if they'd still play the games if they knew their money was being used on machine guns and drugs. Shit, he thought, maybe that's why they gambled their money, with hopes they would win enough to buy machine guns and drugs.

He pulled around back of the casino and parked in a reserved spot. He walked in the back door and took the elevator to the eighth floor where he stepped out on a vermillion red carpet. The ceiling was high, easily twelve feet, with embossed gold foil. He walked to the end of the hall and pounded on the door that said *Warrior Suite.*

A young woman answered. She had dark hair, almost black, that flowed below her waist. She was scantily wrapped in a robe that was transparent white which made her skin look radiant and glow from the dim light behind her. The robe looked so soft, Eddie imagined if he held it between his fingers he wouldn't even feel it. She smiled and kicked her hip out to the side. "You must be Eddie. Lynch said I'm supposed to make you some coffee and tell you to chill the fuck out. Come on in."

The room opened into an affluent view. Every lamp was made of crystal and gold. The counters and tables were thick slabs of exotic wood. The furniture was of hog skin leather, tanned dark with a gold braid around the seams. There was a full-bodied moose stuffed and standing erect by the bay windows. The television set was more like a movie screen that filled an entire wall. Eddie followed her into the kitchen. "What's your name?" he asked.

"Lulu. They call me L. How do you know Lynch?"

"We go back. Is he really asleep?"

"Probably. We partied pretty hard last night." She pushed down the French press and poured him a cup. "Sit tight kid, I'll go check on him."

Eddie walked over to the moose. Standing beside it, the beast towered over him. He reached out his arms and the antlers were wider. He saw a moose once when he was a kid. His dad had taken him and Steve on a camping trip in the mountains. They snuck right up to the thing and it just stood there in the stream without a care. Its wet fur glistened in the sunlight.

Lynch entered the room. "I killed that bastard with a crossbow," he said. "Dumb thing just stood there, I had to shoot it three times."

Eddie turned and looked at him. "Surprised you didn't use an Uzi."

"I have, but that thing tears up the pelt. So what the fuck are you doing here so early?"

"Some shit went down yesterday."

"I see that. Looks like a moose kicked you in the face."

"Remember Darnell? He set me up. Brought me over to his cousin's place and they jacked me for everything."

"Blunt? I know that fool. Always starting shit."

"You know him?"

"Yeah, he tried to get me to front him some of the good shit. I told him to fuck off. I don't trust that fool, thinks he's a big gangster."

"I need a new stash. Get back on my feet."

"How much you got?"

"Shit. They took everything. I need you to front me some. You know I'm good for it."

"Now Eddie," Lynch walked up close to him and put his hand on an antler, "when I agreed not to sell to any other kids at your school, it's because I thought you were smart. I only do business with a few big timers, and I thought you were one of them. Getting jacked is bad for business. I will find somebody else, if this becomes a problem."

"It's not a problem. Just front me a pound. I can flip it by tomorrow."

"Alright, but I'm adding an extra hundred interest a day, starting today. Go down to the lobby and ask for Scooby. I'll tell him you're coming."

"Cool. One other thing. I need a gun."

Lynch turned away and walked to the window. From up here he could see the city stretched out through the long basin, and the mountains beyond hid in a blue mist. "Those mountains were here before any of us. Back in time that's where the people lived and hunted, where the children grew. That was long before this city. Now people are soft and lazy." He turned and looked back at Eddie, who was rubbing the moose's nose with one hand. "I suppose you are going after Blunt. Retribution. It always sounds like a good idea. Believe me, I think about it often. We all have enemies who deserve revenge. I think you should forget about it this time. Learn your lesson and stay outta the Bad Town. You got enough clientele with those school kids."

"I'm not going to let it be. I don't even care about getting my shit back, they've probably smoked most of it by now. He needs to be taught a lesson."

"Think you're the one to do it? Shit. You are a hard ass." Lynch sat down on the couch and flipped on the television. "Tell you what Eddie. You need a gun I'm not going to stop you. I'd rather you got a proper piece from me than some worthless shit off the streets. But I'm not in the business of fronting guns. You sell that stash. It'll make you enough to pay me for it and get you a down payment on a quality piece."

"I'll have your money by tomorrow."

"You will. Now hold tight a sec." Lynch stood up and walked over to the far wall where opened the lid on a wooden box that sat on top of a marble table. "Come over here, Eddie. I've had enough of you sending me these coded pages. It's time we make you proper."

Eddie walked over and looked into the box. Inside were a dozen mobile phones. "Are you serious?" he looked up at Lynch. "Those are fucking cool."

"Don't think this means I'm happy with you. Take your pick of one and never page me again."

"Tell me about this one." He picked up a cobalt blue flip phone.

"That's the slimmest one in its class. Motorola Timeport flip phone. Digital screen. You'll never need a pager again. This thing can send full text messages. Use the letters on each number key to type out the words. Keep it short and simple. No more of those damn pager codes."

"Damn man, are you serious?" Eddie's eyes lit up as he flipped open the phone. "I can have this?"

"Send me a text message when you need something. Now take it and get out of here. L is waiting for me."

"Sure thing. But first, you got a pipe? Those fuckers took mine."

"Shit. You're a needy little punk. Don't smoke the whole pound. Grab the little glass piece from the drawer on your way out. I need the money tomorrow. Now get the fuck out of here before I change my mind."

Eddie took the elevator down to the lobby and asked for Scooby. What a ridiculous name, Scooby. Then he saw him, and it fit. A tall lengthy dude with a giant nose and droopy eyes. Scooby carried a burlap coin bag and handed it to him. "Rent's due tomorrow, don't blow it on the games," was all he said.

. . .

Eddie drove to school and parked in his usual spot, then packed the bowl and pulled a couple hits. They had an open lunch policy, which meant some of the kids ate in the cafeteria, but most of them either ate outside or drove to a nearby fast food joint. Lunch hour was Eddie's best business. Within thirty minutes he'd sold enough to pay Lynch for the stash. Eddie watched his clients as they loaded up their pipes in the cars, laughed with their friends, and looked out their windows with nervous eyes as they blew out clouds of smoke. Most of them smoked because they wanted a connection, something they could do with each other. An action to feel rebellious. Eddie smoked because it helped him cope. It calmed his nerves and pushed the past further away.

Scott popped in the passenger door and bought a dime bag. Eddie was a dealer of the first-come first-served mentality, which meant, unlike other less successful dealers, he'd sell whatever size bag was requested, and this allowed him to move weight faster than those who only sold in designated sizes. If you came to him with thirty-six dollars he'd give you thirty-six dollars worth. Plus, he only sold the top notch neon green sticky, and he always had it. This stuff gave his clients a cleaner, translucent high, without the after effects of ditch weed.

"Want to match me for a smoke?" asked Scott.

"You know it."

"So, you ever coming back to class?"

"What the fuck for?"

"Good point. How's that eye doing, thing looks wicked."

"Don't worry about it." Eddie handed him a generous pinch and Scott rolled it up.

"So, what happened with you and Christine last night? She was asking about you today."

"Shit, wish I could remember."

"Yeah, that was pretty fucked up."

"What do you mean?"

"Shit, you don't remember anything. I confided in you man. I told you I was going for her, and then next thing I see she's all over you. I should probably tell you to fuck off." This was a sensation Scott was not accustomed to feeling. His position among the ranks of his class generally meant he was the one girls were attracted to. But Eddie had something else. It was more than just being easy access to great weed, they were attracted to his ability to truly not give a shit. Or at least give that appearance. "Don't you remember anything from last night?" Scott asked.

Eddie started to remember. He remembered her hand on his leg and her lips on his neck. He could have pulled away but didn't. It was fucked up. He knew the only reason Scott didn't completely dismiss him was because of the weed. Scott got good grades and was a star player on the hockey team, but he got his street cred by being friends with Eddie.

"I gotta bolt," said Scott, "fucking Geography test next hour."

"Good luck with that."

"I'll hit you up later."

Scott got out of the Rover and Eddie sat in the parking lot. He blasted the stereo and watched the kids file into school. What was he going to do now? He put the car in drive and started to pull out. Then he saw her, Vanya. Today she was wearing a red plaid dress that went to her ankles. He watched her walking in alone and noticed her high heel cowboy boots with clumps of mud caked around the soles. She didn't seem concerned about this. Funny, every other kid always looked awkward if they were alone, but she seemed perfectly comfortable. He watched her until she was inside and then drove away.

. . .

He was getting hungry, so he pulled into a drive thru and ordered a double cheeseburger with large fries and a large soda. Ever since Carl was born his mom only stocked organic food in the house, and wouldn't buy anything unless it was all-natural. She stopped cooking with oils, and even tried to make him eat things like lentils and cauliflower. This wasn't too bad, but Eddie liked the taste of a fast food burger and greasy fries with extra salt. It was just one of the many secrets he kept from her. He kept secrets from everyone.

The pager vibrated in his pocket, it was a message from his mom, "424" which was code for "Call me back."

Shit, why couldn't she just leave him alone? He ignored the message and ate his food while he drove downtown. The skyscrapers were tall and the streets loaded with cars and taxis. He pulled into a parking spot and fired up a joint. This city was always so damn busy. He watched through the windshield how it moved and changed shape.

He saw the tall buildings which were bound to this earth by sinews of cement dug into the ground, pillars of steel pounded and buried by raw hands and breaking backs, by people whose lives have been lost and forgotten or never even known. Rooftops hung higher than the trees, near enough to scrape the low clouds. Pyramids of a different form, but lacking the ritual or permanence. Contemporaries of the satellites and mobile phones. Temporal designs on the landscape that scream we are here. A composition of what was natural, now dismembered and then recomposed as something new. A landmark that will weather away and be replaced with new growth and changing ideas of the manmade world.

He rolled down his window to let the smoke out, and kept his stereo blasting. Men and women walked in and out of the buildings and along the sidewalk. They wore suits and ties and carried fancy bags. Not a single one of them looked happy. What the fuck were they doing in these tall buildings with reflective windows? He watched the people on the corner in their ragged clothes and hands held out. There must be something more.

Many days he could sit in his car and watch this scene for an entire afternoon, but today it bored him. He drove to Bad Town and turned off the radio. He'd been jacked before, and certainly jacked others, that was part of the game, but he was sick of it. One thing he knew about this world was that you couldn't be weak and expect to survive. If one person took advantage of you and got away with it, then others would. That wasn't going to happen.

Eddie parked on Blunt's block and watched a group of ten thuggish dudes on the front porch. They were drinking large bottles of beer and looking tough. People like these were the reason his brother died. Steve had been a pretty good student, and a damn fine fisherman. When they were young and lived in the country, it was Steve who took Eddie fishing and taught him how to read the water, predict where the fish were hiding, and then cast a delicate fly. Steve was only three years older than him, so they attended the same small country school. When Eddie was twelve and Steve was fifteen, they would rush home after class each day and then be left mostly alone to explore for a couple hours. There was a stream on their property where they'd catch trout and go swimming. It was their spot, nobody else had access, which made it seem larger and more grandiose. The entire world existed in those hills and in that cold crystalline water. Eddie hadn't felt the tug of a trout since they moved to the city five years ago when he was thirteen.

Steve was sixteen when they moved to the city, and this difference in age felt greater than it had in the country. At their country home it was just the two of them playing outdoors or sitting around the bookshelf in the evenings. The nearest kids their age lived nine miles away, and even though in the country that distance was considered a neighbor, they rarely visited. When they moved to the city Steve quickly became consumed with the going-ons of other teenagers, plus he had his drivers license, so he spent most of his evenings away from their home. Eddie didn't know much about his brother during those years. He only knew that he had changed, and that he kept secrets from them.

The police never caught the fucker who shot Steve in the head. Eddie remembered that night clearly. He was fifteen, and Steve was one month away from graduating high school. His mom rushed him to the hospital and his dad was already there when they arrived. Dad wouldn't let them in the room, Steve wasn't going to make it and they didn't need to see what happened. Eddie thought it was fake, a movie skit, and he pretended it wasn't happening. His mom was crying and his dad held her tight. These were his parents, they had super powers, and they would fix this. Steve would be alright. They would go fishing again when they were both older and had children of their own. They had too many experiences together, too many more to come. It wouldn't end like this. Steve was too good, too real, and had always been there.

The official report was that it had been a random act of violence, that Steve looked like somebody with money, and somebody without it killed him. That wasn't good enough for Eddie. Steve was his big brother, the one he looked up to even more than their dad, and he was too good to die randomly. There had to be more to the story. His big brother couldn't be a statistic, an unknown, he was a real person. They would find the killer, hang him in the street, make an example out of him. That would bring his brother back. Steve's life would mean something. This fucking city.

Eddie clinched the steering wheel tight and let a cloud of smoke from his nose. He looked at the gang on Blunt's porch and wanted to put the Rover in gear and run them over. He cranked up the stereo and at the first sound of booming bass they looked his direction. Gunner, that mother fucker, pointed at the Rover, and Blunt started walking towards it. Eddie put it in gear and pushed the pedal hard. He held up his middle finger and Blunt flashed a gang sign. What a fool.

Eddie continued to drive. He would get those fuckers another day. He would enact a super hero vengeance worthy of any comic book. They'd call him Eddie Rover, or Eddie the Pain Dealer, or Ed You're Dead. Damn, he was really stoned.

It was only mid-afternoon and he had to find something to do. He drove to the west side and pulled into Elk Hill Apartments. Who the hell named this place? There weren't any elk within forty miles. His buddy James lived here. James was a year older than Eddie, and had been friends with both he and Steve. Now all he did was smoke weed, eat shrooms, play video games, and deliver pizza. That was alright with Eddie because it gave him a place to go in the afternoon. Any place other than school was alright.

Before walking in he called his mom from the mobile phone. "Hey mom. Sorry I didn't reply sooner, was in class."

"That's okay. I figured you'd call me after school. I don't recognize this number on caller ID. Did you go someplace?"

"I'm just calling you from one of the new pay phones outside. You asked me to call?"

"Yes, I was just hoping you and I could talk. Alone."

"Sure. How about I take you to dinner tonight? Just us." She was the only real family in his life. His dad lived on the east coast, but he hadn't seen him in over a year. Eddie was happy that she found Cole, that they had Carl, but he missed the way they used to be a family.

"That sounds great. How about six o'clock at the Prince?"

"See you there," he replied. The Prince was her favorite place. It's where they had taken Steve on his last birthday. They didn't know then it would be the final birthday he ever had. The food was Mediterranean, one of the only places in this city that had organic dishes, and was a popular place for middle-class families. He flipped the mobile phone shut and walked up to the apartments.

"What's up Eddie," said James as he opened the door. James was a few inches shorter than Eddie and wore his hair long, down past his shoulders. Always kept a clean shave and wore nice clothes, but he was a scrapper. Whenever he spoke he made erratic motions with his arms. He had bright blue eyes that presented an image of innocence, but these were deceptive. James had been on the wrong side of the law for longer than Eddie, had a rap sheet with more tallies than years he'd been alive, but he kept his cool and stayed hidden these days. He was in that vortex of knowing he should change, but the best he could do was to keep himself cool by the use of street prescriptions. Eddie could always tell when James was tripping on shrooms by the way his pupils seemed to move independently of each other.

"Just making the rounds. How about you?"

"Fucking killing it man. Have you played the new *Ninja Knight* game?"

"Not yet. Let's check it out." Eddie sat on the couch beside James. The place was littered with beer bottles and dirty laundry. Hanging on the wall above the television was a Samurai sword in an emerald green scabbard with a dragon head handle. He once saw James use it to chop up his shrooms. That could work, he thought, and imagined slicing it through Blunt's neck.

"Oh man, that fucker didn't even see me coming. Sliced him in two. You see that shit?"

"You're a bad ass man."

"Fuck yeah. Slicing fools is what I do. You got any weed?"

"Way ahead of you." Eddie pulled out the glass piece he got from Lynch and packed it. He took a deep pull and handed it over.

"You gonna tell me what happened, or am I left to assume you got beat up by a chick?"

"It's nothing man, just part of the game."

"Looks like more than nothing. Come on, tell me about it. You know I got your back."

"Just some shit that went down yesterday. I got it under control."

"If you say so. Probably wouldn't have happened if you were in school, instead of fucking around on the streets."

"Whatever dude. Besides, if I were in school, who the hell would keep your dumb ass company?"

"You got a point there. But I'm serious man, you've come this close to graduating, may as well finish."

"Why? So I can deliver pizza and slice fools? I got better things to do."

"Give me a break man, at least I graduated. Steve would've too, you know. That dude was smart. Must not be genetic I guess."

"You're right, he was. Do you think about him much?"

"Fuck man, that dude was like a brother to me. You both were. Are. That's why I play these games man. In my head every fool I chop up is the bastard who shot Steve."

There was a knock at the door and James started hiding his paraphernalia. "Why you so paranoid man?" said Eddie as he got up and answered the door. It was Casandra, Lynch's sister. She was tall and narrow, thin faced with nervous eyes. Hair long, straight and dark that reached down to her boney elbows. "Cassie, what are you doing here?" asked Eddie.

"Shit, that's right," said James walking to the door. "Come on in. I almost forgot you were coming."

"What are you boys doing?" she asked. "Smells like you're killing some skunk."

"You know it," James pulled out a roll of fives and ones and handed it to her.

"Here you go, this is primo stuff," she handed him the shrooms. "So tell me true James, you putting that shit on people's pizza?"

"That would be hilarious. I'm too broke to go wasting it though. You got time to stick around?"

"Not today, got a few more deliveries to make." She started to turn around, then said, "You boys know about my end of year party, right?"

"We haven't heard anything," said Eddie.

"Well shit, it's gonna be my biggest party yet. The usual crowd times ten. I'm having a couple of baby giraffes flown in. It's gonna be a fucking circus."

"Alright, we'll be there," said James.

"Cool. Catch you fools later." She walked out the door and James started to shut it.

"Actually," said Eddie, "I've gotta bolt too."

"Whatever you say bro. But seriously, we should chill again soon and talk. This is some deep shit."

"Sounds good." He gave James a bump on the shoulder and walked out.

Deep shit. James didn't know the half of it. Eddie watched him retreat into a cave after Steve died. What a waste, sitting around his little apartment eating shrooms all day. They used to have a good time, but now Eddie felt sorry for him whenever he visited.

. . .

There were still a couple hours before he had to meet his mom for dinner. Eddie did a quick inventory of his stash, and figured he could make another twelve hundred bucks on top of what he owed Lynch. Drop five hundred on a down payment for a piece, and he'd still make a little pocket cash. There were always good clients at the uptown mall, so he headed that direction.

He parked the Rover and walked inside. The arcade was some of his most reliable business. This was where most of the stoners went when they skipped class, and where many more met up after school. This dim lit room, video games, dome hockey, skeet ball, and neon lights. These young people with nothing else to do. Eddie could save them, elevate them, provide for them a greater experience. These were the mouths he fed, these were his people, and he treated them well. Eddie was known, and that was almost as good as the easy money. Maybe better.

His pockets were loaded with cash when he walked out of the arcade. He had one more delivery, then the stash was sold, save for the bag he kept for himself. He always kept enough for himself at the end of the day. The mall concourse was full now and Eddie felt like he was the only one here who mattered. He watched them pass – young girls dressed in high fashion, families with strollers and department store bags, old people shuffling along in no rush – they all passed by at slow speed. It seemed like they were watching him, not as spies, but as paparazzi. Watching him so they could tell their friends who they saw at the mall. He was known, and his head was high.

Stephanie worked in the book store at the other end of the mall. Stephanie was what the kids called Grunge, and she smoked a lot of weed. She was the first girl Eddie ever kissed, the first bare ass he ever felt in the palm of his hand. This gave him confidence amongst his peers, as she was two years older than him. That soft cool skin is what he thought of alone in his room many nights. A hit of the weed and the memory of her became tangible. They had a good thing for a while, but he lost interest in her when she started getting into heavier drugs. Heavy drugs weren't for him, but they still ran in the same circles, with some of the same crowds, and she was a good client. Plus, they had an arrangement.

Eddie walked into the book store and saw Stephanie behind the counter helping a customer. She saw him and discreetly rubbed her left breast, slow circles around the nipple. This was the signal that she was open for business. He walked down the aisle and found the Staff Picks section. Under Stephanie's name was *Flappers and Philosophers* by F. Scott Fitzgerald, *The Waves*, by Virginia Woolf, and *Inherent Vice* by Thomas Pynchon. Eddie thought her selections to be generic, but this didn't matter. He leaned the two copies of *Inherent Vice* forward and placed an eighth-ounce on the shelf behind them. Nobody ever picked up the Staff Picks.

Eddie enjoyed reading, but didn't share this fact with many people. He had a reputation to keep, and being a book geek might change their minds about him. He often stayed in his bedroom for an entire night devouring pages from classic literature and pulling hits from his bowl. Books were so much simpler than real life. These characters were defined by a linear purpose, and they either won or lost, it was that simple. It was never that simple in his life. It was never clear if he was winning or losing, he only knew the game continued. It continued until he died.

Eddie perused the aisles until there were no customers in line, and then he laid a copy of *Candide* by Voltaire on the counter. Stephanie picked it up and said, "Are you getting into gardening?"

"Why would I do that?" he replied.

"I guess you've never read this book. I think you'll like it."

"If I already read it, I'd have no reason to buy it."

"Well, you're not exactly buying it."

"That's not true. Weed is money in my world. It's green currency."

She voided the sale and put the book in a bag. "Did you hear about Cassie's grad party?"

"Yeah, just bumped into Cass. Sounds like it will be crazy."

"I'm so excited. I heard she's gonna have a buffet of coke. Maybe I can get you to take some with me."

"That's not my game, you know it."

"Whatever. It will expand your mind." She touched his bruised eye, "I do crazy things on coke."

"I'm sure you do." He pulled away and said, "I need to be some place. See you around."

"Think about what I said."

Eddie got in the Rover and blasted the radio. Hard drugs weren't for him. He remembered a presentation by the guidance counselor at school who said marijuana was a gateway drug. For Eddie it was a gateway, but not to harder shit. It was a gateway to comprehension. Getting stoned was the only way he could make sense of anything. Lots of his friends were into shrooms or coke or E, but he always thought they looked ridiculous. If he wanted to look ridiculous, he'd drink. Getting drunk worked pretty good for that.

Cops were cracking down on the dealers of the hard shit. Coke, shrooms, and E had taken a foothold in their city, and took some of the law enforcement attention away from weed. Everybody smoked weed, and everybody had it. Eddie hid in that plain sight. He knew there was more money in the hard shit, but he was making good cash selling weed and getting his smoke for free. Plus, he was known.

. . .

The Prince was already packed when he arrived fifteen minutes early. He put in their name and started thumbing through *Candide* while he waited. This was a small book and he'd likely finish it tonight. "His countenance was a true picture of his soul."

"Eddie, you're here early." His mom sat down at the waiting bench.

"This place is busy, but our name should be next."

"Your eye looks horrible. Are you ready to tell me what happened?"

"It's nothing mom. It will heal in no time."

"Well, if you don't want to talk about that. What are you reading?"

"Just some old book."

"Is it for Mister Bonnell's class?"

"I doubt it."

"What do you mean? Didn't you go to class today?"

"Yes, of course. I just doubt he would assign a book like this."

"Young for two," announced the hostess. "Right this way."

Eddie watched his mom as they followed the hostess. He was sixteen when she married Cole, it had only been three years since Steve died and barely more than a year since his dad left. He resented that she took on Cole's last name – Clemens. Cole asked her to convince Eddie to share their last name so they could be a family, but Eddie refused. He said he had always been Eddie Young, and used the excuse of not wanting to change all his identifications and have to go through the hassle of telling his friends his new name. But his mom knew that wasn't the real reason. She understood her son, better than he would ever know, and she knew he was a sentimentalist. He kept his last name because that was Steve's last name. It was that simple. It was that complex.

They were seated at a small booth in the corner. Above them hung a painting reprint of a village by the sea, with stucco houses painted beige and orange. Across the blue and white water was a mountain range. "Do you know that artist?" asked his mom.

Eddie looked up at the bright colors and distorted landscape. "Should I?"

"Your brother would have. He always wanted to visit Greece. Remember that coffee table book he had at the ranch? With all those full color pictures of the Mediterranean, its history and culture." She looked away from the image and smiled.

"He was a daydreamer," said Eddie.

"I miss him too, you know." She wiped a tear from her cheek.

"Why don't you ever visit him then?"

She put her face in her hands a moment and then looked up, "I see him every day. He is twenty-one now and so mature. He manages a fly fishing shop. You remember how good he was at tying flies? He was an artist."

"I see him too, mom. But I see the way he was before, when we were kids."

"You remember the tree fort he built? Of course you do. He was so proud of it. He wanted to make that a store front to sell his fly fishing lures. You're right, he was always a dreamer."

"I think when we moved to the city he missed that tree fort almost as much as the trout stream."

"This city was never good for him. It wasn't good for any of us." She looked off across the room. "But we had to sell the ranch, you understand that. Once your dad got the job offer here in the city, that was the only way we could make enough money. He wanted you both to go to college, something he never could afford working the ranch."

"I wish we could've just stayed. I don't care about college. I miss the country, the ranch, the wild animals, the fishing."

"I know you do. I know it's been hard. We need to make the best of what we've got. If you work hard you can give yourself whatever life you want in the future."

"Are you ready to order?" asked the waitress.

"Yes," said Eddie. "Can we get organic Moussaka for my mom, and I would like the Souvlaki."

"Absolutely."

"Thanks." His mom got the Moussaka ever since they put it on the organic menu, and he liked ordering for her. "You don't need to worry about me mom, I've got everything under control."

"I know you think you do, Eddie, but I am worried. Skipping school and letting your grades slip is just the beginning. What's going to happen if you don't graduate?"

"I'm resourceful, I can find a job."

"Are you just going to load UPS trucks the rest of your life?"

"Who knows. Why does it matter?"

"I want something more for you Eddie. You deserve better. But if you don't work for it, nobody's going to give it to you."

"And you think if I pass some ridiculous classes, maybe keep a journal, that will give me a better chance?"

"Yes, I do. I know you don't see it now. I want you to do something. I think it will help."

"What's that?"

"I want you to fly out and spend a couple days with your dad."

"What?"

"I know he hasn't been there for you lately, but he does love you. Cole tries to give you direction, and I understand it's difficult for you to take him seriously. I think spending time with a grown man will be good."

"Have you asked him about this?"

"No. You know we haven't spoken in almost two years since he moved east. He left us, Eddie. And while I don't forgive him for that, I understand why. He needed to separate himself from the bad memories here."

"Don't let him off the hook that easy. He hasn't even contacted me in almost a year. If I had a son who was a senior in high school, I would want to know what's going on with him."

"He has his reasons, even if we don't fully understand them. That's why it will be your responsibility to contact him and make arrangements. I have spoken to Cole and he's agreed to pay for your airfare. Do you have your father's phone number?"

"Yes, assuming it's still the same."

"Good. So will you contact him?"

"I don't know. Who says he even wants me to visit?"

"I'm sure he will. He only stopped loving me, not you. After Steve died it was as if our connection was broken. Steve was our firstborn, he's part of the reason we got married, and without him …"

"I know mom. I'm not stupid. Steve was your favorite, I get it."

"Eddie, it's not like that. The firstborn is the one that taught us to be a family, and when he died your father and I could no longer even communicate. Everything between us for eighteen years had been based on the existence of Steve, and now that connection was gone. We had to move on, both of us."

"So you want me to record a journal and visit my father. This is great."

"Will you do it?"

Eddie looked up at the painting on the wall. The placard said it was a limited reprint originally painted by Paul Cezanne. Steve would've known that. "Yes, mom, I can do that."

"Good. Thanks. Are you coming home after dinner?"

"Yes. May as well."

Eddie watched his mom eat. She looked so happy here with him, but he sensed it was an illusion, or a masquerade. How could she be happy with all the shit she's been through? Maybe a new husband and a new son completely reset everything. That was all she needed in life, a man to hold her and a child she could hold. It seemed quite primordial to Eddie, which he was okay with, but he wasn't okay with being the outsider. He felt farther away and more alone than ever. He wondered if this was what the start of manhood felt like, a deep sense of separation from what he had always known and trusted.

"How was everything?" asked the waitress.

"Oh it was fabulous," replied his mom.

"Can we get the bill please?" asked Eddie.

"Eddie, let me take care of this one."

"That's alright mom, I've got it. This is my treat."

. . .

When they returned home, Cole had already put Carl to bed. Eddie snuck in and watched him sleep. Carl was really into dinosaurs. He wasn't talking yet, but whenever they held one in front of his face his eyes lit up. Eddie looked down at this tiny little human wrapped in a dino blanket. They were too far apart in age to ever be close, at least not close the way he had been with Steve. This made him feel like a stranger, or at best a distant relative. Seventeen years apart, some of Eddie's classmates had kids closer in age. Even with this separation, he knew some day Carl would learn about him, would hear rumors in school or on the streets. Eddie was known, but he didn't want his family to know why. He sat on the chair by the nightlight and read all 84 pages of *Candide*.

"Want to watch a movie with us?" asked his mom when he walked out of Carl's room.

"What are you watching?"

"Good Will Hunting."

"Ha. Nice try mom. I'm probably just going to read tonight."

Eddie walked into the den and over to the bookshelf. He thumbed through the books, the yellowing pages, the coffee stains, the wine stains, and tobacco stains. Time stains. He thumbed through them all and felt the past moving around him. Books were the past and they never changed. Moments trapped and people immortalized. He thumbed through the pages but never read a word, he only looked at the stains.

APRIL 1999

SUN	MON	TUE	WED	THU	FRI	SAT
				~~1~~	~~2~~	~~3~~
~~4~~	~~5~~	~~6~~	~~7~~	~~8~~	~~9~~	~~10~~
~~11~~	~~12~~	~~13~~	~~14~~	~~15~~	~~16~~	~~17~~
~~18~~	~~19~~	~~20~~	~~21~~	22	23	24
25	26	27	28	29	30	

He packed the glass piece full and sat up in bed. A long deep pull made his lungs feel crisp. He exhaled slowly through the nostrils, felt it tingle, and his thoughts grew higher. He looked at the copy of *Candide* on his nightstand, and opened it up to a page he marked: "We must cultivate our garden." Today, that's exactly what he would do.

Eddie walked upstairs and saw his mom wiping the kitchen counter and Carl sitting in his highchair. "Good morning mom. Is Carl enjoying his breakfast?"

"He sure is. They've got organic oatmeal at the super market now." She turned and smiled at him. "Did you have company last night?"

"No. Why?" He sat down at the table and put his hand gently on Carl's head.

"I heard someone knocking on the door around midnight. I figured it was a friend of yours."

"That's strange. I didn't hear anything."

"Hmm, maybe it was the wrong house."

Now Eddie's head spun, but he tried to hide it as he sat at the table. Who the fuck would come knocking at midnight? He had a strict rule never to deal from their house, and everybody knew it. If he found out it was one of his clients jonesing for a midnight hit, he'd cut that fucker off for good. "Did Carl sleep alright?"

"Didn't hear him all night. I woke up several times to check on him because I was worried, but he was sound asleep in dreams."

"Alright, well I better get going. Don't want to be late." He stood up and kissed his mom on the forehead. "I work tonight so don't expect me home early."

Eddie got in the Rover and started to drive. The sunrise was pushing shadows across the pavement. He kept the stereo down and paid attention to his neighborhood. There were mini vans, trampolines, metal-framed deer, automatic sprinklers and houses with red shingled roofs that had chimneys connected to gas powered fireplaces. This was an artificial world, but nobody seemed to care. Maybe he shouldn't care either. Perhaps he was an artificial man. He felt mechanical in this programmed routine. Stop lights and honking horns. Coffee shops with lines around the block. Fast food joints with lines even longer. Nobody knew what the fuck they were doing. Wake up each day and guess the best that they could. Let the routine guide them. At a red light he looked east and saw the sun cresting over the mountains. A thin blue film of clouds hung there and he knew the air must be cool. It would also be fresh, almost sweet on the tongue, loaded with aromas from pine trees and cobble stone streams.

Lynch seemed pissed yesterday when he showed up early, so today he'd kill some time before heading over. He needed to pay up and get a new stash. He also wanted to see what kind of piece Lynch had for him. It would likely be something big and shiny and fully automatic. A gun any gangster would be proud to use for blasting fools.

With nothing better to do, he pulled into the parking lot at school. Maybe he'd go to class, just the first one, then see Lynch after. He saw Alex approaching and rolled down the window. "What's happening boy?"

"Oh you know, just need something to try and take my mind off these damn allergies." His eyes were swollen, red, and teary.

"Sorry dude, but I'm dry until lunch hour."

"Shit, really?" He sneezed and wiped his nose with the handkerchief from his pocket. "You got nothing?"

"I didn't say that. Jump on in and we can smoke a quick one."

They rolled up the windows and packed the bowl. Alex was a mess, he always looked like one. Damn kid was allergic to oxygen and sunlight, that's what he said. He looked more stoned than Eddie, with those puffy red eyes and bloodless complexion. Eddie kept the stereo down, he didn't want any attention today, at least not until he got a new stash.

"What's up with the radio, why don't you crank that fucker up?"

"Not right now man, just trying to chill a while."

"Shit, that's the best damn stereo in town. I'd keep it cranked all day."

"Typically do." He pulled in a hit and puffed out a cloud of smoke that suspended between him and Alex.

"You hear about Cassie's party?" asked Alex, after sniffling and making frog-like noises in his throat.

"Shit, graduation is more than a month away and all anyone's talking about is her party. That chick doesn't even go to school. Don't you think it's strange that she's the one throwing a big grad party?"

"Yeah, maybe, but she knows everyone. It's gonna be awesome."

Eddie looked out the window. "Could be," he replied. Shit, he didn't even know if he was going to graduate. Two more months of sitting in a classroom was an eternity. Time began to weigh down on him, compress him, when it should do the opposite. Time was supposed to open up and expand him. Wasn't that what they said, that the future was full of opportunities? The world was his oyster, and all that shit.

"You going to class today?" asked Alex.

"Thought about it." He looked towards the front door, the worn push bar and flaking orange paint. Vanya was walking towards the entrance, alone again. "Actually, yes, let's get in there." He shoved the pipe into the ash tray and popped out of the door without grabbing his bag, then started jogging towards her. There were no exact words in his mind, he just knew he had to talk to her. "Vanya," he yelled from fifty feet. She stopped and looked his direction. Damn, there was something fine in the way she stood so straight and her hair followed perfectly down the contour of her back. "Hang on a sec."

He got closer to her and then saw Darnell from the corner of his eye. Fuck, he didn't want her to see what was about to happen. "Yes?" she said looking right at him. She held a thick book over her chest and wore a long dress.

"I just wanted to say hi. I'll catch you later." She cocked her head slightly and continued inside.

"Eddie, I've been looking all over for you," said Darnell.

"What the fuck man. I should kick your ass right here."

"I know, I know. But for real dog, I didn't know they were gonna jack you. That shit was fucked up."

"You're damn right it was. You're the one who brought me there. Why'd you do that if you knew they were into jacking people?"

"Shit dog, you asked if I knew any dealers. I didn't know that was gonna go down. But there's more. I heard he's looking for you. I saw Gunner yesterday and he said you were creeping on Blunt's place. You better watch yourself dog, for real."

"What's it to you?"

"Shit dog, just letting you know."

"Blunt?" asked Alex, with a surprised look on his face. He turned towards Darnell, "As in *Big Bad Blunt*?"

"That's my cuz and you don't want to fuck with him. And if you fuck with me you're fucking with him." Darnell walked past them and into the building.

Eddie looked at Alex, "You know that guy? His cousin."

"I know *of* him. There was a full article about him in the paper a year or so ago. Some reporter was doing a piece on Bad Town, trying to figure out if it's really as bad as they say. They used Blunt as a case study. Called him Big Bad Blunt."

"Yeah, so? That doesn't mean shit. So he had five seconds of fame. Big deal."

"Man, if I remember correctly," Alex's eyes drifted off and looked past Eddie, "he's been built the hard way by those streets. When Blunt was a kid, like fifteen or something, his mom was murdered in their home by some crackheads. When his dad found out who did it, he went all fucking mass murderer on them. Found out where they lived and shot seven of those fuckers dead. But that wasn't enough. After they'd all been shot to hell, he cut them up into pieces and then threw their parts all around the front yard. Cops found him just sitting on the rocking chair in the yard with body parts all round. Talk about fucking creepy shit."

"I remember hearing about it. Happened when I still lived out in

the country, but it made all the papers back then. What'd they call him? It was some goofy sounding name."

"The Body Soup Banger. Yep. He was executed a little over a year ago. Guess that's why they featured Blunt in the story. Apparently Blunt's been living alone in that house ever since, raising himself on the streets since the age of fifteen." Alex turned his head and sneezed three times. "Been getting into bad shit ever since. You remember that scar on his face? The one across his left eye."

"Yeah. So?"

"SWAT team raided him. But instead of cooperating or whatever, he rushed them. That article had a quote from him bragging about knocking out one dude before another one smashed his face in with the butt end of their rifle. Guy's fucking crazy, Eddie."

"Hmm." Eddie turned his head away from Alex and looked down the long brick wall. He thought about what his mom said this morning, about hearing a knock on the door at midnight. There's no way Blunt knew where he lived. Unless somebody told him. Fuck. He had to get over to Lynch, get a piece. Nobody was going to threaten his family. He turned around and got in the Rover. School would still be here tomorrow.

. . .

Lynch opened the door, and the first thing he said was, "You got my money?"

"You gonna let me in first?" Eddie walked past him and straight into the kitchen. He dug into his cargo pocket and pulled out a wad of cash. "This covers the stash from yesterday, plus a down payment for another pound. I also need the piece."

"Just slow down there Rambo. Let me count this shit. Looks cool." Lynch stuffed the cash in the pocket of his baggy sweatpants. "I can flip you another pound, but you're gonna have to wait for the piece. Shit's been hot right now."

"Fuck, man. You said I'd get it today. You've got to have something for me."

"You're a hard ass, Eddie. I like that about you. Tell ya what, give me the cash, and I'll get you one ordered. May take a few days, but you'll get it."

Eddie handed him another roll. "That's five hundred dollars. I can give you more if needed. I want something big."

"You'll get it." Lynch stuffed the roll in his other pocket. "Scooby will meet you in the lobby."

"Cool. Another thing, know where I can score a fake ID?"

"Shit fool, you always want something." Lynch ran his hand through his long ponytail. "I don't mess with that nonsense, but I know a guy. He's legit, used to work at the courthouse or some shit. Now he's a librarian. I can make a call. Will text you details."

"Alright, bet." Eddie turned towards the door.

"Eddie, you pay me for the weed tomorrow."

"Yep." He continued out the door, met Scooby in the lobby, then hopped in the Rover. The streets were loud and busy. This was the way streets must always be, in every city, he thought. This is what he knew now, that people lived in their cars, and drove from event to event. Whatever the place of work or type of roof over their head, they lived at a slow crawl on four wheels. It didn't matter a damn if they had a diploma or street training, a bank account or cash under the mattress, a family or alone, this was where they ended, this was the divine and demonic manifestation of civilizations progress.

There was no freedom here. Not for Eddie, and not for these strangers. One hand on the steering wheel and an extra-large soda in the other. The great discoverers, entrepreneurs, inventors, past and present, is this what they wanted? Progress had always been in the name of simplification, of tricks to make survival easier, but he

watched them in passing or at a stop light, and he thought this must be the most difficult time in history. Nothing had changed in the minds of men since *Candide's* time. Nothing had changed except new ways to destroy each other. New ways to destroy oneself. He would take cold nights and near starvation, rival clans and wild animals, feast and famine, over this intoxication, this social deprivation of knowing too much and living too easy. There was no strength here and he was part of the weakness. Had it ever been another way? Lightspeed in his lifetime were the changes. The rapidity of progress and he saw a bleeding world. There was nowhere to look, nowhere to go, the streets were a maze, a rollercoaster, a torrent that only gained momentum, never relief. He was too small to fix it, he was only a spectator, perhaps like everyone else, and this rollercoaster was gaining speed.

The stereo blasted and Eddie pulled a hit. He pulled into the school parking lot and waited for lunch hour. He had to do business, that was the only reason to push ahead, to move forward, to walk through each day. This fast-paced world and he was a hustler. Class was still in session and nobody was around. His mind became full, rambling, tumbling, falling like rain over a mountain. His thoughts moved fast, he held them all briefly, and wanted more. He wanted to remember, to hold each feeling and idea forever. He opened his backpack and pulled out a pen and notepad. Why the fuck not?

He held pen to his face and wanted to release his mind. There was too much, it was all so confusing, incomprehensible as a single unit. There was Steve, Carl, his mom, Cole, his boys, Lynch, the party, Blunt–that bastard, Vanya–that girl, strangers, revenge and lies and love and dice on cobblestones. It all rolled together and he couldn't separate each as a single thought. There was more, so much more, the details, the changes, the pain, the hope, it all tied together, wound so tightly, single braids on a thick rope, and he was hanging. He couldn't unravel the words and push the ink down on paper. Instead he waited, and pulled another hit from the bowl.

He waited until the crowds emerged from the orange and flaking doors, until the life-pulse and energy of youth, of others like him but so different, filled in the spaces around him. He rolled down his window and business was good. He felt high, not only from the weed, but from being known, needed, admired. He stepped out of the Rover and joined a crowd of peers passing a joint hidden behind their cuffed hands. These were his people, he had known most of them for several years, since they were young. Or younger. He was still young, but that wasn't his fault. His experiences were grown, and the counting of age, the tally of years, could not define them.

How many of these kids would remain, be a part of his life, and continue in the same circle after the finality of graduation? Not many, or even less. He thought about his mom, her solitary life raising her children, the man she spent evenings with, but few friends. That seemed to be the epitome of adulthood, the grand future that waited for them all. But here they were standing in a circle getting stoned and thinking of nothing further than tonight. He would enjoy this now, as they were, as they never would be again.

Eddie followed the kids into school and attended class, he attended every class for the rest of that day. He listened to the teachers, and the quieter remarks of the students. He tried to pay attention, even took notes, but his mind wandered. There were things happening in this city and no text book spoke of them. There were lessons that could never be learned without walking through the shadows and cutting through alleys. He could never believe it unless touched with his fingers and breathed through his lungs.

"What are you doing after this?" asked Scott as they walked out the building.

"No plans. You?"

"Sounds like a bunch of people are going down to the river park. You should be able to sell some shit, if nothing else."

"I'm game. Couple things I need to do first, then will see you there."

Eddie hopped in the Rover and checked his phone. There was a text from Lynch. He read it from the small digital screen. "Go to the library at 4. Old dude with grey hair and a goatee. His name's Chuck. He'll hook you up."

The library was not what he thought libraries should be. There were only a few people reading books, or looking studious. There were more people in the DVD aisle than searching for books. Shady looking people sat at the computers taking advantage of free high-speed dial-up internet. He found the man who fit the description. "Chuck?"

"Yes," the man replied.

"Lynch sent me."

"Of course. Follow me." They walked into a back office and down a dark set of stairs. It was musty, smelled a little like old furniture and wet dogs. There were piles of books stacked on the cement floor in no apparent order. In the far corner was a steel desk beside a white wall. "Stand over there," directed Chuck.

Eddie stood in front of the white wall and Chuck snapped a picture with a digital camera. "That eye of yours is pretty ugly, but don't worry, I can use my Photoshop program to correct it. What's your name?"

"Eddie."

"Is that your real name?"

"Yes."

"What name do you want on the ID?"

"Shit, I don't know. Does it matter?"

"I will create one for you. Payment is due now. I will have it ready next week."

"Next week? Any way to get it sooner?"

"You can pay an extra fifty for rush service."

"Fine." Eddie pulled the cash from his pocket. "I need it to say I'm at least twenty-one."

"Kid, I can make you as old as you want. Stop by tomorrow and pick it up."

Eddie walked upstairs and towards the door. There she was, Vanya, sitting at a desk with several books laid out before her. He hid for a moment behind a nearby shelf. She was consumed, fully engrossed in whatever she was working on. He pushed the nerves all the way down, from the uncertainty of thoughts, through the rapidity of breath, past the hollowness of knees, and out through steadfast feet. He approached her desk and said, "Are you following me?"

"Excuse me?"

"Never mind. I just didn't expect to see you here. What are you working on?"

"Political Science. I find it fascinating. Aren't you in that class?"

"Yep, well, supposed to be. I haven't made it in a little while."

"I've heard about you. If what I've heard is true, I find it odd to see you here."

"I don't know what you've heard, but I like books. I'm no stranger to a library. Though, it's usually my own."

She looked at him with deep brown eyes. Darker than pine bark in the evening. Provoking, yet restrained. He imagined she didn't have much of a social life, but thought about getting one. Everybody needed a social life, even if they weren't any good at it. Hers would be acquired through the passages of fables. Eddie imagined she only knew about life what she read in books. There were certainly less accurate ways to learn about the world. All he could think to ask was, "So, how do you like the new school?"

"It's not that new. I started here in January. It's much more crowded than my previous school. But I'm no stranger to crowds."

"I know what you mean. If you ever want someone to show you around, I mean, maybe not school, but the town, let me know."

"Sure. But I'm usually pretty busy with homework. And the only time I come to town anymore is for school."

"And the library?"

"I wait here for my dad to pick me up. We live out of town a ways."

"That sounds nice. Maybe I'll see you tomorrow."

"You mean if you come to class?"

Eddie forced a laugh but didn't reply. He nodded his head and walked out the door. There was something about that girl, mysterious and yet familiar. He wanted desperately to touch her hair, to confirm if it was as soft as it looked. He had never thought about a girl's hair this much.

. . .

It was still light out when he got to Lost Horse River Park. There were a lot of cars and people, mostly families with younger children, and he knew the group he was looking for would be hiding up in the woods. This wasn't a forest, but several acres of trees nestled in the city provided plenty of space to do what they weren't supposed to do, and that was the reason they came. It wasn't a secret place, youth from all walks of life met here, smoked bongs beside a fire, shot-gunned beer, kissed girls behind the bushes, and got in fist fights. He filled a backpack with the rest of his stash, it would be easy to sell it all here, and he kept a small bag in the Rover for later.

Before walking into the trees, Eddie stopped beside the river. The water was wide, deep, dark, and dirty from the miles of city and prairie upstream. It was moving fast with spring runoff, hurtling large trees downstream. He knew this river at its source in the mountains where it was steep, clear, and shallow enough to wade across. Up there the only deep spots were around bends and that was where the larger trout hid. Mountain trout were the best. Steve had taught him how to drift a stonefly nymph, let it follow a natural course, and watch for a subtle strike.

There were several people fishing from shore where there was a deep eddy protected from the torrent. It looked like they were casting worms, marshmallows, and corn. These murky waters held catfish, carp, and perhaps other fish, but no trout. These waters were of no interest to Eddie, and as he turned to walk away, he thought about how immensely the river changed in a relatively short distance, a distance short enough that he could see from this spot the mountains where it sprang from the rocks, collected from the snowmelt, and was always pristine. Those mountains weren't far away, but it had been a long time since he held a slippery trout in his hands.

The footpath was narrow as it cut through the trees, and when he came to the clearing there were over fifty people. The park maintenance crew had given up on trying to keep this place clean, and so some of the regulars dug a deep pit and instructed everyone to throw their beer cans and bottles there. This excited the drunken youth, and they made spectacular and grandiose displays, making announcements such as, "Three seconds left for a Hail Mary pass," or "Approaching the target and missiles locked on!" It was expected for you to cheer if they hit the pit, or boo and ridicule if they missed.

"Eddie!" announced Scott from the crowd. He felt like every eye amongst them turned his direction. Yes, he had arrived. He smiled and held his backpack up high. People swarmed around him, reaching out, announcing their order. He was a god damn rock star. He broke off a large cut and gave it to Scott with instructions to sell it on the other side of the clearing. Scott was excited to do this, and the crowd separated. The stash moved quick, and Eddie gave Scott fifty bucks for his work.

"That was a rush," said Scott as they lit up a joint. "The only time I get attention like that is on the rink."

Eddie pulled in a hit. He had gone to a couple hockey games, watched Scott dangle the puck around opponents, fire slapshots and make laser sharp passes. He had been featured in their local paper more than once. Rumor had it he was being scouted by some of the top colleges in the country. This kid was going places, maybe the pros, but Eddie didn't envy him. Scott was too clean. Sure he smoked some weed, hung out with Eddie for street cred, but he lacked the rough edges, only wore name brand clothing, couldn't tell you anything about books other than what he learned in Bonnell's class, and, as far as Eddie knew, he never had a black eye. Eddie had his reasons for keeping Scott around; mostly because Scott reminded him of what he would have been if Steve never died and his family never split up. Pristine like a mountain stream. Known, but for a different reason. This was a source of great wonder in his young mind, the influence of time, the uncontrollable and often imperceptible changes. The waves and the winds. The great divergence and a course unknown.

The crowd circled and swayed and shifted. A group of dudes were shadow boxing near the fire. This was a game they played meant to demonstrate their courage and agility, swinging fists but never making contact. It was for display only, like the showy feathers of a Lady Amherst pheasant, but it wasn't working to gain the attention of the girls, who were mostly consumed with taking pictures of each other with a wind-up disposable camera.

Someone brought a potato rocket made from PVC, and was launching potatoes into the sky. A Sony boombox was blasting Dr. Dre's album *The Chronic* and a group was dancing near the fire. Eddie stood alone on the far side of the clearing and watched. He could be the socialite when business was good, but was just as comfortable outside of the circle.

The sky grew dark but the stars remained hidden behind the city light. The light was a dome, they lived in a terrarium, and after dark, there was nothing else, nothing to be seen beyond the yellow haze. The fire was burning larger now, and the people, drunk and stoned, maybe worse, were getting louder. Their voices carried themes of happiness, drunkenness, and courage. They were immortal and above any law or judgement. There were no concerns for who was worrying about them, or what their curfew was, or if this was a night they'd remember on some lonely night in the distant future. Then a spotlight hit the crowd and a voice announced, "This is the police, everyone stay where you are!"

That's all the crowd needed to run as fast as their intoxicated legs could carry them. They dispersed in a frenzy through the surrounding trees. Some of them fell and were promptly swept up by the cops. Eddie and Scott paused inside the tree line and watched. There were at least fifteen cops now, and those who weren't busy with one of the fallen crowd were making their way into the trees. Eddie picked up a rock and chucked it at a cop who he hit in the leg. The flashlight quickly turned in his direction, so he and Scott fled deeper into the trees.

They paused behind another tree and looked back to see three flashlights gaining on them. "Butch and Sundance baby," said Eddie as they turned into the darkness.

"Wait, didn't they get killed?" said Scott as he tried to catch up. Then, in the darkness of thick trees, Scott tripped on a twisted root and fell to the ground. "Shit, Eddie!"

Eddie turned and saw Scott tangled on the ground. The flashlights were getting closer, and he knew Scott wouldn't make it. There wasn't much time to get away, so he turned back to help. "My fucking shoe's stuck," said Scott. The two worked together and pulled so hard Scott's foot came right out of the shoe. No sooner than they got on their feet, Scott was tackled by the first cop. Eddie broke free from another and continued to run. He looked back and saw Scott being held by two cops, and the third was heading his direction. He ran until the trees cleared and he stood at the edge of the river. Shit, he went the wrong way. The flashlight still followed, so he dove into the raging water and swam to the other side. The current was fast, the deep weight of it carried him downstream, until he finally emerged on the far side. The cop wasn't following him, but what the fuck was he going to do now? Plus, they got Scott. Shit, what a night.

He stood on the shore wet and cold, and reached into his pocket for the stash. He packed the wet weed into the bowl but couldn't get it to take flame. Fuck. He crouched down beside a bush along the river and watched. The river was wide, but from this spot he could see the parking lot, the lights, and the cops loading kids into their patrol cars. One of them was surely Scott, but he couldn't tell. All he could think was that nobody better mention his name.

Eddie took the long walk upstream to the next bridge, and back to the park. It was all clear now, save for the cars driven by the ones who had been arrested. He hopped in the Rover and sent a message to Scott's pager, "911-???." It was a good thing he left a bag under his seat, because everything in his pockets was drenched. He loaded a bowl and smoked while driving. There was still no reply from Scott when he pulled in the driveway at home.

APRIL 1999

SUN	MON	TUE	WED	THU	FRI	SAT
				~~1~~	~~2~~	~~3~~
~~4~~	~~5~~	~~6~~	~~7~~	~~8~~	~~9~~	~~10~~
~~11~~	~~12~~	~~13~~	~~14~~	~~15~~	~~16~~	~~17~~
~~18~~	~~19~~	~~20~~	~~21~~	~~22~~	23	24
25	26	27	28	29	30	

First thing he did was put a flame to the weed, and then looked at his mobile phone and pager. No new messages. Shit, what happened to Scott? He sent him another message but got no reply. He packed the bowl again and pulled another hit. He couldn't remember if Scott had any weed on him when they ran. Surely one of the arrested kids was holding. What would they tell the cops?

Eddie was in a rush to get out the door, he had to get to school, talk to someone, anyone that could give him details. His mom was in Carl's bedroom, which was perfect because he could sneak out quick. Then he heard her say, "Eddie, can you come in here a minute?" Shit.

"I'm in a rush mom, supposed to meet with a study group before class." Sometimes he didn't even know where these lies came from.

They manifested as a predestined script in his head. All he had to do was act the part.

"It'll just take a sec."

Eddie sighed out loud and turned around. His mom was examining the contents of a heavy diaper. "Can you hand me the wipes from over there," she said as he entered.

He handed them to her. "Is that all you wanted?"

"No. I didn't see you last night. We were supposed to talk about you visiting your dad."

"Sorry mom, I thought you knew I had to work."

"I know. I just thought I'd see you. Anyway, we got your plane ticket for tomorrow."

"Mom, I never even agreed to go. Besides, I haven't called dad yet. Can't this wait until next week?" There was too much going on, he couldn't leave.

"Just call him today, okay. I'm sure he'll be happy to see you."

"Fine." The quickest way out the door was to agree with her. He popped in the Rover and blasted the music loud all the way to school. There was a crowd of kids standing in the far corner of the parking lot, and he knew what was happening. The events from last night would be the talk of school. He pulled up next to them, not even in a parking spot, and jumped out with the music still blasting.

Scott was standing near the center of the crowd but acted like he didn't see Eddie. "Scott, what the fuck happened?" Scott looked at him but not directly.

"Shit man, I got arrested."

"Obviously. What'd they do?"

"Fuck dude, they took my fingerprints, mugshot, and kept me in a holding cell until my parents got me. They called my fucking parents."

"Shit. Did they find anything on you?"

"I had a little bit, plus my papers. Now my parents know. My dad was so fucking pissed."

"Damn, that sucks. What'd you tell them?"

"I said it was my first time. Bad luck. I wasn't going to do it again. He didn't believe me. Said if the scouts found out I'd lose my scholarship."

"Not your parents, the cops. What'd you tell them?"

Scott looked away and replied, "I didn't tell them shit. Who do you think I am?"

"That's my boy. And don't worry about the scouts, there's nobody better than you. Criminal record or not."

Eddie jumped back in the Rover and pulled out of there. Everything would be alright, so long as nobody else talked. Maybe he should lay low for a while, take a break from dealing. Visiting his dad started to sound like a good idea. Then he got a text from Lynch. "I got business this morning. Scooby will have your stash. Bring my money." Fuck. May as well load up, just keep it quiet for a few days.

After paying Scooby and getting his new stash, he sat in the Rover at the Casino. Lynch was big time, in more than just the drug game. He was second oldest in the family that owned this place. They were fucking loaded. So loaded that every relative was given twenty-thousand bucks a month once they turned sixteen. Fifty-thousand when they turned eighteen. Lynch didn't have to sell drugs, he could just coast, get high, shoot shit if he felt like it. Eddie figured he liked being known. They knew all kinds of people owning a casino, most of them bad. He figured they had connections for all kinds of shit, and since they didn't have to work, they played the dope game. Maybe it was their way of saying fuck the man. Who knows. Eddie wasn't too good at figuring people out. They were all a damn mystery.

When Eddie arrived at the library, Chuck waved him downstairs again. Eddie followed, but they stopped halfway down the steps. "Here you go kid. Or should I say, Edward Abbey." What the fuck. Leave it to a damn librarian to use the name of a famous author. Shithead. Oh well, the places he would use this, nobody was likely to know who that was. "Your name's still Ed, just better."

Edward Abbey, twenty-three years old, from some town he never heard of before. Eddie went back upstairs and sat at a computer. He memorized the ID, the license number, and researched the town he was supposed to be from. Population just shy of ten-thousand, out in the high plains somewhere. Their claim to fame was an abandoned oil rig, supposedly the first of its kind and the first one to draw oil from this state. Sounded like a damn boring place, he could probably sell a shitload of weed there.

It was still early, so he dug in his wallet for his dads phone number. It rang seven times, and just as he was about to hang up, "This is Dennis Young."

Eddie stood up, surprised to hear his dads voice. "Dad, how are things? Haven't heard from you in a while." He started pacing around the library.

"Eddie? Hey. Surprised to hear you call. I didn't recognize the number. Is everything okay?"

"Everything is fine, dad. What are you doing tomorrow?"

"Tomorrow? Why, what's going on?"

"Mom thinks I should visit this weekend. I know it's short notice."

"Your mom thinks you should visit? Why, are you in trouble?"

"Everything is fine dad. I thought maybe I'd check out some colleges while there, you know, just walk around the campus or something. Can you pick me up at the airport tomorrow morning?"

The phone went silent. Eddie waited, trying to imagine his dad's face. It had been nearly a year since they talked and almost two years since he saw the old man.

"I can pick you up, Eddie. But I've got things going on tomorrow night so you'll be on your own."

"That's fine. My plane lands around eleven AM your time."

"I'll be there."

Eddie hung up the phone and looked around. He was standing in the middle of the history books aisle. At the end was a lady who made a scolding face and put a finger to her lips, "Ssshhh." He walked around the corner and thought his dad didn't want to see him. Shit, he didn't even know what the old man was doing with his life. Last time he saw him was before Carl was born. He didn't even get a birthday card from the old man for his eighteenth birthday.

Eddie looked at the clock on his mobile phone. Lunch hour was approaching, so he rushed outside and drove towards school. There was a cop car parked in the far end of the lot. Shit, he quickly turned down the stereo. He'd never seen a squad car parked here like that. They had to know something. He was already in the parking lot, and it would look suspicious if he turned around, so he parked and got out. He tried to not look at the cop, but shit, maybe not looking appeared even more suspicious. He had to know if they were watching him. He was nervous as hell, carrying a backpack full of weed. A fresh pound of the best shit in this city. He figured he'd carry it with him, in case he had to run again. He turned his head towards the car, two men inside, and both watched him. Fuck. He smiled and gave a half-wave. What the fuck was he doing? Every instinct told him to run, get out of there quick, but he held fast, and walked inside.

The class bell rang as he entered the front door. He stood inside the entrance and waited, he'd walk out incognito, just another bobbing head in the crowd. Then he heard a kid sneezing and Alex came up and asked him for a bag. As tempting as it was, he couldn't take the risk. He'd meet up later. They walked out together, Alex had his face in the handkerchief, but Eddie looked over to the far end of the parking lot, and the squad car was gone. Eddie joined the line of cars headed towards the nearest fast food joint.

He got on the road and drove. Shit, what did they know? Surely they were looking for him. Maybe it was a coincidence. Maybe he was just stoned. He drove around and thought, he needed a plan, a strategy. Big timers didn't carry all their weight around in a school bag. He needed a safehouse, someplace to keep his stash in between deliveries. Kathy's could work, people were always coming and going, and her dad was clueless. But he didn't trust her, not that much. James would be happy to host him, probably only charge a small amount of weed per day as rent, but he didn't want to put James at risk.

Then he remembered a place on the north side at the outskirts of town, and headed that direction. When he pulled up, he saw a sign that read: "Weekly rates available." It was the last commercial building within city limits. This was the place where the cultivated lawns and gridlock pavement met the buffalo grass and winding gravel roads. Prairie Wood Motel, family owned and operated since 1915. Shit, Eddie thought about all the changes this place had seen. It was probably a country resort when they first opened, might have even had horses, the kind of place where families went to get away and play nice with each other. Now the city was upon it with a heavy foot on its pathway of expansion. This city would probably reach the mountains during Eddie's lifetime. This motel wasn't much to look at now, but it was nice to see the prairie grass, and he still had easy proximity to his clientele.

This could work. It would cut into his profits a little bit, but he was moving a lot of weight and making enough cash to drop some in the name of safety. He popped out of the Rover and reserved a room, paid cash for a month. Edward Abbey now had a safe house. This shit was awesome.

First thing Eddie did was lay on the bed and smoke a bowl. He was a fucking kingpin now. A god damn drug lord with his own crib. This was the stuff of movies, and he lived it. This room wasn't exactly the Hilton, but it was better this way. He could lay low here, keep his stash safe. Shit, he'd probably have girls lined up outside just waiting for their turn. He fell asleep on top of the blankets, fully clothed with his shoes still on.

When he awoke he started to work. His first assignment was to find a proper hiding place. It couldn't be something generic like under the mattress or behind the TV. It had to be big enough to accommodate all the weight he was going to move. He had his own place now, with bills to pay. It was time to get serious.

He dismantled the space heater mounted on the wall. There was plenty of room in here for a couple pounds, but shit, if that heater kicked on it would cook his weed and send the skunky pine aroma wafting out the door. The large old microwave could work, it would conceal the smell, but too obvious. He walked in the bathroom, pulled on the wall mirror and looked under the sink. Then he looked up at the ceiling. That could work. He brought in a chair and popped off the bathroom fan. It came off easily, and the ceiling hollowed out behind it. There was plenty of space, so he stashed the weed and most of his cash, and spent the rest of that afternoon flipping through TV stations.

This was a boring way to spend the afternoon, but Eddie needed a break, and to lay low for a little while. Most of these stations were playing reality TV or sports. He spent five minutes watching a show about some chick whose cat died the same day she filed for bankruptcy. That was the entire plot. He wouldn't have watched it that long if the chick hadn't been so damn attractive. Maybe they had some good old-fashioned porn stations on this TV.

As he flipped through the stations, he found a fishing network, but these actors treated fishing like a competitive sport. Always the angle of selling some new name brand rod or ugly lure. There was not the slightest inclination towards fishing as leisure. Not that Eddie knew, he hadn't fished in so damn long, but he suspected, if memory served correct, that fishing was more about the silence and challenging himself, than it was about showing off. He clicked off the screen, double checked that his stash was safely hidden, then got out of there.

It was early evening now, and the sun was bouncing angles over the mountains that reflected off the tops of the highrises. Friday night and he had nothing to do. Nobody would be at the park for a couple weeks after the bust. Kathy's basement would be popping, but he wasn't going to show up there without anything for sale. He wasn't going to sell anything until he got back from his dad's, give it a weekend to cool down. James was likely gaming in his apartment with a couple of dudes, they'd be fucked up by now, but he couldn't deal with that scene. James made him depressed.

Fuck it. He drove. Cut squares through this gridlock. Blast the stereo and inhale the smoke. Stoplights and vagabonds. Bimmers and business men. These were real people but sometimes he forgot that. Sometimes it was easier to pretend they didn't matter. They were scenery, like postcards or wallpaper. He could never know them all, never feel their lives or understand. There was so much mystery and that's what hurt the most. That was the source of his longing, his discomfort, and his intoxication.

He felt so damn hollow. There was nothing to fill it. Driving these streets to kill time. Brought him no place but the places he'd already seen. So he angled the Rover towards home. A young man lost was neither half full nor half empty. It was both a consumption and an extraction, fighting eternally, internally, at war like the last few angles of sunlight pushing against the darkness.

APRIL 1999

SUN	MON	TUE	WED	THU	FRI	SAT
				~~1~~	~~2~~	~~3~~
~~4~~	~~5~~	~~6~~	~~7~~	~~8~~	~~9~~	~~10~~
~~11~~	~~12~~	~~13~~	~~14~~	~~15~~	~~16~~	~~17~~
~~18~~	~~19~~	~~20~~	~~21~~	~~22~~	~~23~~	24
25	26	27	28	29	30	

It was 5:00 AM when he awoke in his bedroom, and he figured if he smoked enough weed before getting on the plane, he'd be able to sleep through the entire flight. Eddie hated flying. He wasn't too interested in falling, either. But it was more than a primal fear for his life. He suspected everyone made peace with death whenever they got on a plane. For him it was the separation between where his feet were, and where they were supposed to be. He remembered the last time he flew, and the feeling of his feet on the floor of the plane. It felt solid enough if he didn't think too much about it, but he was burdened by thinking too much about things. He thought about all of the empty space between the floor of the plane and the ground beneath. He felt that hollowness like a vacuum. He could imagine falling, freely through the troposphere, and this part actually sounded fun, weightless and high. But that infinite emptiness, that sky of nothing solid, his feet too far from earth, that thought made him dizzy.

On the kitchen counter was a card with his name on it, and on top of the card was a small white box. He opened the card first and found the plane ticket, plus a note from his mom. The note said she had scheduled a taxi to pick him up at 5:45 AM. He was to keep his Rover parked in the driveway. Fuck. He'd have to pop in the garage and smoke a fat joint quick. He continued reading the note, it said she bought him a pocket-size voice recorder, he was to use it for starting his journal.

He opened up the box and removed the voice recorder. It was silver and slender, could easily fit in his pocket. He noticed there was a file already saved, so he hit play. It was his mom "Eddie, I want you to know how proud of you I am. I know these last few years have been difficult for you, but I want you to know that I love you and am so proud of you for not giving up. I hope this voice journal helps you find your way." What a bunch of reverse psychology, he thought. Implanting the idea that he wasn't giving up. Shit, he didn't need to be told what he was or wasn't doing. He had control.

He snatched up the plane ticket and his small travel pack, then fired up a joint in the driveway, kept it cupped in his right hand, and when he exhaled the mild breeze blew it away. He twisted up another one and left it in the glove box of the Rover, it was always good to have something waiting for him. When the taxi arrived he hopped in the back seat and said, "Airport, but need a quick detour first." The streets were already full and the sun hadn't even begun to crest over the eastern horizon. A quick detour led him to his motel. He told the driver to wait five minutes. When he got inside, he thought nobody would know if he stayed here for the weekend. He could lay low, smoke his weed, maybe call Christine. He didn't care too much about her, but this motel room should be used. It was always easy for him to find a girl to fool around with, and he knew they only wanted his image. His image and his weed. That was okay. What the fuck was he going to do at his dad's place anyway? He couldn't even bring his weed on the plane.

The stash was safe and secure above the ceiling fan. He packed a one hitter, pulled a hit, and called his dad on his mobile phone.

"Morning dad."

"Eddie, it's early here, which means it must be super early there. Everything okay?"

"Yes, I just wanted to let you know that I'm almost to the airport so make sure you're there to pick me up. I've got a bunch of things I want to do there this afternoon."

"I'll be there Eddie. But remember, I won't be around this evening. I've got a gig tonight, so won't see much of you, but I can pick you up at the airport and then drop you off someplace. We should have time for lunch together."

"Okay dad, that's fine. I'll be there in a few hours."

A gig? What the fuck was that about? His dad had tried to teach him to play the guitar when he was young, sitting on the back steps of their ranch looking out over the prairie. One night a week for a year they would sit back there, just the two of them with their guitars, watching the sunset and practicing cords, but it never really took. Eddie was too fidgety, always wanting to run out and see where his brother was. His dad was pretty good at strumming old country songs, but certainly not a rock star. Eddie couldn't imagine his father, the quiet rancher, the nine-to-five grinder, the man who never left the house after work and didn't have any friends, he couldn't imagine him playing a gig. A triple check of his stash to make sure it was safe, and a handful of cash to get him through the weekend. He packed one joint in his shirt pocket, hung the *Do Not Disturb* sign from the door, and got back in the taxi.

. . .

The airplanes were loud overhead, and there were so damn many of them. He watched them rise, and he watched them come in. All the people in there must be crazy. Was there any place so important that they had to fly? So damn loud, and so damn high. Look at all of the empty space in between. His legs began to feel restless as he sat in the backseat. The cab driver parked by check-in and he paid his fare. There was still enough time so he walked to the parking lot, hid behind a cement wall, and fired up a joint. He tried to think about something else. Surely there were cameras here, and armed security would come rushing at him any moment. Fuck them. This was his life and if he wanted to get stoned before flying, before paying their paycheck, before losing his mind, then give him space.

He extinguished the joint with several hits remaining, and then hid it in the mounting hardware of a No Parking sign. It would be better if there was something waiting for him when he returned. He didn't know what the hell he was going to do at his dad's place, but he knew he'd have to find some weed. Get out of the parking lot and walk inside. He could do this. A simple flight and he'd be there. A million miles between him and the ground, but that didn't matter. He'd have time to think. Maybe pick up a book inside. Okay, it was getting easier now.

The line at security was long and moved slowly. All these damn people going someplace, leaving and returning, not really changing, nomads still like the days before. Nomads with mobile phones and gas powered winged machines. One of the security guards made eye contact with him while speaking into his walkie. Fuck. They were on to him. Someone had talked, the motel manager found his stash, they were on to him, and he was trapped in this line. He put his head down and moved forward, made it through check-in. Surely this was a trap, they were following him, waiting until he entered a restroom or gift shop, someplace confined where they'd capture him, charge him with distribution of narcotics, possession of an illegal weapon. At least then he wouldn't have to fly.

At the bookstore he crept through the aisles looking over his shoulder and watching people pass. It seemed clear now, but just in case, he pulled out his mobile phone and paged his mom, "831," which was code for "I love you." At least he got that out of the way, in case next place she saw him was in jail. He could do time, he was tough enough. Could probably get Lynch to smuggle weed in for him. He'd make a killing. King of the cell block.

Now he needed a book. Flying sucked, so it would have to be a good one, a story that pulled him in until the end. Most of the titles here were generic mystery novels or self-help bull shit. Then there was the small shelf with the best sellers. These bored him, all written with the same formula, and he imagined the writers sitting at a desk with their professor watching over their shoulder correcting each comma and instructing them that creativity didn't sell. In the back of the store was the literary fiction section. This section was much smaller than the best sellers or the mystery novels. He found this ironic because these were the only books that mattered. Maybe nothing mattered, and that's why there were so few good books.

He laid a copy of *Homer and Langley* by E.L. Doctorow on the counter. The back cover said something about two brothers living together, but he didn't have time to read the full synopsis. He paid the cashier and realized he hadn't paid cash for a book in a long time. Weed was better currency. If the entire world switched to the barter system, he could trade his weed for whatever he wanted. But this was better, the risk and rebellion. The potency of being young and wanted by the law. The absolute intoxication of being known. The adrenaline of being jacked and having enemies. A man should always have a few enemies. It kept him alert.

Eddie made his way to the terminal and waited in the boarding line. The young woman up ahead checking tickets was quite sexy. Something about her long hair lapped over the back of that dark blue suit. Maybe she'd be on the flight and give him something to look at. Then it occurred to him that's why stewardesses were typically attractive, a strategic attempt to distract the passengers from how far away the earth was beneath their feet. He got closer to the ticket check and started to feel the separation.

"Your seat's halfway down the aisle on the right." Damn, she had a really pretty smile.

"Thanks," he said, and stepped into the tunnel. Not a single window in here, as if they were trying to hide the plane from him. Nobody could see the bird guts and rusty propellers.

He had a window seat, so he closed the shade. Now was the time to take his mind somewhere else. Four hour flight, and he didn't have any weed. If he started reading now maybe he'd fall asleep for the second half. The stewardess said some shit over the intercom, but he wasn't listening. His eyes were already scanning the pages of the book, trying to force himself to jump inside of it.

The seat rumbled now and he heard the engine accelerating. That moment when they left the surface of earth, when they disobeyed all laws of gravity that man had respected for millennia, that acceleration pulled the breath from his lungs and he read with greater ferocity. The plane climbed and climbed, and he knew the mountains would be looking small by now. If he looked out that window all he would see was empty space. There were two seats next to him and both were vacant, so he switched to the one in the middle. Two extra feet from the window made it a little easier, but his mind was still rushing, and it was difficult to focus on the book. Fuck, Fuck, Fuck. Four more long hours. He pulled his voice recorder out and held it to his face. Talk about something else. Anything else to change his thoughts.

Voice Recording #1

Hello. Hey. It's me, Eddie. This is my first recording. Guess I should start with the basics. It's Saturday, I think April twenty-fourth. I'm in an airplane. Haven't been in a plane for a long time. It's super easy.

I'm not going to lie, this is pretty ridiculous. I don't even know what you want from this assignment. So I'm just gonna record some shit. Suppose I'll have to edit out all the swear words when I type this out, I tend to swear a lot. Maybe I'll leave them in. You just wanted my true thoughts, at least that's what you said.

You wanted me to talk about my thoughts, or study my emotions, or some shit like that. Well this plane just took off, we're probably a few miles up and past the first mountain range by now. Flying is some pretty cool shit. I mean, just thinking about how high I am. I'm really fucking high right now, Mister Bonnell. One of the stewardesses was really sexy. I suppose you'll say that's a normal thing for a young man to think. But what if I told you that I wanted to fuck her and forget her? I wouldn't even be polite about it or add some artificial romance. I'd just come out and say it. What would you think about me then? Would you ask for details? I could give you a long list of details, believe me.

This is foolish. I'm talking to my teacher on a voice recorder while sitting alone on an airplane. Really, I'm just talking to myself. I'm the guy on the plane sitting alone and talking to himself. These people probably all think I'm weird. But they don't know. Shit, they don't know the half of it. If they did know, they'd realize that they were the weird ones. People are all pretty weird. Especially you. How about that? Maybe if I piss you off right away you won't even read the rest of this. I could just copy and paste a bunch of random text, maybe from a Penthouse website or something. Then you'd really like it. I bet if you assigned Penthouse as required reading material then people would actually like your class. Damn it, now I'm thinking about naked chicks. I think about naked chicks quite a lot actually. It's really one of my favorite things to think about. But it's difficult to think about naked chicks while strapped to an airplane seat at five million miles above the earth and traveling seven thousand miles an hour. So here's the deal.

I'm going to visit my dad. I haven't seen him in over a year. You'd probably like to know why, and say it would be good for a young guy to study his feelings. I fucking hate that word, *feelings*. Why should I waste time feeling something when actions are all that matter in this world? So here's what will happen. I'll see my dad, we'll give each other a big old hug, and then I'll fill him up with a bunch of lies about how good I'm doing and everything. That's all he wants to hear, right? It's not like it was my choice to visit him, and he certainly didn't invite me. It's my mom, she said it would be good. I try to make her happy, she's really a sweet lady. It's easier if I lie to her. If I told her the truth about things she'd probably commit suicide for having created a monster.

There's that sexy stewardess, she's walking down the aisle. Maybe she's giving away free peanuts. I don't know if they even do that anymore. Maybe she's giving away free handjobs, but only to me. I bet she's wearing a red lacy thong. I'm going to pretend like I'm saying something smart, so she doesn't think I'm a weirdo talking to himself. I'll just read a couple lines from this book until she passes.

How can you make an ontological distinction between outside and inside? On the basis of staying dry when it rains? Warm when it's cold? What after all can be said about having a roof over your head that is philosophically meaningful?

Excuse me sir. But all electronics are required to be turned off during flight.

This is just a homework assignment. What's it gonna hurt?

It's our policy, sir. Please, it's for the safety of you and the other passengers.

Fine.

PAUSE.

I'm back. Just walking through the airport. There's about a million people here. That flight wasn't too bad, but seemed long. That's alright, I read about half of my book. It's pretty good so far, real slow character development. There's no super etchy or scandalous plot. It's just about a couple brothers, pretty normal people. That is, normal in the way everyone's weird. It's pretty dull, so you'd probably never assign it. I like it though. Even though there's no action. I get enough action in real life. Although I wouldn't mind reading about a good old-fashioned Russian duel. I wonder if Blunt would accept a challenge to a duel. I'd propose sabers at dusk. That fool would probably bring his whole gang loaded with machine guns. They're a bunch of cowards. Seems to me that most people who are always in a crowd are cowards.

Fuck. I'm rambling. Don't get me started on Blunt, or cowards, I could ramble for hours. I'd fill up this whole damn memory drive just ranting about them. I still don't know what you expect from this assignment. It's bull shit, really, Mister Bonnell. I think you must be bored. That's it, isn't it? You're bored and you heard about what an exciting life I live. This entire assignment is just a way to bring some entertainment to your boring existence.

Suppose I could clue you in to the details of my surroundings, since that's what you wanted. Right now I'm walking down this damn corridor. It's so fucking packed in here. There's so many people and it's so loud nobody would even know I'm talking to myself on this voice recorder. It's like a god damn cattle show in here, everybody just moving in lines not really looking at anything. It's kind of pathetic, if you ask me. How'd there ever get to be so many damn people anyway? There's also something antiseptic about this place, which seems weird since there's all these damn people. I guess it's because of the bright lights and white floors, or maybe just a lack of anything beautiful. It's like the waiting area at an emergency room, these people all look like they're ready to die, or have accepted the death of a loved one. Believe me, I would know.

I'm heading to the baggage claim. Not that I have any bags to pick up, I just don't know where I'm supposed to meet my dad. There are so many damn people here, I would've been better taking a taxi. I wonder what the weather's like outside. I hope it's warm so I can go to the beach and scope out some chicks. They'd probably think I'm some weirdo hanging at the beach alone. Fuck that, I'd be the mysterious guy from out of town. As long as I score some weed first.

This is super weird, walking around talking to this voice recorder. Maybe people think I'm a journalist or something. You better pass me for this, Mister Bonnell.

Wait a sec, I think that's my dad. Son of a bitch. He's sitting there on one of those uncomfortable airport benches. Not even holding a sign with my name or anything. If I wasn't looking for him, I wouldn't have recognized him. What the fuck's up with his hair? It's long, not quite hippy Woodstock long, but longer than I've ever seen it. That goofy looking goatee, what's he thinking? It's more than that though, more than the larger belly and grungy clothes. It's mostly his eyes. Not quite the eyes of a whiskey drunk, a little different than some star-gazed poet. Can't quite place it, but there's more wrinkles, they're narrower, almost squinty, with a hint of desperation. Maybe he's stoned? Suppose I better go talk to him. I'm not going to walk up to him holding my fucking voice recorder. You probably want to hear this though, don't you? Shit, I'll put the damn thing in my shirt pocket, leave it recording. I can't promise much.

What am I doing? What the fuck am I doing here? Truth is, I don't really want to spend any time with him. I'm sure after this weekend I'll go home depressed. He's probably going to want to talk about Steve, and ask how my mom's doing. He'll probably be all psyched about me telling him I'm looking at colleges. Then he'll get all serious and explain why he was never able to pay for my college. It'll be a whole long boring discourse that will depress the hell out of us both. Tell you the truth, I'd rather go back home and sign up for the baseball team, wear tight pinstripes, and practice my high-fives, than deal with him. Well, maybe not that. Fuck it, here I go.

Dad. Hey dad. What the fuck's he doing? Dennis. Dennis Young.

Eddie. There you are. I was just thinking I must've missed you. Wow, what happened to your eye?

My eye is fine. Don't stand up, dad. Here, I'll just sit down for a while.

Oh no, you've been sitting all flight. Here, give me a hug.

PAUSE.

Well shit. My recorder turned off, must've bumped the button when he hugged me. It was really an awkward hug, usually is when two men hug. Now I'm just waiting outside the doors, he went to get the car. Wouldn't even let me walk with him. Not much happened. He asked how my flight was. I told him it was great, gave me lots of time to think about the college I want to visit. I don't even know why I said that shit, it's not like I needed to. Sometimes I don't even know why I say shit, I just do. It's not like I could tell him about how I daydreamed of fucking the stewardess the entire flight. Seriously, I could hardly even focus on my book. I thought about a few other things too, don't want you to think I'm a complete pervert. I thought a little about revenge. I'm not gonna tell you too much about that, but there's this dude who I've a got a score to settle with. But that's not really any of your business.

So I asked my dad where he lives and everything. He said he lives on the water. Big deal. He probably lives in a damn trailer home or something. I don't know why I even agreed to come here. Honestly, I don't know why I'm bothering to talk into this damn recorder. It's not much different than thinking, I guess. Thinking out loud. I suppose everyone just assumes that I'm narrating a novel or something. Either that, or they don't even care. They're probably too busy to even notice. Although there's this dude standing about twenty feet away who keeps looking at me. I'm just standing outside, can't remember if I already told you that. He's over there leaning against one of those cement pillars, I don't know what the fuck you'd call them, some sort of support beam. Anyway, he's just leaning there looking all crazy, and keeps eyeing me. He's got this whacky look in his eyes, probably on crank or something. I bet he knows where I could score some weed. Shit. Well, I'll probably definitely edit out anything I say about weed. Don't take it personally, I just don't really trust anyone.

All my dad told me when he walked off was that he drove a red car and he'd honk when he got here. It sure is taking him long enough. Probably drove off and forgot about me. I'll give him five more minutes then I'll just get in a damn taxi. I could spend the day on the beach, shouldn't be too difficult to find some weed. I could just sit and watch the ocean all day, maybe even sleep there. Shit, there he is. That is one ugly looking car. He truly is an example of the middle age man in crisis. Maybe I can get him to stop at an electronics store, someplace I can buy one of those new age microphones for my voice recorder, so I can record our conversations. Not that I expect anything super exciting to be said between us.

PAUSE.

Well, this isn't what I expected. I'll give it to the old man, he could be on to something here. He lives in a houseboat. It's nothing spectacular, basically a trailer home on pontoons. Keeps it tied up here at this crumby old marina. I mean seriously, this place looks like a movie scene where they catch somebody importing heroin or Chinese slaves. I'm in my room, guess in boat talk they call it a cabin. I don't fucking know. It's a damn tiny room though, with this bed that's about as big as a small couch. It's got a comforter with the print of a tropical shoreline. That's a joke. This place isn't scenic at all. There is a small window, right above the waterline. I can look out and see all kinds of water. That's kind of cool, I guess. It's not a damn postcard or anything. I don't want to get you all excited and think my dad's a rock star living in luxury or anything. But it is kind of cool, for a lonely old bum like my dad, I suppose.

So I picked up this microphone thing. I'm not much of a techie, but it seems pretty simple. It's got this long wire that connects to my voice recorder, so I can keep the recorder in my pocket, run the wire up under my shirt, and clip the mic on the inside of my shirt where it's not super obvious. Just like you see in the spy movies. I'll connect it and give it a try.

Hello. Hello. This is Eddie-oh-seven, signing in. Seems like it's working. At least, it created a new file on the recorder. Now I can keep the thing recording without having to hold my voice recorder up to my face. This is some spy shit. Although I feel like I'm wearing a bug, like I'm a narc or something. If I ever wore a bug it would be because some super-secret government agency needed my street skills to foil a big terrorist plot or something. I'd probably be responsible for rescuing the president's hot daughter. If the president had a hot daughter. I think of the strangest shit sometimes. I don't even know why. It's not like I care too much about the government, or even terrorists for that matter. Maybe the hot daughter, a little.

It's still pretty early in the day. My dad's out there making lunch. I'm sure it will come from the microwave. I brought five hundred in cash. Figured any more than that would look suspicious. After lunch I'm gonna get my dad to drop me off somewhere. I haven't been this sober in a long time.

This is even more ridiculous. Now I'm just talking to myself without even holding a recorder to my face. Guess I'll walk out there and hang with dad. Something actually smells good.

Are you ready for lunch Ed?

Ed? Nobody ever calls me that.

I know. I figured since you're a man now. Ed sounds more mature than Eddie.

Whatever you say dad. So what are you making?

Redfish. Ever had it?

Nope. You catch them or something?

Yep. Last night after you called, I pulled the boat just right over there past the point and caught them on a streamer fly. These two were about twenty inches a piece, which is the size they taste the best. I had a bigger one landed but let it go. Once they get above thirty inches they've accumulated too many toxins from the water. These aren't the pristine waters of the mountain streams that you and Steve used to fish.

So we're eating toxic fish? No thanks. I'll probably just hit a fast food joint.

Are you serious? What are they teaching you in school? A fast food burger is worse for you than ten of these fish. Besides, they say if you only eat one of these a month the toxins are so low they're not even going to affect you.

Now you're starting to sound like mom.

What do you mean?

Oh you know, ever since Carl was born she's gotten all into organic food and everything. I can't even eat good stuff anymore.

So how do you like having a new baby brother?

It's nothing really. All he does is cry and poop.

Yeah, that's what baby's do. That's what you did. I changed a lot of your diapers back then. So how's your mom's new husband? His name's Cole, right?

It's alright dad. Listen, I don't really want to talk about all this. Truth is, mom just told me I'm supposed to come out here and visit. I'd rather not start talking about all that gushy stuff, you know.

So you only came to visit because your mom asked you to? I thought you were looking at colleges.

I am. But she thinks I should spend time with you, or something.

Why, are you getting into trouble?

Nothing serious dad. It's no big deal. I'm just supposed to be working on this special assignment my English teacher gave me. He said I'm far more advanced than the rest of his students, and I needed a new challenge.

That sounds pretty interesting. I'm not around too much on the weekends, but you're welcome to come back here anytime if it helps with your homework.

We'll see how it goes dad. Is that fish ready yet? Cause if it's not I might just go wait up top.

It'll be ready in just a minute. We could go up top and eat on the aft deck.

The what?

Back of the boat, Ed. You should learn this stuff, if you're planning to spend time here.

Maybe tomorrow. I just need you to drop me off at the college today, if you could.

Any time you want. Let's go up and eat. It's a beautiful day out there.

It is nice out here. So you caught these fish just right over there?

Yep, just this side of the point. You can see where the waves break over submerged structure. Right on the near side of that.

That's pretty cool. I haven't fished in a long time.

Why not? You're so close to the mountains. I'd take fishing the mountains any day over this salt water stuff. Cleaner fish. Cleaner air. No people.

You know how it is dad. I get busy with school and work and stuff. I haven't even seen my old rod since we moved in with Cole.

I take it Cole isn't a fisherman?

I doubt it. Who knows? He's more of a city guy. Always wearing a suit and tie, that sort of thing.

Yeah. Well. Tell you what. I've got Steve's old fly rod around here somewhere. You remember that bamboo rod he built?

I think so.

It's a nice rod. Too light for these salt fish. Good for the mountain trout though. How about I send it back with you?

I don't know dad. Like I said, don't really do any fishing.

Well you can take it, just in case. If you decide not to use it, bring it back. I don't want it getting ruined, or lost, or anything.

Fine.

Good. I'll dig it up later and leave it on your bed.

Okay. Well I'm gonna head down to my bedroom and get ready. Think we can leave soon?

Sure thing.

Alright. Actually, since you mentioned it. What do you call a bedroom? In boat terms, I mean.

It's a stateroom.

Alright. I'm going to the stateroom then.

PAUSE.

See Mister Bonnell, I told you that wouldn't be too interesting. The fish was pretty good though. I wonder what the hell he does all day. Just sit around on the boat alone? Old men are weird. It seems like all they want to do is be alone. I'm never gonna get that way.

Well shit. I'm gonna probably turn this thing off now. Just going to have him drop me off at that college. At least if I can't find some weed right away I've got this fake ID. A beer buzz would be better than nothing.

PAUSE.

That was a pretty boring car ride. My dad pointed out places he likes to eat, or get his fishing gear, but we didn't really talk too much. He said he was proud of me for coming out here to look at colleges, even said it would be nice to have me around. Sometimes I feel sort of bad about lying. But mostly not. Mostly it's the best way. It's for his own good. If I told him the truth he'd get too stressed out, probably feel inadequate as a parent and everything. If I ever really started to hate him, I'd tell him the truth.

I asked him about his gig. He was kinda mysterious about all that. Almost seemed embarrassed, like I wouldn't think he was cool enough, or something. All he really said was that he plays the local bar circuit. I can't imagine that pays much. Maybe free drinks, at best. I don't even know if that's his real job. Can you make enough money playing at bars to live in a houseboat? I probably should have asked him where he worked, and shit like that. It just never occurred to me. I always think about those things after it's too late.

So I had him drop me at this college. It's about thirty minutes from his house. Or his boat. Whatever. I figured this would be an easy place for me to walk around and find some weed. It's the east coast, after all. Alright, well I'm gonna turn this damn thing off. Maybe I'll check back in later, if something exciting happens. Or I might not.

PAUSE.

Alright, I'm fucking stoned. This is much better. It was easy as hell, too. I just took a taxi down to the boardwalk. Place was busy as hell, with chicks and low life dudes all over the place. Smelled like salt, but mostly dead fish. I just hung out for a while, watching the people. I was looking cool as hell. These beach bums probably never met someone as cool as me. Then I saw these dudes passing a cigar back and forth. Nobody shares a damn cigar, so I knew it was weed. I just walked right over and told them I was new in town and needed a hookup. Said I'd smoke them up for free if they could find me an ounce, but that it had to be primo shit. I think my black eye helped prove I wasn't a cop or something.

They brought me over to this dude at a paraphernalia shop. Can you imagine that? Selling weed right out of a paraphernalia shop. I'm telling you, it was that obvious. But nobody gives a shit about weed. It's not that high quality or anything. At least not as good as the shit I get back home. It'll work though.

I bought an ounce, not because I'm going to smoke all of it today, though I could, if I wanted to. Figure I'll sell some of it here at the beach. That's always a good way to meet chicks. Nothing else for me to do.

So I smoked a blunt with the dudes for hooking me up. They were weird, talked like idiots. Said they were meeting some girls, actually they called them bitches, but anyway, they said they were meeting some chicks at a bar later. Told me I could roll with them, acted like it was a big favor they were offering. Bunch of ass holes. Might be a good way to practice with my fake ID though. I'm not even going to think about that until later. Right now I'm just gonna hang at the beach and sell some of this shit.

Man, there's a lot of fucking weirdos in the world. Bunch of dudes, maybe six or seven of them, its broad fucking daylight, and they've got a bonfire going on the beach. Plus most of them are wearing black sweatshirts with the hoodies pulled up. I bet if there were goats here they'd be sacrificing them. And don't even get me started on those guys pumping weights over there. Who the hell would bring dumbbells to the beach? Then there's this group of super tanned dudes all wearing bright neon swimming shorts, I swear it looks like every one of them bleach-blondes their hair, and they're just kicking this little bean bag around like it's some giant display of athleticism. There's quite a few chicks around, but most of them are wearing jogging pants and t-shirts. I haven't seen a single string bikini yet. This place is lame.

So I've been walking down this boardwalk for a while. It's packed, lots of little shops and tons of people. One thing I should warn you, if you're ever walking on this boardwalk, and its broad fucking daylight on a Saturday, keep your eyes open. I just about got run over by some freak on a unicycle. Who the hell rides a unicycle? I'm telling you, this world is weird as hell.

Think I'll find a spot to sit for a bit. Maybe a get a beer. There's all kinds of sports bars and night clubs on this strip. I want something more chill. You know, dim lights and good mellow music playing. I'll probably check out the night clubs later, but right now I just want to sit down and not see any more damn weirdos. Plus, I've got that book in my pack, wouldn't mind reading a little more. I try to read a little every day. You probably don't believe me, not after what you've heard about me, but it's true.

STOP.

Eddie stood in an alley beside a large blue dumpster and fired up a joint. He inhaled deeply and smelled the rotting flesh of restaurant trash. The alley was narrow, with metal escape ladders that dropped down along the brick walls of the buildings. Farther down the alley, he saw several guys laying on the ground with wet cardboard and raggedy blankets for beds. Looking the other direction, towards the main drag, people streamed past in crowds, loud, obnoxious, oblivious to what existed down this alley. He was invisible here, just like the men sleeping on the ground. He held a breath of smoke deep in his lungs and realized he enjoyed being hidden. Something about not being seen made him comfortable, but this alley smelled rotten, so he walked to the main drag and turned out with the crowd.

He walked down the sidewalk, grey concrete, he was part of a crowd all moving together, had all predetermined an acceptable speed, uncommunicated but subconsciously agreed to, and most of them followed this unwritten rule, but not all. Eddie was glancing in the windows of buildings as he passed, looking for the right place, and as he had his head tilted up to read a neon sign, he felt a body knock into his back with enough force to make him fall to the ground. A man was running full speed through the crowd, dodging and weaving, and shortly behind him came two policemen in their blue uniforms, yelling for the pedestrians to get out of their way. Eddie watched this scene move past him, a spectator this time, and wondered which he'd rather be; the pursuer or the one being pursued.

He got back on his feet and looked up at the neon sign on the red brick building. It read "Murphy's" and it reminded him of Murphy's Law. That was pretty cool, he thought. He was familiar enough with things going wrong. At least the place wasn't named something cheesy like "Sea Side" or "Big Wave." The entrance was an extra wide wooden door, no windows. He entered into a room dimly lit by several beer signs on the walls and a billiards lamp hanging over the horseshoe shaped bar. He saddled up and sat on the high stool. When the bartender approached, Eddie pulled out his ID and handed it to him. The man looked down at the card, looked up at Eddie, handed the ID back and said, "Edward Abbey, huh. Wasn't he the guy who blew up some dams or something?"

Eddie smirked, surprised the name rang any bell, and replied, "It wasn't me."

"What are you drinking?"

"I'll start with a light beer."

Eddie surveyed the room. There were two older men spaced equidistance around the bar. The room behind him was outlined with tall booths fixed with red-padded backing. In the center of the room was a single pool table, and on the far wall there were several dart boards, but no people. He reached into his pack and removed the copy of *Homer and Langley*. The first beer always helped him focus and he became fully immersed in the pages.

Without knowing how much time had passed, he was jolted from the story by a long light that stretched from the doorway across the room. It felt like a movie scene or an illusion, a woman's form outlined in shadow. The door shut behind her and Eddie blinked his eyes to adjust. The way her body moved when she walked made his heart feel higher in his chest. He calmed his breath and looked back at his book to play it cool.

She stood at the bar on the opposite side of the seat to Eddie's left.

Eddie knew this meant something, because there were a dozen other places she could have stood. When the bartender approached, he said, "Who's heart are you breaking today, Terrible Cheryl?"

"I'll keep breaking hearts until I find one that can't be."

Eddie was watching her from the corner of his eyes. She put her elbows up on the wooden bar counter and leaned forward on her tippy toes. She was wearing short white volleyball shorts and he noticed her tan legs and the outline of a pink bikini underneath. Eddie turned the page to pretend he didn't see her.

"What are you drinking today?"

"I want a scotch with no rocks," she replied as she sat on the barstool two down from Eddie.

Eddie turned the page again without having read a single word. He was thinking this must be a pretty cool chick to come into a bar alone on an afternoon and order a warm scotch. When her drink arrived she looked at Eddie's drink and said, "That looks like a glass of straight up piss."

"What?" replied Eddie, caught off guard by her statement. Then he composed himself, lifted his beer, and said, "This is pure virility juice. Gatorade for men." He smiled and swallowed down the rest of his drink.

"I'm almost impressed," she said, and shot down her drink. "Almost."

"I thought scotch was made for sipping."

"It's made for however I want it to be."

"Nothing wrong with that," replied Eddie as he nodded at the bartender. "Are you drinking another?"

"Shit baby I just got here."

The bartender approached, and Eddie said, "I'll get another round."

"Same thing?"

"Yep. One for the girl, too."

"Whatever you say bud." He poured them each a drink and leaned on the counter between them.

"Is Buck giving you a hard time?"

"Buck? Oh, this guy? Nope, not yet anyway."

"If you stick around here long enough it'll happen." She sipped down half of her drink.

"Whatever you say, Cheryl. Terrible Cheryl. So bud, did you know they call this girl Terrible Cheryl? And she's earned it, too."

"Doesn't sound so bad to me. Cheryl. I'm Edward. You can call me Eddie."

"Eddie. Eddie Eddie my teddy. You new around here or something?"

"Just landed today. Kind of passing through, you could say."

"Is that right? So you're one of those rambling men. What did you do, get a girl pregnant? Looks like she kicked your ass. Let me guess, you robbed a bank and have a fat wad of cash in that bag of yours." She shot down the rest of her drink.

Eddie looked at Buck and pointed at Cheryl's drink, and then gave a thumbs up. While Buck was pouring another scotch, Cheryl looked at Eddie and said, "I'm gonna sneak off to the drainpipe real quick. Don't you go anywhere."

Buck returned, set Cheryl's drink on the counter, looked at Eddie and said, "None of my business, but just keep your expectations in check with this one. Keep your expectations in check and hold your wallet tight."

Eddie pulled another sip from his beer, "It is none of your business." Cheryl returned and sat at the stool directly next to him, but turned slightly on the swivel seat, so that her knees were facing him.

She took a sip from her drink, and Eddie said, "So Cheryl, is this your hometown?"

"Born and raised. I know every inch of this shoreline. That's how I can spot a newbie. You don't look like any other newbie I've seen though. Kinda cute, if you don't mind me saying."

"I've been called worse."

"I bet you have. You're probably some kind of bad boy back wherever you came from. Where'd you say you're from?"

"West of here a ways."

"Ooh, and you're mysterious. I'm glad I met you." She took another sip from her drink, and let her foot bump against Eddie's shin.

A ringing came from Eddie's bag, and it took him a moment to remember his mobile was in there. He retrieved the phone, and as he flipped it open to answer, he heard Cheryl say, "Oooh, that's cool."

"This is Eddie. Who's calling?"

"Who the fuck you think is calling?" came Lynch's voice.

"Hey man, yeah, what's going on?"

"Rent is due. I know you didn't skip work yesterday."

"Man, I'm tied up right now." He looked at Cheryl and winked. "I'm gonna get that to you though." Eddie promptly hung up the phone, knowing he'd have to deal with that later.

Cheryl swiveled in her stool, flung her hair from her shoulder, and said, "So you just planning on hanging out in this bar alone all day?"

"I'm too busy to make plans. Just take it as it comes. What about yourself?"

"It's Saturday night. The fun is just starting. What do you say, will you let a local girl show the new boy around?"

"I could think of worse things to do with a Saturday night. What did you have in mind?"

"I always go dancing on Saturday nights. I just love the loud music and flashing lights. A room full of bodies bouncing and sweating. No other cares in the world. But first, I'm going to check out the new brewery. It's called Plank Walk. You know, like Boardwalk, but for pirates. They're supposed to have some amazing specialty beers. You're drinking beer. Want to join me?"

"If you're ready to switch from scotch to beer, I'm ready to check it out."

"Excellent. We're gonna have a ton of fun. You're gonna be so happy you met me."

"Hey bartender. Buck, can I clear the tab."

"All on one?"

"Yep. So Cheryl, Terrible Cheryl. Where is this place you're taking me?"

"It's only a few doors down."

"Alright. Let's get out of here."

. . .

"What a beautiful day," said Cheryl as they stepped into a sunny afternoon. "Have you ever been to a beach town?"

"First time. But I've been a lot of other places."

"What do you think? So far, I mean. You'll get the real experience after dark."

"No complaints so far. It's much different than living next to the mountains."

"The mountains. So that's where you're from. Yep, I can see it now. I bet you're a regular outlaw. I would love to visit the mountains. I bet they're beautiful. All I ever see is the ocean. If you want to know the truth, I've never been more than twenty miles from the coast."

"No shit? Man, well, I'll have to get you out to the mountains sometime."

"Now you better take it slow Eddie, just cause I'm showing you around and drinking together doesn't mean I'm gonna run off with you right away."

"No rush here. So let me ask you something. Do you like to get high?"

"Oh I thought you'd never ask. I usually do E on Saturdays, makes the clubs so much fun. I do crank sometimes too."

"Yeah, well, I've got some killer weed. I mean, it's nothing compared to the good shit I get back home, but it does the trick. Want to smoke some with me?"

"Weed? No way. Weed's a downer for me. It's Saturday night man, I need something with energy."

"Like beer?"

"Alcohol just keeps me from going over the edge. Keeps me loose."

"No worries. I'm just gonna pop in this alley quick and smoke half a joint. You're welcome to join me."

"Sure, I'll come with you. It sounds borderline dangerous, which I'm always down for."

"Sure you don't want a hit?"

"Okay, I'll take just one. Ooh, that is pretty good. Where'd you say you got it?"

"I've got connections. My philosophy is, if a man's always got money, he can get what he needs."

"Oh, I can vouch for that, baby. You ready to take me in for a beer?"

"Show me the way."

"It's just right around the corner. Come on, let me hold your hand. This is nice. I bet you're a regular ladies' man back where you come from. You're kinda shy too. Or maybe stoic. I like a stoic man, seems so solid. This is the place."

"Let me get the door."

"Ooh, and a gentleman. Wow, look at this place, it's wild. Is that a real shark? Incredible. Let's sit right over there, next to the aquarium."

"How are you two doing today?" asked a server after they sat at a tall table in the corner. "Welcome to the Plank. Can I get you something to drink?"

"Ooh," began Cheryl, as she held up the menu, "I'm gonna get the Gusting Gose. Says it's made with real salt water from the ocean. Can you believe that? Fresh New Zealand hops and malts from the Midwest."

"And for you?"

"Shit, I don't know. I'll get what she's having."

"I'll be right back with those."

"So, do you like breweries?"

"They're alright," said Eddie, looking around the crowded room. "Tell you the truth, I'll drink just about any beer. As long as I've got some weed. I can go days without beer, but I can't go five minutes without weed. What are you doing?"

"Just checking my pager quick. I can't go five minutes with checking it. Sounds like the club is going to be popping tonight. Everybody will be there. Are you gonna come with me?" Their server set the drinks on the table, and Cheryl slammed down half of it with one pull.

"Shit, probably could," replied Eddie, after nodding at the server and taking a sip from his beer. "You think anybody there wants to buy some weed?"

"Maybe. If you had some E you'd sell a bunch. But you might be able to find a few stoners. Why, are you a big dealer or something?"

"I do alright."

"Wow. You keep surprising me. I knew when I saw you sitting at the bar reading a book, there was something about you. I mean, I see all kinds of people, intellectuals, dealers, wanna-be's, preps, you know, the whole spectrum. So, do you really like to read? Or was that book just a prop or something?"

"I read a bit. Why, do you like that?"

"I love seeing a man read. I'm a sapiosexist."

"I bet you are."

"You do know what that word means, right?"

"Of course. I understand."

"Good. I'm just gonna sneak over to the drain pipe quick, this beer is going straight through me. Be right back."

Voice Recording #2

I'm back. Only been an hour or so since my last entry. Switched to a new location, but not too far. I'm sitting in this corner booth watching all these people. I have a hard time understanding what they're all doing here. Just wanted to say something quick, because I'm with someone. But she just stepped away.

I met a girl. She is unlike anybody I've ever met. She said she's a sapiosexist. I'm gonna half to remember to look that one up later. Hmm, that's strange. I just thought of something. I remember when I was a kid, back when we lived in the country. Whenever Steve or I had a question about something, my dad would always take us over to the encyclopedia shelf. We had this entire shelf full of encyclopedias. He'd stand there with us looking through them until we found the answer. I usually wanted to look up something from a book I was reading, like if time travel was possible, or how many people did Billy the Kid kill, or if dragons ever actually existed. Steve always wanted to look up something about fish, or some secret fishing destination. Sometimes it would take us a couple hours, but my dad would stay with us, just flipping through pages. We usually learned about ten new things just trying to answer that one question.

Sometimes people surprise me. I mean, take this girl, wearing short shorts that you can see through, and coming into a bar alone on a Saturday afternoon. I wouldn't think she knew too much, just by looking at her. Then she goes and pulls out a word like sapiosexist, and now I'm all mixed up. She likes these fancy beers too, already drank her full glass. I've still got about half left. I don't really care too much for these fancy beers. When I'm drinking a beer I just want it clean and crisp, simple, something I don't have to think much about. Drinking beer is about not thinking too much. This one tastes like shrimp, briny. I don't want to think about shrimp while I'm drinking beer. It distracts me from her short shorts.

She's taking long enough in there. So, Bonnell, I don't know if this is what you wanted me to do with this assignment. I guess I'm thinking about my surroundings and stuff, but I always do. Now I'm recording them, so I suppose that makes me think a little bit more about stuff. I don't know, it still seems kind of ridiculous. I mean you've got me sitting here at a brewery talking to myself at a table alone. I bet you never thought I'd be sitting at a brewery on the east coast when you gave me this assignment. I think that's enough homework for today. I mean, it's fucking Saturday night, and I'm drinking with some hot chick. I'll check back later. Last thing I'd want her to do is find out I'm recording all of this.

STOP.

APRIL 1999

SUN	MON	TUE	WED	THU	FRI	SAT
				~~1~~	~~2~~	~~3~~
~~4~~	~~5~~	~~6~~	~~7~~	~~8~~	~~9~~	~~10~~
~~11~~	~~12~~	~~13~~	~~14~~	~~15~~	~~16~~	~~17~~
~~18~~	~~19~~	~~20~~	~~21~~	~~22~~	~~23~~	~~24~~
25	26	27	28	29	30	

Eddie woke and opened his eyes to see the water line out the window gently tilting back and forth. He closed his eyes again and focused on the motion, awkward and disturbing at first, the way it rose and fell, sped up then slowed down. With his eyes closed he spread his arms, hanging off the edges of the small bed, and imagined he was floating on a wooden raft drifting out to sea. Expansive and lonely. He smiled, opened his eyes, and walked to the window. There was a small roach remaining from the night before, so he pinched it between his fingers and put flame to it. He inhaled and looked out the window at the slow rolling waves.

His window was at eye height and barely above the water line, which meant from his shoulders down he was below water. He pulled the last two hits from the roach and then extinguished it. He stood in front of that window and watched the waves rolling, up and down, and he thought about how simple this was, to be alone and watch the waves. This gentle motion brought a vision from his past. His brother's silhouette standing in a mountain stream. Eddie could only see his back above the river, and the fly rod held at an angle overhead. The water was tumbling all around him and sounded like static on a radio station. Calming and serene.

Eddie caught a glimpse of his own face reflecting from the window, and put his hand up to his bruised eye. He turned around to get dressed, and then he saw it on the far wall, mostly hidden behind a coat rack. He walked over and pushed the coats aside. It was a picture of Steve when they lived in the country. He must've been about twelve or thirteen. Already starting to look like a young man. Funny that Eddie was older than him now, and he would continue to grow older than Steve ever was. Strange sensation to imagine being older than his older brother. How the fuck could that happen? Eddie knew why, or at least, he was beginning to learn. From what he had seen, this manmade world rewarded the wicked and insane, gave the most to those who lied the best. Eddie decided that the truth was a giant damn struggle; he must be wicked to face it and insane to tolerate it. He dug in his pants pocket and removed the voice recorder.

Voice Recording #3

Fuck. That was a crazy night. Alright, so it's the next day, I guess that makes it Sunday. I'm back at my dad's boat. But still downstairs in my room. So here's what happened.

I was hanging with that chick, Cheryl. Terrible Cheryl. What a fucking name. Probably wasn't even her real one. Well anyway, after the brewery we went over to some local dive bar. I actually thought the place was pretty cool, dim lighting and scuffed up hardwood floors. But then we walked into the back room. It was dark and smelled musty, but there were tons of people all sitting around on these old looking chairs. They seemed pretty chill, holding their drinks, whispering to each other, watching the music. At the end of the room was a small stage with some neon beer signs as the only lights. There was my dad, sitting on the stage alone with his guitar. I didn't recognize him at first because the lights were so dim, and the music was good. Caught me off guard, to tell you the truth. Cheryl said she had seen this musician play before, and that he was one of the most popular local musicians. Deep and moody with a touch of cynicism, that's how she explained him. I didn't say he was my dad. She wanted to dance, but I slugged my beer and told her this place was depressing. I don't think my dad even saw me. He's one of those musicians that just stares at the floor in front of him while playing, as if he wants to pretend there's nobody else in the room and he's only playing for whatever memory is going through his mind. He was pretty good though. If it wasn't my dad I probably would have stayed to listen.

So after that we went over to this dance club, I forget what it was called, probably something cheesy. Man, she was all over me. We were having a great time. She knew everyone, too. Except she kept skipping out to the drain pipe about every five minutes. Probably doing ecstasy or something. But we danced a lot. If you can call it dancing. Just a bunch of drunk people all grinding together and jumping around like idiots. There had to be about five thousand people in that place, and not a single one of them sober. But man, I owned that dance floor. I'm telling you, give me a couple of beers and I can really get into the music. We stayed there until about two in the morning and the place was still rocking. Could've stayed longer, but she asked me to leave with her. She wanted me real bad, I could tell. Her place was supposed to be only a couple blocks away, at least that's what she said.

I was feeling pretty drunk, but not so much that I was showing it. I can hide it good when I want to. But just for the hell of it, I fired up a joint and smoked it while we walked. Smoking weed helps me focus. There were tons of people everywhere. The sidewalk was bright, I mean, I don't think those bars ever close, so we walked down some back streets. Man, she was all over me. Kissing my neck and putting her hand up my shirt. She was saying some really perverted things too, like some porn star shit. I'm not going to repeat them for you, but man, girls back home never said anything like that to me. I kept asking her if we were getting close, it seemed like we were walking forever. She just kept saying we were almost there. I don't think she knew her ass from her feet, tell you the truth.

Then the fucking cops pulled up. They flashed the lights but didn't turn on the siren. Pulled up right next to us on this dark street. I tried to run, but she wouldn't let go of my damn arm. Not that I was gonna leave her, I thought she'd follow me and we'd disappear into an alley or something. But man, she would not let go of my arm. I'm telling you, a drunk girl sure weighs a lot. So the cops jumped out and grabbed each of us. Then they slammed us against the hood of their cruiser, and I mean they really slammed us. I flung the joint as soon as I saw the lights, but they must've seen it because they kept asking me what I was holding. It didn't take them long to search through my bag and find the stash. Good thing I sold most of it. Only had about a dime bag left.

Anyway, the cops didn't seem to care too much about my weed, or even the fact I had five hundred cash on me. After I sold the weed, smoked a bunch, and bought a bunch of drinks for everyone, I was right back where I started. I just told them I work a construction job that pays cash. They didn't really care either way. They sure knew Cheryl though, even called her Terrible Cheryl. They kept calling me John. Turns out she's a convicted felon. Chick can't be older than twenty-three and she's a convicted felon. Some people have the worst luck. Cop kept asking her if she was working tonight. I guess she was a prostitute or something. She kept getting pissed as hell when they asked her that. Can't believe I got fooled by some damn hooker. I'm usually quite perceptive, I really am. I can typically read people very good. But that chick tricked me. Her god damn short shorts, and the way she kept putting her hands on me. Fucking Cleopatra, I swear.

Well, as you can probably guess, the cops weren't too overwhelmed by my fake ID. Not that they knew who Edward Abbey was, they just knew it wasn't me. The really sick thing is, when Cheryl heard them say it was a fake ID, she got all pissed off that I lied to her. I couldn't believe that, as if my fake ID were half as bad as her being a hooker and everything. Fucking people.

By this time, there were three other cop cars and about ten cops hanging out. I'm telling you, that dark street looked like a fucking carnival with all those blue and red lights. I just kept watching the lights hit the side of the houses. It was actually kind of pretty. I'm telling you, I can be really cool under pressure, even if I am a little drunk and stoned. Cheryl could learn a thing or two about being cool, I mean, that chick was going absolute ape shit.

Finally they loaded her up in one of the cop cars and took her away. I heard them say she was going to the detox station until Monday. Tell you the truth, I wouldn't mind if they locked her up forever. Then they got me, I'd been sitting on the curb in handcuffs, and loaded me in the back of another car. Wasn't the first time I've ridden in the back of a cop car, but this one really stunk. It smelled like someone had puked or shit themselves back there.

At the station we did all the typical shit, like take my fingerprints and mugshot. The only good part was that since I'm eighteen they couldn't legally call my parents, unless I gave them permission. I didn't give them permission. So finally they threw me in a holding cell, said even though it was just a misdemeanor, I had to stay the night, since I was intoxicated. I thought that was strange, since there's about a million intoxicated people in this city, and they don't have to sleep in a holding cell.

There were two other dudes in that tiny concrete room. They were both asleep when I walked in, but one of them opened his eyes and looked at me. He said something in a language I couldn't understand, so I just nodded. The other one was snoring loud as hell. I just shuffled over to the empty cot and laid down. I had a hell of a time falling asleep. For some reason I just kept thinking about the old ranch house when I shared a room with Steve. I don't know why I couldn't stop thinking about that.

I remembered when we were young, after the lights were out, we'd stay up just shooting the shit in the dark. After a while, we'd have a contest to see who could flick their boogers the farthest. I know that's pretty gross and not what you want to hear. But it's the truth, that's what we'd do. There was a metal shelf equal distance from both of us, and you could hear if a booger hit it, that's how we knew who won. It's not like we did it every night. There were other things to do besides just flick boogers. I felt really sad lying there in that cell. Not because I had just gotten arrested, or that they stole my new ID. Silly shit like that is what I miss. Just lying in the dark flicking boogers with my brother.

I'm gonna sneak upstairs and see if I can grab something to eat without my dad hearing me. It's almost noon and I'm starving.

PAUSE.

Nope. That didn't work. I'm back in my room now. He was sitting up there like he was waiting for me. He was pissed as hell when I walked in. He didn't even know I'd been arrested. Said he saw the taxi drop me off early this morning. I just told him some bull shit about getting lost and having to stay in a motel. I don't know if he believed me. I've honestly never seen my dad that irate before. He said the reason he was mad was because he worried about me, that there's always random murders in this city. He's been pretty paranoid ever since Steve died. He was so pissed he said I'd have to take a taxi to the airport, and that he didn't want me coming back to visit. He said he didn't want to see me again until I got my shit together. He actually used the word shit.

The thing is, when I got up there, he was sitting on his chair holding this fancy wooden fly rod tube. After he got done yelling, he handed it to me. He said it was Steve's old bamboo fly rod. So I just pulled the thing out and had a look. It sure is nice, I mean, from a craftsman perspective. Super light with these olive green threads. The reel looks about as old as rocks. It doesn't fit in the wooden tube, so it's got this other little leather satchel.

Tell you the truth, I'm surprised my old man gave it to me, after he got so pissed and all.

I'm all packed up, guess I'll wait outside for the taxi. Looks like it's going to rain out there, I mean you can see these big dark clouds hanging low over the ocean. I'm not really looking forward to this damn plane ride. I can't wait to get home though, I need to check on my weed. Glad I left that half joint hidden at the airport. The little roach I smoked this morning was all I had left. Think I'll leave this thing recording and plug in the mic while I walk out, just so you can hear how pissed my dad is.

Alright dad, well, I'm outta here.

Listen to me Eddie. I've been thinking, you know, there was a time when I was your age. I was even younger once. Doesn't seem that long ago, really. Yet so much has happened. It's inconceivable how much can happen. That's the funny thing though, we count time as if years are these extended durations or great landmarks. They're so damn short after you've experienced enough of them. Things just pile up on top of each other. Pretty soon you start to forget the sequence of events. It might not seem like it now, since you're young, but every single day is important. If I could wish one thing for you, it would be to take things slow and appreciate the motions. But I understand that won't happen. It's one of those things that can't happen. Life's too damn powerful and we all get swept away by it. I'm sorry I don't have any other advice for you. I tried to be a good father. I wanted nothing but the best for my family. I still do. But it's up to you now. I can't be there for you anymore, and pretty soon, nobody will. That's the hardest lesson you might ever learn, but it's also the truest. I want the best for you, and that's why I'm not allowing you to visit. You need to figure out who you are, Ed Young. Until then, there's nothing I can offer.

Whatever you say, dad.

I know. This isn't something I expect you to understand right away. I see you're taking Steve's fly rod. I wasn't sure if you would, or if I should let you. I want you to use it. Take some time away from your friends, or whatever else seems so important. Trust me, take some time away and find yourself.

I have to go dad, the taxi's here.

Okay. Before you leave, I have one more thing for you. Here, it's a box of trout flies that Steve tied. That should be enough to get you started. If you need more, I'm sure you can buy some at a local shop. Or you can learn to tie your own. That's what Steve did.

You know Steve wanted to be just like you, dad.

Goodbye Eddie.

PAUSE.

Now I'm just waiting in the security line at the airport. They already called my flight, so it's gonna be close. I just keep thinking about what my dad said. I don't know if there's anything to it, like spending time fishing is supposed to help me. I don't know what he even thinks I need help with. And what I really don't understand is why all these adults think I need help or that they're the ones to give it to me. It's not like they're doing so terrific.

PAUSE

Alright, I'm sitting in the plane now, the engines are getting loud so we must be about to take off. I've got a whole row to myself again, so I'll probably read and try to sleep. I just keep thinking about what my dad said. I wish I wasn't. I really don't understand how things got this way. I remember when my father was a hero. At least that's how I saw him. I'd often imagine some dangerous scene, you know how kids are, always imagining shit. Well I'd imagine armed Russian gangsters breaking into our house, and I'd really act out the thing in my head. It was so real I can still see it. They could speak English, but with really terrible accents. For some reason these Russian gangsters had broken into our house and taken us hostage. Sounds crazy when I think about it now, why would Russian gangsters want to take my boring old family hostage, but it seemed pretty reasonable to my young mind. There was always a scene when we'd fight back and break free. It never went down as it was supposed to, but no matter what happened, my dad would always take a bullet for us, to save his family. He never died or anything, maybe just shot in the arm or gut. I remember thinking it actually happened, like the next time I saw my dad he was going to have a big old bandage on his arm where he got shot. That's how real it was. Now my dad just lives in a dirty old house boat and plays gigs at the local dive bars. He doesn't seem so heroic to me now, though, even though I still remember him that way. Fucking time.

STOP.

The sky was cloudy and grey when Eddie walked out of the airport. Off in the distance, beyond the clouds, he saw the sun dropping below the mountains. There were so many colors on that horizon, and they all melted together where the mountains and the clouds met the sunlight. He remembered what his dad had said, about finding himself, and those mountains looked too far away for a self-searching quest. His place was in this city, on these streets, where he was known and peopled depended on him.

He found the half-joint hidden behind the sign and lit it up. This time he hid behind a pickup truck, last thing he needed was to get arrested twice in one weekend. He pulled the smoke in deep, and it sure tasted good. Sunday night and it was still early enough to do business. He called a taxi and made a stop at the motel.

Eddie stepped out of the taxi in front of the motel, and as he walked into his room, he spoke to himself, "Mother fucking Scarface." The room was untouched, nothing changed since he left it. He grabbed his duffel bag from the closet, popped off the ceiling fan to remove his stash and cash, and then, after loading it into the duffel bag, he hung the bag around his shoulder and stood in front of the mirror. The black eye was starting to heal, but still noticeable. For a moment the reflection was that of a stranger. He blinked his eyes and saw himself as a young boy, chubby cheeks, messy hair, clothes dirty as they always were when he lived the country life. Then he blinked again and saw himself as he was now. Tall, clean, mature, and then he added another mental note to the list—registered criminal. He smiled and walked out of the room.

On the way home he sat in the backseat of the taxi looking out the window at the city streets and people passing in a blur. This was alright, having a driver take him wherever he wanted to go. This was something he could get used to. Maybe he'd buy a limo. Shit, then he'd really be a kingpin. Lynch would respect him and Blunt would fear him. Just ride around in back smoking joints and making stops to sell his primo shit. He'd have his choice of high-class women. People already knew him, but if he started doing business out of a limo, fuck, they'd make movies about him. That limo would have the best damn stereo in the country. Neon lights illuminating the interior. He'd be such big time that the cops wouldn't even fuck with him.

He was enjoying this image, it made him excited, and created a sense of ambition. He started to plan the rest of his night. First, he would go home, give his mom a kiss on the forehead, and tell her how grateful he was that she suggested he visit his dad. Then he would pick up Carl, give a playful dinosaur growl, and hold him high in the air. Shit, he might even go so far as to thank Cole for buying the plane ticket. After the household niceties were complete, he would hop in the Rover, crank the stereo – damn, he really missed that thing the past couple days – and then pay James a visit. James really was like a brother to him, even if he was rather depressing. They'd hang out, play a few video games, reminisce about Steve, and then Eddie would leave. He would roam the streets, make some sales, and see some friends. This was his town. He was really getting into this idea now, so he pulled out his mobile and sent a page to everyone on his list to let them know he was back: 420-420-420.

The taxi pulled up along the curb in front of his house. The neighborhood was quiet, and lit peacefully by the street lamps. It was the type of cool spring evening that existed in proximity to mountains – he could see his breath in the air, but his body felt warm. He carried his bag and Steve's old fly rod case towards the front door with his head held high, and then noticed something wrong. This couldn't be possible, and for a brief moment he refused to accept the obvious. He rushed up to the Rover and saw the shards of glass scattered across the driver's seat. The receiver had been ripped out of the dash and torn wires dangled loosely. Shit. Maybe they hadn't gotten the speakers. He opened the backdoor and looked into the trunk. Gone. Everything. Fuck.

He threw his bag and rod case on the ground and paced up and down the driveway. He wanted to kick something, or growl ferociously into the air, but he restrained. Who the hell would do this, in this neighborhood? The city was full of crime, but rarely did it touch these streets. Cole had done his research when selecting this house, knowing Samantha needed safety after what she had gone through. This couldn't happen here, somebody must've seen something. Who the fuck would have done this to him?

His pager kept beeping with messages from people wanting some weed, so he turned the damn thing off. He was creating a mental list of suspects, but it could have easily been random. It was no secret that his stereo was the best in town, and someone could have easily followed him home, scouted the place, and waited for the right time to steal it. It could have been some great conspiracy enacted by a rival dealer, or even a client. Mostly though, he suspected Blunt. It wouldn't have been difficult for him to find out where Eddie lived. All he knew was there were more possibilities than certainties.

The funny thing was, he didn't really care too much about the stereo, he would make enough money selling the weed in his bag to buy another, even a better one. No, what really pissed him off was that they stole from him, Eddie Young. It was becoming a theme, and he had to put a stop to it. First thing tomorrow, he was going to see Lynch, get his piece.

When he entered the house, he found his mom, Cole, and Carl in the living room. There was an obvious energy of excitement in the air, and he quickly learned why. Carl had one hand on the coffee table, and was standing up on two wobbly legs. His mom looked towards Eddie briefly, and said, "Watch this." She was knelt on the ground about two feet from Carl with her arms open. "Come on Carl baby, show Eddie how big you are." Carl looked around the room as if he were gathering his bearings, and then released his hand from the table. He took one unbalanced step, composed himself, and then took two more, landing in his mother's arms. Cole clapped his hands from the couch nearby, and Samantha gave him a big cheerful hug. "Isn't this great Eddie, three days before his first birthday and he's walking. This might be the happiest day of my life. Aren't you proud of him?"

"That is amazing mom." For a moment he forgot about his stereo and the broken glass. He forgot about his weekend getting arrested, and his thirst for revenge on Blunt. That was the power innocence had over him, an ability to see something truly beautiful, and replace the darkness with light. He set his bag and rod case by the top of the stairs, and walked into the living room where he knelt beside his mom. "Let me try." He opened up his arms and said, "Come over here big guy, let's see what you've got." Carl gave him a hesitant look, and then smiled and took two steps into his arms. "You're a mobile little dinosaur now. Carl the T-Rex." He picked him up and gave him a big hug.

Cole was still sitting on the couch when he said, "So, did you see your car?"

Eddie raised Carl above his head, "Now you're a pterodactyl." Then he set him down.

"I'm really sorry about your stereo, Eddie," said his mom. "It's truly terrible that this happened."

"Don't worry about it mom. Carl's walking." This simple act transformed the young boy in his mind from something small and unrelatable, to an actual animate human being, a person who he would know the rest of his life, a person who would look up to him the way he used to look up to Steve.

"Well, okay. I did call the cops. They came and filed a report. Said the burglars probably used a spark plug on the window, I guess that can break glass without making much noise."

"You should know Eddie," began Cole, "that the likelihood of them catching the people who did this, or them retrieving your stereo, is highly improbable."

Eddie stood Carl up on his feet, held him by the hands, and then slowly released him. "Now walk over to your mommy little dinosaur."

"Come here baby Carl." She opened her arms and he walked in. "So, how was the visit with your dad? What did you two talk about?"

"Oh you know dad, he's basically a stoic. Talking was never his priority."

"That's mostly true. But you spent an entire weekend together. Didn't he ask you how things are going or say anything to you?"

"He basically said he wished I was more like Steve."

"I doubt that. Your father was very proud of you."

"*Was* is the key word there, mom."

"What did he say, exactly?"

"Exactly? I don't remember exactly. He gave me Steve's old fly rod. Said I should go fishing alone in the mountains to slow down time. He said every single day is important and that fly fishing would teach me to appreciate the motions."

"You're right, Eddie. Your father never opened up much. He wasn't a very expressive guy. But it's the men who rarely say sentimental things that say them best when they do. Are you going to take his advice?"

"About fishing? I don't know mom, I'm pretty busy with work and school and everything. Maybe later."

"Let me know if you'd ever like me to take you fishing," said Cole.

"Sure thing." Eddie imagined this would include a visit to the Lost Horse River Park, where they'd sit on lawn chairs by the shore, drink apple juice, eat brownies his mom made, and cast corn into the water then stare at bobbers for an hour. Probably talk about golf or bowling.

"So he's doing okay? Your dad, I mean."

"He's doing just fine mom. I wouldn't worry about old Dennis Young."

"And he's okay with you going back next weekend?"

"Absolutely. We've already got a long list of things to do."

"That's great. Don't you think you should thank Cole for buying the tickets?"

"It's no big deal mom, I'd be happy to buy my own tickets. I do have a job, you know."

"Eddie, it's my pleasure," said Cole. "Anything I can do to help."

"Well, I think I'd better get down to bed. It's been a long weekend and school's going to come early. Goodnight little dinosaur." He gave Carl a hug, his mom a kiss on the forehead, and nodded at Cole, then proceeded to gather his rod case and bag and walk downstairs.

APRIL 1999

SUN	MON	TUE	WED	THU	FRI	SAT
				~~1~~	~~2~~	~~3~~
~~4~~	~~5~~	~~6~~	~~7~~	~~8~~	~~9~~	~~10~~
~~11~~	~~12~~	~~13~~	~~14~~	~~15~~	~~16~~	~~17~~
~~18~~	~~19~~	~~20~~	~~21~~	~~22~~	~~23~~	~~24~~
~~25~~	26	27	28	29	30	

Eddie swept the shards of glass off the driver seat onto the floor of the Rover. He hopped in and fired up a joint, then backed out of the driveway. The smoke was pulled out the broken window as he drove through the crowded streets. He heard the engines of cars rattling, poorly tuned stereos blasting, and that ubiquitous energy which flows through all cities during morning rush hour. This was the source of great frustration for him, and these sounds reminded him of his anger.

He parked in the far end of the lot at school where no one would notice him. With a broken window he couldn't lock the doors, which made his stash vulnerable. He wasn't going to bring it inside because you could smell the fresh buds seeping out of his backpack. There wasn't going to be any business until lunch hour, so he had to find a safe place to hide it. He popped the hood and stepped out of the car. There was nobody around, and he made sure nobody was watching. The 3.5 gallon Ziploc bag fit snugly beside the battery casing. He locked the doors out of habit, and walked inside carrying a backpack that only contained one notebook and a couple of pens. His cargo pocket bulged from the cash inside.

He found Scott who was standing in a circle of other hockey players. Circles of people always confounded Eddie and made him uncomfortable. They all looked so confident in their tight jeans and form-fitting shirts. You could almost believe that by passing the puck around on the ice made them superior beings. Eddie wasn't fooled, in fact, he felt sorry for them. Not because they played hockey, everyone needed a hobby. No, he felt sorry for them because in this circle none of them actually existed. Circles were predictable, rolled at definable speeds, and had no individual points, no singularity, and only occurred in uniformity. Maybe they were lucky that way. Eddie didn't know, and none of the books he read gave him an identifiable system for judging better or worse when it came to human behavior. He only knew they were different than him.

"Scott. Hey Scott," said Eddie. It must be a game day, he thought, as he noticed each of them were wearing hats with their jersey number embroidered on the front.

"Scott, who's that?" asked the kid wearing number fourteen.

Scott turned around and looked at Eddie. "Shit bro, I didn't see you there." Then he looked back at number fourteen and said, "Don't worry about him, I'll handle this."

"Come on Scott, I need to talk to you for a second. Some serious shit happened while I was gone."

"You were gone? Oh yeah, that's right. What's up?"

"Just follow me a second." Eddie guided him down the hall, past the lockers and class rooms, around the circles of kids standing with others like them. They went around a corner and stood near the Principal's office, nobody ever hung out here. "Have you heard anyone talking about my stereo?"

"Your stereo? You mean other than every kid in school wishing they had one as bad ass? Not lately. Why?"

"Shit man, I got home last night and my Rover was all broken into. They took everything."

"Fuck. Well, I suppose it was bound to happen. People are always jacking systems around here. Did you call the cops?"

"No, but my mom did. It's not like they're going to do anything. I've got to find these people myself."

"What are you gonna do?"

"Get my shit back of course. Then teach them a lesson."

"Whatever you say Eddie. Listen, I've got to get back to the team, we've got our first state finals game tonight. I'll keep my ears open though."

"You do that. And tell people I'm offering a reward. An ounce of the primo shit for any information."

"Sure thing Eddie." Scott turned to leave.

"And Scott, good luck at the game tonight man. I predict you score five goals." Scott turned his head and winked at Eddie, and then made a motion with his hands like shooting a puck. Eddie nodded, and then went back down the hall, stopping to talk to every familiar face he saw. He told them all about his stereo and the reward. Sooner or later, somebody would talk. Nobody could keep something like this a secret. He suspected that if someone from school jacked his stereo, they did it for bragging rights. They'd be the leader of their crew to say they jacked Eddie Young.

Down the hall he found Alex, just as the first bell rang. The kid was always nervous as hell, a poet with allergies. What a mess. His home life wasn't exactly the greatest, hadn't been since he first entered foster care. Soon he would be eighteen and swore he'd leave. Eddie suspected the allergies were more of a psychological defense, developed from all the shit he's dealt with, rather than an actual physical ailment.

"Hey Alex, we need to talk man."

"Sure thing Eddie, but let's wait until after class. I can't be late for first hour."

"Fine. But meet me right here after."

Eddie continued down the hall and entered Mr. Bonnell's class. Even though he was known, he felt like a stranger walking into this room. Bonnell gave him a nod and a faint smile as he walked in. Eddie sat in a desk at the far corner and pulled out his voice recorder. He looked at it and thought about the journal he'd started. What the hell would Bonnell think about his rambling words? It seemed too personal to him now to ever be shared with another person, let alone an adult, a teacher. His thumb hovered over the *delete* button, and then Bonnell stood up and addressed the class. Eddie put the recorder back in his pocket and listened.

"I hope everyone had a great weekend. By a show of hands, who finished the reading assignment?" Half the class raised their hands, the other half shuffled in their seats. Eddie crossed his arms over his chest, feeling bored already.

"Good. Now, for those of you who just raised your hands, can anyone give me a brief synopsis of this book?" He held up a copy of *The Red Badge of Courage*, by Stephen Crane. He looked around the room but nobody spoke, either they didn't know the answer, or were too embarrassed because they did.

Eddie remembered that book. The year after Steve died he had spent most of his time in his bedroom reading. He read so much that his dad bought him a line of credit at the local bookstore so he could pick up as many books as he wanted. He spent that year reading in his bedroom at their old house on the east side, while his mom and dad were growing further apart. He read one-hundred and twelve books in eleven months, and even kept a book journal where he recorded the title, author, date read, synopsis in his own words, favorite quote, and a rating on the zero-to-five scale. *Red Badge of Courage* got a four.

Eddie started to raise his hand, but then decided to just speak instead. "He had been out among the dragons, he said, and he assured himself that they were not so hideous as he had imagined them."

He felt the eyes of everyone in the class turn towards him. That's when he noticed her, Vanya, sitting in the front row. She was the only one who didn't look at him, instead, she was writing something down on her notepad. Eddie felt a hollowness in his stomach, and his heart beating in his chest. A reaction not from all the eyes upon him, but from the only pair in the room that weren't.

Bonnell rubbed his eyebrows, and then said, "That's good Eddie. However, it doesn't answer my question. I asked for a synopsis, in your own words. Can you do that?"

"Certainly. I think that book was about…"

"Eddie, please stand to address the class."

Fuck. What was Bonnell's problem? Surely he was just messing with him, punishing him for all the times he'd skipped class. Didn't matter. Eddie stood up and calmed his breath. He was looking towards Vanya, who still had her head turned away. Nobody else in the room mattered right now. He spoke his words confidently, imagining her hair in his hands as they sat alone together beside a mountain stream discussing literature. It would be a sunny day, but slightly cool, so she'd sit really close, and there'd be birds chirping in the pine trees and trout rising in the river.

"The term red badge of courage was used as a symbol for being wounded in battle, like if you had bled on the battle field that meant you were courageous. But the book was deeper, because the protagonist was never actually wounded in battle, at least not physically from the enemy. His wounds came from an understanding that could never be reversed, an understanding of the evil in men that would no doubt haunt him and direct his future existence. It's a lesson that once learned, can never be reversed."

"Well said Eddie." Bonnell rubbed his eyebrows again, apparently deep in thought, or at least trying to give that impression. "I have to ask, since you weren't here last week when I gave the assignment, when did you read this book?"

Eddie sat down and looked back towards Vanya's soft brown hair. It was braided in long pigtails today. Nobody wore pigtails anymore. He wondered if she knew this, or just simply didn't care. "I don't know, probably two or three years ago, I guess."

"Two or three years ago," reiterated Bonnell, now directing the class. "You see students, a good book will stay with you for longer than the time it takes to read it. For the rest of class today I want everyone to write a three-hundred word synopsis about this book. If you haven't finished it yet, spend this time reading. The assignment will be due tomorrow."

After class, Eddie rushed out to the hall to the place he was supposed to meet Alex. The halls were crowded and loud, similar to the streets of this city. He kept popping up on his toes to look for Alex, scanning the faces left to right. The next bell rang and the halls thinned out. Alex never showed, but Eddie wasn't too surprised, that kid was nervous as hell.

When lunch hour arrived, Eddie jogged out of the building and hopped in the Rover. He made it half a mile down the street before remembering his weed was stuffed in the engine. He pulled into an alley and retrieved the bag. The plastic had started to melt from rubbing against the engine block, and a couple of buds along the edges were burnt. Not a big deal, he removed the burnt buds and smoked them on his way to the mall. Business was good, a lot of kids skipped class on Monday's, and he sold most of the stash within twenty minutes.

Now he had enough money to pay Lynch. First, he wanted to get this damn window fixed. He pulled into an auto shop and walked inside. There was a line at the reception window, so he stood and waited. He looked around the room at the patrons sitting on red vinyl chairs. The television on the wall was playing an old black and white rerun of the Andy Griffith Show.

When it was his turn, he walked to the receptionist and said, "I need someone who can replace my driver's window. It's been completely busted out."

"Can you leave it with us? Windows take a few days."

"Several days? No, no, that won't do. Can you get to it quicker?"

"No promises. Our local distributor typically has to order them."

"Can I talk to your manager?"

The receptionist sighed, said, "Sure, just a minute, I'll see if she's available," and then she disappeared into the back office door.

A moment later the manager walked out, approached the window and said, "Sir, I'm sorry, but we don't have the ability to rush windows."

"I understand," replied Eddie, "but can you just come out and take a look at it with me?"

"Sure. I'll meet you out front."

Eddie rushed out to the Rover, removed a large handful of sticky buds from the bag, and stuffed them into a smaller bag. When the manager approached, he said, "See, they completely smashed my window. Damn criminals. Jacked my stereo," he pointed inside at the dash with the wires dangling out.

"That sucks," began the manager, "and I feel for you, but windows take time."

"I understand, but would this help speed up the time?" He held the bag of neon green buds out, and opened them up. "Have a sniff."

The manager paused, looked at Eddie, then gave a faint smile and put her face in to take a whiff. "That's good stuff."

"It's yours if you can have it ready by tonight."

She looked at her watch, and then back at the shop. "I've got a guy who always has Toyota windows in stock. Shouldn't be a problem."

Eddie smiled and said, "You're the best. I'll be back late so just leave the keys on the rear tire." He handed her the keys, grabbed his pack, and then called a taxi to take him to the casino.

. . .

Lulu answered the door at the Warrior Suite. "Eddie, come on in." She gestured him into the room, and then whispered, "I should warn you, Lynch is pretty pissed."

"Why?"

"I don't know, said something about you owe him money."

"Well, that's why I'm here. See, I've got plenty of money." He pulled out the thick wad of cash.

"Don't show me, bring it to Lynch."

He found Lynch sitting on the couch watching a basketball game on the 64-inch television. "You better slam that shit!" he yelled at the screen. "These players are a bunch of wimps now-a-days. I'm telling you, get a game going here on the rez, and people know how to play. None of this throwing your hands up and crying every time somebody touches you. Do you play any ball, kid?" He still hadn't looked at Eddie, who was standing behind the couch.

"Not too much, you know. A little bit here and there."

"Do you play tough? Or do you play like one of these professional sissies?" He didn't wait for an answer. "I bet you play tough. Shit, see me on the courts, and fools give me space."

"I brought your money."

"What the fuck was that! I'm telling you, this game's gone to shit. Fuck this." He switched off the television and stood up to face Eddie. "You're late. I was gonna give you to the end of the day before sending Scooby after you for collection. I don't like it when people are late."

"I was out of town."

"That isn't my business." He pulled his long pony tail around to the front of his chest and started caressing it like a pet snake. "You owe me two grand for the pound, plus five hundred interest."

"Five hundred? It was only three days, you said a hundred a day."

"I changed my mind."

"Shit man, you're really cutting into my profits. I need the money, shit has happened."

"That's not my concern. I've got a mind to keep the five hundred you gave me for the piece. Kid like you needs to learn how this business works. Don't mess around with me."

"Don't worry about it man, it's no problem. Here," he reached into his pocket and counted out the money, "that doesn't leave me much. Did you get my piece or not."

"You'll get it this week." Lynch snatched the money out of his hand and sat down on the couch.

"Alright. I'm going to need another pound."

"Figured you would. Scooby's waiting for you downstairs. And Eddie, interest is now two hundred a day."

Eddie called a cab and went to his motel room. He rolled up a fat joint and held it in his hands. He looked out of a window that faced north, and he saw the miles and miles of prairie that stretched to the mountains. He watched the clouds roll over the mountains and drop down. It would rain tonight. The prairie grass bent and rolled and caught sunlight with every motion. He must have stood beside that window for an hour before realizing the joint was still in his fingers, unlit. He held it up to his nose and the aroma reminded him of how sage brush smelled when he and Steve gathered it for kindling. He put a flame to the joint and took a deep pull.

APRIL 1999

SUN	MON	TUE	WED	THU	FRI	SAT
				~~1~~	~~2~~	~~3~~
~~4~~	~~5~~	~~6~~	~~7~~	~~8~~	~~9~~	~~10~~
~~11~~	~~12~~	~~13~~	~~14~~	~~15~~	~~16~~	~~17~~
~~18~~	~~19~~	~~20~~	~~21~~	~~22~~	~~23~~	~~24~~
~~25~~	~~26~~	~~27~~	~~28~~	29	30	

Eddie spent Thursday morning in class. He decided to rotate every day; today he would go to his morning classes, tomorrow the afternoon, and so on. This seemed like a tolerable plan and would provide him enough credit to pass his classes and maybe even graduate. Graduating wasn't his highest priority, but if it could fit into the rest of his life, then he figured may as well do it.

At lunch hour he waited outside the front doors for Alex. Alex was one of the few kids he knew that he actually trusted. Mostly because they had committed crimes together, but also because he was fucked up. Being fucked up seemed more relatable to Eddie. Then he heard a loud, squeaking, snot infused sneeze from up the hall.

"Alex, what happened to you the other day? I waited for you."

"Shit Eddie, I totally forgot. After class I rushed into the library to write down this new poem. I've been having all kinds of crazy dreams lately, and it's given me tons of inspiration. Probably from the new medication."

"Yeah? Is it working?"

"Does it look like it?" He was a damn mess.

"I guess not. Maybe it'll kick in. So, you got anything for me to read?"

"Not yet. I'm working on putting a collection together though. I'll let you know when it's ready."

"Absolutely. But listen, I need to talk to you about something."

"Let me guess, this is about your stereo."

"How did you know?"

"Everyone's been talking about it. I must of heard them or something."

"What have you heard? I need some intel. Whoever took it, well, let's just say they'll regret fucking with me."

"Why, what are you gonna do?"

"I've got a plan, don't worry. Now, what did you hear?"

"Just that your shit was jacked man. Nobody knows anything. It was probably some random thing, you know. Maybe those punks from the south side who we fucked up last summer."

"Could be. But I doubt it."

"Why, what do you know?"

"This type of shit isn't random, and those other bastards have no idea where I live. I'll find the fuckers, whoever they are."

"Don't get your hopes up, that's all I'm saying."

"Don't worry about it. Listen, I'm ditching the afternoon. Did you need any weed before I bolt?"

"I'll take a quiper."

They went to the Rover and Eddie cut him off a quarter ounce. Several other people approached and he made a few sales. When he popped in and fired up the engine, out of habit he reached for the stereo dial, but only saw the red, yellow, and green wires dangling out of the dash. He put it in reverse and noticed a piece of paper on the windshield. He grabbed it and sat back in the car. It was a note from Vanya.

"Eddie, It's been nice to have you back in Bonnell's class. I was really impressed by what you said on Monday. Sorry it took me a few days to write this. Truth is I'm not very good at making new friends. I didn't know you were into books. I like books too, but it seems like very few other kids here do. Maybe we could get together sometime and compare notes. Give me a call." She left her home phone number at the bottom, and drew a large heart around it.

Okay, so this chick was a little weird, he thought. Nobody wrote notes any more. They sent coded pager messages. But he actually liked that, something old fashioned and refreshing, from someone who either didn't know, or didn't care about the social normalities of her generation. He saved her number in his phone, and then shoved the note into his glove box.

He swung out to the motel to check on his stash. The front door of his room was ajar, so he grabbed the small pocket knife he kept in the center console and crept inside. The maid was tucking fresh sheets tight into the corner of his bed, and it smelled like bleach in the room. "Oh, hey," he said, surprised to see her. "I meant to leave the do not disturb sign on the door. Must've blown off from the storm last night."

"My apologies, sir." She spoke with a northern European accent. She was kind of cute too, he thought. But this thought didn't last very long, as he became more concerned about her finding his stash. As if the maids ever cleaned the ceiling above the bathroom fan.

"It's not a problem at all. Truth is, I just like doing my own cleaning. Gives me a task in the evenings."

"Yes, I understand." She gathered up her things, collected the garbage bags, and walked out.

"Thanks," he said, and shut the door.

He popped off the ceiling fan and pulled down his stash. Business had been going good, and yesterday he saw Lynch for two pounds, doubling his possession and his profit. It also meant he had to work twice as hard, which required a revised strategy. Now he had a couple of employees, or rather, sub-contractors who sold weed for him at a reasonable split. He was careful to select people who had their own list of clientele, and wouldn't try to sell to his customers. James was one of them, and even though he and James were good pals, James mostly knew different people. Plus, his pizza delivery gig was a perfect cover. It was easy for him to meet a couple customers while on a delivery run, and his manager wouldn't be the wiser. Shit, if anything, his manager would be one of his best customers.

Lynch still didn't have his piece when Eddie saw him yesterday. Said it would arrive today. Eddie was getting sick of the damn run-around. He could have gone to the pawn shop and had something by now. But the pawn shop would leave a paper trail, something doing business with Lynch never had. So he was patient. Patience gave him more time to plan his revenge.

His mobile rang. He had only given a few people his number. It was a call from James. "I'm working tonight and need something from you."

"I'll be there in five," he responded. It actually took closer to twenty minutes for him to drive through the traffic of this city. James already had his work uniform on and was waiting by the front door. He paid Eddie for yesterday's supply and requested another half pound.

"You're killing it, man," said Eddie.

"Shit, if I knew it was this easy, I would have started slanging a long time ago."

"It's not always easy. Just stick to your simple route, and you'll do fine."

"Don't worry about me. Listen, I need a favor."

"What's up?"

"I was supposed to go over to Cassie's. She fronted me some shrooms yesterday. I would've had time to stop there before work, but it took you so damn long to get here."

"Not a problem. How much do you owe her?"

"Nothing really, just five hundred."

"Five hundred? Are you selling shrooms now too?"

"Not at all. Now that I've got a little extra cash, figured I'd just buy larger quantities for myself. You know how it is, the more you buy, the more you save."

"Sure thing. Give me the money and I'll run it over."

Eddie hopped in the Rover and hit the streets. The trees in the city were budding, and he knew the prairies would be teeming with wild flowers soon. Up in the mountains, they'd be sparse yet, as there was likely still patches of snow at higher elevations. The rivers would be gaining momentum, probably already at their peak, and would begin to recede as there became less and less snow pack in the mountains. He continued to drive, through the reservation, around the casino, and to the west end of town. The city was located in a big basin surrounded by mountains. The mountains to the north were the largest, and even though the ones to the west were smaller, they were still pretty to look at. He watched them get closer as he drove towards Cassie's house on the outskirts of Rez Land.

Cassie's house was not even a house, it was a palace. The driveway was long and winding, with statues of exotic animals shaped in bronze. The yard sprawled out in all directions from the house, lush and full like a golf course, with particolored flowers and fruit trees. From his parking spot Eddie could see several maintenance crew members hustling around with lawn tools and doing work. There was a small pond on the east side of the property with a water fountain that shot high into the air. Eddie got out and walked towards the house. Near the front door was a fenced in area with nine Rottweilers who barked ferociously at him as he rang the doorbell and waited.

"Edwardo!" Cassie answered the door in nothing but a long t-shirt. He wasn't even sure if she was wearing panties underneath it. "What a surprise!" She jumped up and gave him a hug. This chick was always out of control when she was on coke. "So, what are you doing here? Come to party with me?"

"That would be great Cass. Would if I could. Actually, James asked me to stop by and drop off some cash for you."

"Oh Eddie, that's a drag. Not that I don't like the money, but that's all just for pretend. When are we gonna party again?"

Eddie couldn't remember ever directly partying with her, though he had been to a dozen of her parties. He was surprised she even remembered him being there, since it was usually a couple hundred people or more. "I'm open to suggestions," he replied.

"You absolutely have to come to my end of the year party. It's going to be the greatest one yet. Have I told you about the giraffes?"

"I seem to remember something about it."

"Guess what. They're here! Yep, arrived just yesterday. I haven't gotten to show them to anybody yet. Please, won't you come see them?"

"Show me the way."

She hopped outside barefoot and skipped across the lawn. Around back of the house was a large shed. Calling it a shed was a joke, it was bigger than the house Eddie lived in with three other people. "They're right in here," She swung open the large door. "I used to keep my Corvettes in here, but Lynch is watching them for me until I can get a new car garage built. Aren't they beautiful," she gestured towards the two young giraffes.

"Wow," said Eddie. "You actually did it."

"Of course I did. Don't worry though, I don't keep them in here all the time. I take them out for walks twice a day. They love prancing around the big yard."

"Do they have names?"

"Of course they do. I couldn't have two baby giraffes without giving them names. I call the boy over there Tillicum, and his sister is Ahote, which means the restless one. She's like me."

"They're really great. What are you gonna do when they get bigger?"

"Oh, they'll be outside. I'm going to have the entire south plot fenced in, I want them to feel free. I might even get some rhino's or something, make them feel at home."

"What about in the winter?"

"They'll be fine. I can have all kinds of heaters everywhere. Now stop being such a downer."

"I'm just trying to help."

"Oh, it's going to be so beautiful here. Just imagine coming over and seeing all these animals playing in the field, with the mountains right there. It'll be like my own private zoo, except I won't charge anyone to see it. If you're cool with me, you get the free exhibit. Don't you think that's a great idea?"

"You could be on to something." He thought she was absolutely insane. Only an eighteen-year-old girl living alone with too much money would concoct some crazy plan to have her own zoo with safari animals on the edge of a big city. That's okay, he thought, you had to be a little crazy and fucked up to survive this world. "And nobody cares that you have giraffes? I mean, is it legal?"

"Legal, ha, as if you're one to talk. But no, since you ask, nobody cares, at least, nobody can stop me. This is the rez after all."

"I see."

"So, are you going to stay and party with me?"

"I'd love to, but actually I need to go see your brother."

"Lynch? That wannabe gangster. You tell him I said that, he's a big old wannabe gangster. And don't let him fool you, he's really not all that tough either. You can tell him I said that, too."

"Sure thing." Eddie couldn't imagine a scenario where he'd ever say something like that to Lynch. Not that he was afraid of the guy, even if he did have tons of connections and even more machine guns. No, he just needed the steady hookup for weed. They were all using each other anyway. "I gotta go Cass."

"Okay. But listen, tell everyone you know about my party. I want it to be the wildest time ever."

That poor girl might be the loneliest person he knew, even if she did throw the biggest parties. He pulled out of there and within five minutes was at the casino. He did a quick count of his cash in the parking lot. Yep, he had enough for two more pounds, plus a little extra to cover the piece. He still had half a pound in his motel room, too. His business was booming, a god damn entrepreneur.

"I've got a surprise for you today, Eddie." Lynch seemed in much higher spirits than the last time he saw him. "Follow me."

Eddie followed him into the kitchen. His eyes lit up at the sight of three machine guns spread out on the marble countertop. "Wow," was all he could say.

"Aren't they beautiful. I selected them especially for you. Keep up the good work, and I'll keep treating you right."

"Man. Those are something. Which one's mine?"

"You choose. They're all top of the line, and guaranteed to kick some ass."

Eddie already knew which one had his name on it. He picked up the jet black one with a matte finish. The steel felt cool in his grip. He extended the telescoping stock until it made contact with his bicep. The gun itself wasn't much longer than his forearm. The thing was light as hell, too. It had a long magazine that he grabbed with his left hand, and put his right finger on the trigger, applying just enough pressure to ignite the laser beam that hit the fridge door.

"Watch yourself, that thing is loaded."

Eddie removed his finger from the trigger. "What do you call this one?"

"That's the Sig Sauer MPX. Best in its class. Government issue. I had to use one of my classified connections to get that piece. Here, hand it over." Eddie passed it his direction. Lynch ejected the clip. "This one's nine mil, fully automatic, with the extended thirty round clip. If my brothers had this gun back in time, you white boys wouldn't be here."

"I like it. How much?"

"What'd you pay me already, five hundred?" Lynch rubbed his pony tail, pretending to be deep in thought. "Tell you what. Since you're doing so good, I'll cut you a deal. Another grand and it's yours. Shit, I'll even through in a box of ammo."

Eddie did a mental inventory of how much money he had. There was enough in his pocket to cover two pounds, plus this gun, but he wouldn't have much left. That was alright, he needed a piece, and this looked like the right one. Money didn't really mean much to him, he could sell a bunch of weed tonight and have a fat roll in his pocket before morning. "You've got a deal."

Lynch put the machine gun in a duffel bag with a box of cartridges, and handed it to Eddie. He told him to meet Scooby downstairs for his weed. Eddie exited the casino with a fully automatic machine gun in one hand, and two pounds of primo weed in the other. They didn't teach him anything about this in school.

It was four PM now, and Carl's birthday party was at six. Eddie still hadn't gotten him a gift. He swung into the mall, made a couple quick sales, just enough to afford Carl's gift, and then went to the music store. Carl was turning one, a huge milestone, plus he was walking. Eddie didn't want to get him any old generic gift. No, he was going to get him something awesome, something to rock his little world.

He found a youth-sized Ibanez acoustic-electric guitar, with a cut-away shape, made of spruce and mahogany, painted denim blue with black trim. This thing said rock star all over it. Certainly much more than his one year old half-brother needed, but he wanted to get him the best. Shit, this thing was taller than Carl, but he'd grow into it. The salesman said it was the best guitar they carried for beginners. The only difference between this one, and a guitar professionals used, was the size.

. . .

Eddie entered the front door, saw his mom preparing dinner in the kitchen, and Cole and Carl in the living room playing with dinosaurs. He started to take off his shoes, and then realized he brought the wrong bag inside. In his hand was the duffel bag with a machine gun. Fuck, he must be really stoned. He stood in the entryway wondering if anyone noticed. Neither his mom, Cole, nor Carl seemed to know he was there. They hadn't noticed him in a while. He was the invisible member of this new family. He went back out to the car and swapped it for the guitar.

"Eddie, you're late," said his mom after he entered the kitchen. "We were wondering if you'd make it."

"Sorry mom, I was at work. I told my boss it was my little bro's birthday, and he said I could take an extra-long break. I need to be back at seven."

"Well, that doesn't give us much time, but at least you made it."

"That smells delicious. What did you make?"

"Red lentils with Basmati rice, a few spices. You probably smell the coconut milk. It's all organic, of course. Plus, it's really soft food, so Carl can eat it. I made a crustless apple pie for dessert."

"You've been busy. Did you give him his presents yet?"

"Of course not, you know we always do that after dinner. Let's sit down and eat." She called Cole and Carl into the dining area. They set Carl in his highchair and all sang happy birthday.

"So, how's work Eddie?" asked Cole.

"Oh you know, always busy."

"I bet. I still don't understand how I can order something from clear across the country and have it at my door the less than ten days."

"It's truly an intricate system. A lot of hands and minds involved."

"I believe it. I just ordered a new work shirt, from that catalog you gave me, Samantha," he looked at Eddie's mom, smiled, and then continued. "You know I'm meeting some real important people from the governor's office tomorrow." He looked at Samantha again and gave her a big proud smile. "Anyway, I just ordered the thing last week, and it arrived today. Actually, the driver was just pulling up as I got home. You might know her, said her name was Jen."

"Sounds familiar. There's a lot of people there though."

"Yeah, I asked her if she knew you, but she said pretty much the same thing. Too many people."

"Is everyone ready for pie?" asked his mom. She served them all a dish, and Eddie used a baby spoon to feed Carl. Nobody said much more until they were all done with the pie.

"So, can we do presents quick? I do have to get back to work."

"Let's do it," answered Cole.

"Great," Eddie got up and retrieved the bag. "I didn't have a chance to wrap it." He laid it on the table in front of Carl. It was in a large plastic bag, and the upper frets stuck out the top.

"My gosh Eddie, what did you do?" exclaimed his mom. Carl started playing with the plastic bag, enjoying the sound it made. Then he started slamming on the guitar, really hard, so you could hear the strings vibrating.

"Here, let me help you with that little buddy." He removed the guitar from the bag and gave it a quick strum for Carl. "Now this is how you do it," he strummed it again. "If you can learn to play the guitar, you'll never have a problem getting a date for the rest of your life."

"Is that an Ibanez?" asked Cole. "Those things are expensive."

"Nothing but the best for my baby bro."

"Eddie, you didn't have to do this," said his mom. "He's not even going to be able to play the thing for a few years." Carl was smacking the wooden face of the guitar with one hand, and the strings with the other.

"Nonsense mom, look, he's a natural."

"Don't you think he's too young for a guitar?" asked Cole.

"I don't expect him to start strumming a song for us right away. I thought it would be a good developmental tool for him, you know, to learn that he can use something as simple as wood and strings, and have it respond to his influence."

"That's a really sweet thought," said his mom.

"I don't know," added Cole, "that's an expensive piece of equipment. We might want to put it away until he can respect it."

"What's your problem?" asked Eddie.

"What do you mean? I'm just trying to be the voice of reason here."

"All I wanted was to buy my little brother a gift." He stood up and brought his dishes to the sink.

"Eddie ..." started his mom, but she couldn't finish the sentence. "I'm glad you made it for this. I'm sure Carl will love his present," then she looked at Cole, and continued, "when it's time."

"I've got to get back to work." He patted Carl on the head, and said, "Happy birthday little bro. Enjoy this time while you can, pretty soon everyone will expect something from you."

MAY 1999

SUN	MON	TUE	WED	THU	FRI	SAT
~~25~~	~~26~~	~~27~~	~~28~~	~~29~~	~~30~~	1
2	3	4	5	6	7	8
9	10	11	12	13	14	15
16	17	18	19	20	21	22
23	24	25	26	27	28	29
30	31					

Saturday night, and Eddie had a plan. He thought about the people he knew, friends and acquaintances, others of his age. They were probably out partying, or driving around, definitely getting fucked up one way or the other. There might be a few who were at home studying, or working a part-time job somewhere, but not many. Eddie was onto something different.

He took the plane ticket off the counter this morning, and left a note for his mom saying he was going to drive to the airport, instead of taking a taxi, and keep the Rover parked there. They had security cameras in the parking lot, and he didn't want to risk his Rover getting broke into again. He'd be back Sunday night, after spending the weekend with his dad. So, he spent the early part of today making the rounds and selling his weed. He's been in the motel room for several hours now, planning his revenge.

Eddie dressed in black from head to foot. He stood in front of the bathroom mirror and looked deep into his own eyes. He leaned his hands upon the porcelain sink, and spent many long moments there in a trance. This was not a gaze into the colorful reflection of vanity, it was a stare of studious introspection into the vacuity of his soul. Then he noticed the bruise on his eye was mostly faded, but still a prominent feature on his face. He looked deep until he no longer saw himself or the bruise, but rather, the person he imagined the world saw. Young and dangerous. Unpredictable and powerful. He started shaking his hands to a song in his head, and then turned back to the bed.

Spread across the comforter was his Sig Sauer MPX fully automatic jet black machine gun with telescoping stock and thirty round clip. Also upon the bed was a pair of chrome handcuffs, shiny brass knuckles, a Spider Co pocket knife, and two fully loaded blunts. He fluffed up the pillows, laid down upon the mattress, and smoked one of the blunts, taking his time, feeling every cloud of smoke fill his lungs.

He loaded his gear in a duffel bag and popped into the Rover, then peeled out of there. The sky was dark above this yellow city. The streets were loud, and without his stereo, he was forced to hear every noise carried by the pavement, echoing between the highrises, shopping centers, and convenience stores. He pulled into Bad Town, parked in an alley two blocks from Blunt's place, and unloaded his gear.

He walked in the shadows and stayed out of sight. Not that it would have mattered, this city was so loud and busy that nobody would have noticed him even if he were wearing hot pink and shooting off bottle rockets. Everyone was too busy and wrapped up with their own shit. But he had more fun this way, imagining himself on a movie screen, and this was the final showdown, the gunfight where the hero earned his retribution.

He approached Blunt's house from the back, hopped over a loose chain-link fence, and scrambled slowly across the small yard. There were lights on throughout the house. He calmed his breath, and peaked into a window. Nobody. All he saw was a fucking mess.

There was less than ten feet between Blunt's house and the one next door. Eddie crept lowly between the two, and peaked into another window closer to the front, but only saw more shit scattered everywhere. Then he heard voices on the porch.

"Those fucking punks, they've got nothing on us," said Blunt.

"Taught them a good lesson boy," sounded like Gunner.

"Did you see the look in that fools eyes, when we scared the shit out of his dog?"

"They won't come around here again."

Eddie slid up near the front of the house. From the window nextdoor he heard music, a classic R&B rhythm, "…wishing only good for you, all you gotta do, is just want it, and it's gonna come…" He knew that song. It was *Brother, Brother*, by the Isley Brothers. He sat down with his back leaning against Blunt's house, and rested his machine gun across his knees. The brass knuckles were in his front right pocket, and he gripped the handle of the gun. He continued to listen to the conversation happening on the porch. It sounded like there were only two of them.

He stood up and hid behind a dead shrub and watched them on the porch. Gunner was a big dude, likely the one who had knocked him unconscious and gave him the black eye. He wasn't sure, couldn't remember too much about that day. What really pissed him off was the stereo. That happened at his house in proximity to his family. His mom and Carl were inside, probably sleeping, and these fucking thugs thought they could come onto his property and rob him. There'd be no reasoning with them now, they had to learn the hard way.

Eddie came low around the bush towards the front of the house. Traffic crawled slowly on the street only thirty feet away. He stayed low until reaching the front of the porch, and popped up with his gun aimed on Blunt. "Get in the fucking house!" He rushed up the tattered steps towards them, onto the small old wooden porch. He waved the barrel back and forth between the two, and guided them into the house.

"Fool, you better get that gun off of me," said Blunt as they stood inside the front room.

"Get back, get the fuck back!" said Eddie, and guided them down the short hall to the living room. "Now get on your fucking knees."

"I kneel for no one," said Gunner. Eddie saw a look in this man's eyes that expressed no fear, only anger. Certainly not the first gun ever jabbed in his face. In front of him Eddie didn't see Blunt or Gunner, he didn't consider the bag of weed stolen. This wasn't an issue of petty revenge. It had escalated, joined forces with something greater in his mind. What he saw was the criminal infection that contaminated this city. What he saw was his brothers smiling face now buried.

In one swift motion, Eddie hit Gunner square in the nose with the butt of his machine gun. Blunt tried to make a move, and Eddie turned the barrel back on him, two inches from his face. "I said get on your fucking knees!"

"You're gonna regret this fool," said Blunt as he knelt down and kept his eyes on Eddie.

"Now where is it?" exclaimed Eddie, hovering over the two and waving his gun back and forth.

"Where's what?"

"My fucking stereo."

"What the fuck are you talking about fool?"

"You know god damn well. Think you can come to my house? You better think again."

"Kid, I don't know a fucking thing about your stereo or your house.

But I can tell you one thing, I'm gonna find out where you live and fuck your shit up. You're dead. Your family's dead."

Eddie reached into his pocket for the brass knuckles, and tightened it around his fist. He swung at Blunt's face and made contact with his temple. This sent Blunt bent over on the ground for about five seconds. When he rose back to his knees, there was blood on his face, and fire in his eyes. His eyes spoke volumes about the pain he had received in life, about the pain he had given. Eddie knew then that this was a man who would never stop, a creature born of the darkness, a darkness Eddie had been introduced to, so he understood the hatred it caused. He believed this man would never stop until him and his entire family were dead.

He released the safety and held the barrel to Blunt's head. There was only one way out of this now. Then Gunner spoke, "Pull that trigger and I will rip you apart."

From outside came the loud booming of subwoofers. Eddie turned his head slightly to listen. He knew that sound unmistakably as his system, it was the only one so clean and crisp. An amp matched perfectly to the size and scope of the speakers, and empowered by a receiver that could handle the task. The bass vibrated low and powerful, and even at a distance Eddie could feel it vibrating the cartilage in his knees. This was the first time he had ever heard his system from a distance. He felt a moment of envy for creating wreckage in the ears of strangers.

He saw the lights of a car park in front of Blunt's house, and the music kept pounding. The paneling in this house which hung loosely from the walls vibrated from the bass, then it went quiet. He heard two car doors slam shut, and he inched back a step, barrel still aimed at Blunt's chest. After a moment he heard the front door open.

Eddie kept his gun aimed on Blunt, and turned his head towards the door. In walked Darnell who was holding a cigarette in his fingers, and he was followed by Alex who held a flip phone up near his face with one hand and a hankerchief in the other. Eddie was surprised for a moment, and in a state of disbelief. He made eye contact with Alex, and the entire room paused.

"Alex?" he said, but unable to develop any further question. Alex stood stock still holding his handkerchief halfway up to his face. His swollen eyes moved down to the machine gun in Eddie's hands.

"Eddie, what the fuck?" said Darnell, who's eyes were also locked on the machine gun.

Then, from the corner of his eyes, Eddie caught a movement. He turned towards his hostages. Gunner had jumped up in a bolt and removed a pistol from the back of his pants. The barrel was aimed directly at Eddie. Fuck. He should have patted them down. Next time he's ever holding two thugs hostage, he's going to remember to check them for weapons. Things never went the way they were supposed to.

"Give me your fucking gun!" said Blunt, now standing beside Gunner.

"No way. No way! Give me yours," said Eddie, waving the gun back and forth.

"Gunner, you better shoot this fool."

Eddie directed his barrel at Gunner. Less than two feet of air between them. Tight quarters, this had become more of a sword fight. He was a samurai with a machine gun. "Put your fucking gun down!"

Gunner cocked the hammer back and extended his arm. "Two seconds and I blow your head off."

Eddie started shuffling his feet towards the back door, never taking his eyes or his gun off of Gunner. With a back-kick, he flung the door open, and started to slide outside. Gunner was inching towards him, and Blunt yelled, "Shoot that fool!"

Eddie fired a round that hit the wall beside Gunner's head. He ducked outside just as the return fire came. He ran, fast as he ever had, hurdled the fence in a single motion, and hit the alley. Gunner fired a couple shots out the back door that hit the gravel beside Eddie's feet. He pushed farther down the alley with Gunner and Blunt rushing upon him, both now armed. They fired at him, and he fired back.

He turned left and across the busy street, cutting through the slow-moving cars. He caught the eyes of a driver, a middle-aged man in a blue dress shirt buttoned all the way to his neck. The man looked absolutely horror-stricken by Eddie running across the street with a machine gun. Eddie imagined that the man just now realized everything he had heard about Bad Town was true. He'd have a hell of a story to tell his cubicle neighbors back at work.

Eddie ran into another alley, getting short on breath, and looked back. His pursuers were not far behind. They exchanged more gun fire. The shots were bright flickers of lightning with immediate thunder clasps. A hundred feet apart and running, they all missed their targets.

Eddie stopped at the end of an alley and ducked behind a steel dumpster. He peeked his head around to view his pursuers who were gaining ground. The alley was narrow, about the width of a vehicle, with tall wooden fences on both sides. This looked like a good spot for a gunfight. As good as any.

He took two deep breaths, and then popped up and sprayed fire. Three rounds shot out before he heard the *tat, tat, tat* of an empty clip. Fuck. His shells were in the Rover, three blocks away across the busy street. He hadn't imagined needing more than the thirty rounds in the clip. Gunner and Blunt were still approaching, but noticeably tiring, and had slowed to a medium pace. He concealed himself behind the dumpster again, took several deep breaths, and then bolted.

He lost them through the jungle of lawns and the tangle of side streets. When he returned to the Rover, he tossed the machine gun on the passenger seat, and pulled away. In the distance he heard sirens coming. There was something he had to know first, so he drove past Blunt's house, and sure enough, it was Alex's car parked in front. It was Alex's car that housed his stereo. He waved a middle finger at the house and headed out of town, sticking to the back streets, weaving his way north.

He continued to drive out of the city limits. The prairie was only darkness in the night, and above him hung the flickering beams of starlight. The mountains were barely visible on the horizon, etched with sharp blue lines into the shadows. He pulled down a gravel road and parked. He replayed the event through his mind, and knew the worst was yet to come. He tried to sleep in the driver's seat, but spent the entire night shifting with closed eyes and remembering the surprise on Alex's face when he entered Blunt's house. He was trying to figure out which of them must have looked more shocked; himself being confronted with the realization it was a friend who jacked his stereo, or Alex entering and seeing him holding a machine gun to the heads of two thugs. He reached over to the passenger seat, picked up the gun, reloaded the clip, and then rested cold steel on his lap while he waited for daylight.

. . .

Sunrise came over the mountains and crashed through his windows. Prairie grass was illuminated and shadows swayed with a gentle rhythm. He scratched open his eyes and saw a herd of antelope grazing in the field nearby. For a moment, however brief, this world was peaceful and old. Last night was a nightmare that clawed its way out of the darkness. He laid his hand upon the machine gun, cold steel on his lap. In his rearview he saw the city, reflective and tall. Through his windshield, the mountains were auspicious and calm. He fired up the engine, and drove north.

He got back on the paved road that bent around the hills and beside the river. He drove slowly, watched the water cut over boulders, and saw a pair of falcons gliding low. Several miles up, the road turned to loose gravel, and diverted from the river. Now the hills grew larger, and narrow driveways jutted off every couple miles like tributaries. It was Sunday, and his mom wouldn't expect him back from his dad's until late this evening.

He pulled off on the shoulder on top of a hill and got out. The mountains were close enough to smell now, and he was taken back to a time long ago. His eyes scanned the landscape, rough and rugged, but also gentle and serene. Just to the west he saw a ranch spread through a valley where a small creek came down. In the field were hundreds of sheep, white, grey, and black. Behind them he saw two horses, saddled and ridden by ranchers. Cowboys still like the days before. Somehow this valley had been unmolested by the city. They had remained in an older time. But he knew it wouldn't always be.

He continued to drive slowly, eyes on the ranch, and his mind replayed memories from his youth. He could see Steve clearly, the day he returned from the river with a twenty-two inch rainbow trout. He held that fish as if it were a bag of gold, and the smile on his face was worth twice as much. They rarely killed large trout from the river, the smaller ones were better eating, but Steve wanted this one mounted. He brought it to a taxidermist who placed it on a piece of driftwood with Steve's custom stonefly nymph, the *Luminous*, hooked into its upper lip. They kept that thing mounted in the tree fort Steve had built, and whenever company came over, it was part of the mandatory tour. Eddie couldn't remember what happened to that fish since they moved away. There were a lot of things he couldn't remember. But he remembered Steve's smile.

The ranchers and flock of sheep were skirting the road in front of him, and he slowed down to let them cross. The horses were saddled with a middle-age man and a younger woman. Aside from the cowboy attire, the man didn't look much like a rancher. His face was clean shaven and smooth, and his back was straight. The woman had long brown hair that flowed out from her full-brimmed hat. She had on big aviator style sunglasses, so he couldn't see much of her face, but as she crossed the gravel road in front of him, he realized it was Vanya.

Eddie gave the horn a short beep, which startled the flock. The man tipped his hat Eddie's direction, and Vanya pulled her sunglasses down. The mountains were pastoral and dim behind her, but her skin was radiant in the sunlight, like rich soil after a spring rain. Then she waved, just now recognizing who he was.

Eddie popped out of the Rover in the middle of the street. Vanya said something to the man, and then turned her horse towards Eddie. She rode light on that animal, long limbs and flowing hair. She looked down at Eddie and asked, “What are you doing here?”

His head was spinning in circles, thinking he had just figured out why she seemed so comfortable being alone at school. Coming home to this, none of that other nonsense mattered. “Oh you know, just checking out the sights. How about you?”

“Well,” she said with a playful smile, “we’re just moving the flock over to the east pasture.”

Neither of them said anything for about thirty seconds. They both looked towards the sheep, slowed down now as the man waited for her. “Is that your dad?” Eddie asked.

“That’s him. What gave it away?”

“Matching boots,” he laughed. “I didn’t know you lived out here.”

“How would you?”

“True. So, have you lived here long? I mean, this is a pretty great place.”

“We moved out here a little while ago.”

“Out here? As in away from the city?”

“Yep.” She looked away, and Eddie noticed the shape of her face change, ever so slightly, as if he had just reminded her of something she preferred to forget.

“I see,” he kicked the dirt on the road. “Well, guess I better let you get back to work then.”

“Ah, he can wait.” She took her hat off and waved it through the air at a fly. "What are the chances of bumping into you out here anyway?" Her horse shifted at the sight of a shadow approaching. A golden eagle drifted across the sky above them, and they each tilted their heads to watch. "So, did you get my note?" she asked.

"I did. I meant to call you, but figured I'd wait until next week."

"Okay," she replied, and watched the eagle glide up the mountain. "Suppose I better get going. Don't be afraid to call me now." She turned and kicked heals into the animal. Trotting up into the prairie, he saw her paused in the sunlight. A painting come to life, as if he had seen it somewhere before. When she reached the flock, he got in the Rover and continued up the mountain. Cutting up the switchbacks of the front range, he saw the city off in the distance. It seemed so far away and inconsequential.

Voice Recording #4

Alright, here I am again. I mean, here I am again on this voice recorder. I'm in a completely different location than last time. Seriously, this is as opposite as possible from the last place I recorded. Last night I slept in the Rover, parked on this secluded mountain road. I woke up to the songs of birds coming through my window. So I guess that makes it Sunday morning. I'm telling you, up here in the mountains, you'd never even know there's a city on the far coast a couple thousand miles away teeming with weirdos and prostitutes. I'm sure there's some good people there, maybe, but they're probably all scared to come out of their homes.

It's only been a week, but man, Mister Bonnell, some shit has happened. I'm going to talk about some of it, but probably won't type it all out when I turn this thing in. If I turn it in. A guy's gotta have a few secrets. So as I mentioned, I'm in the mountains. The ones you can see right out of your classroom window. Have you ever been up here? I doubt it, most people I know in the city have never been here. Like it's a faraway foreign place filled with aliens or something. In fact, that's probably why Big Foot was invented, by some genius as a way to keep people out of the mountains. The mountains wouldn't be the mountains if there were a bunch of people here.

I pulled off on this little dirt road right where it meets the bend in a river. I'm just up past the front range, so as far as elevation is concerned, I'm about halfway up the mountain. Man, I can see a lot from here. I bet if I had some fancy remote-controlled rocket launcher I could hit Blunt's house. Blow that fucker up for good. That wouldn't be so bad. But what I'm thinking about most, honestly, is these little purple flowers that are starting to bloom everywhere. Probably sounds cheesy as hell, right? A young dude alone in the mountains looking at flowers. Truth is, I was thinking about picking a few of them for this girl I know. I'm not much of a romantic, but I think she'd like it. I suppose if I were a poet I'd be able to tell you some sort of metaphor about how these flowers remind me of her. Truth is, I don't even think they do. I just think she'd like them. It's really that simple.

So I've been walking along this stream, probably about two miles or so. It's a pretty nice day, I mean, the sky's blue and everything, but it is a little chilly. I didn't really pack for this sort of thing. When I left the motel last night and set out to Blunt's place, I didn't know what was going to happen. Part of me figured I'd just kill the dude and then turn myself in, be sitting in a jail cell talking to a lawyer right now instead of up in the mountains talking to a voice recorder. You never know how things are going to play out.

So anyway, as I said, I was hiking along the stream, and even though it's chilly, I was working up a pretty good thirst. I didn't bring any extra food or water with me when I left last night. So I just dunked my head into the stream and pulled a drink. It tasted pretty good. Honestly, it tasted much better than the chemical water from the tap at home. My mom says we're not supposed to drink from the tap, but I sometimes do.

Even though I didn't pack for this, I'm still carrying a bunch of shit. Probably too much, actually. I'm going to tell you what I'm carrying, just because you might think it's a funny combination of things. Well I've got the obvious items, a small flashlight and my pocket knife, just this little folding one I've had for about two years. But I'm also carrying a pair of handcuffs, I don't know why I brought them, probably should've used them last night, but I've also got my fly rod, it's in a really cool wooden tube that works good for a walking stick, my brother made it, plus I've got a box of nine millimeter shells. What are the shells for? I'll tell you. They're for my fully automatic machine gun. Yep, you heard correct. What do I need a machine gun for, while hiking in the mountains? I probably don't, but I wasn't going to leave it in the Rover. In fact, since I'm up here all alone, and it's quiet as hell, I might fire off a few rounds, just for practice.

On second thoughts, maybe I won't shoot right now. I got as far as loading the thing up and pointing it at a tree. But then I heard the stream gurgling, so I looked over, and saw some trout rising to the surface. I'm just sitting on this big boulder next to the river now. There's all kinds of insects in the air. I don't know what they're called. Steve would know. I'm just watching them bounce around in groups and fall into the river. It's pretty stupid for them to fall into the river, because trout eat about every single one of them.

And, just for the record, I'm smoking a fat joint. It tastes amazing up here in the mountain air. Maybe in a little while I'll string up the old fly rod and catch a few trout. Shit, there's enough of them in there, I bet it'd be real easy to fool a few. Maybe I'd bring them to Vanya. On second thoughts, I'd bring the flowers for her, and the trout to her mom. Then I'd go on and tell her dad how I used to live in the country. They'd probably want to adopt me. Doesn't sound so bad, living in a ranch at the foot of the mountains. Wouldn't have to deal with all that shit happening in the city. Truth is, sometimes I wish I could just get away. Someday I will, you can count on that. I've gotta deal with a few things first.

It's funny though, seems like every time I'm about to solve a problem, shit happens and the problem only gets worse. I'll figure it out though, you don't have to worry about me. I really am a pretty good guy, Mister Bonnell, despite all this other shit going on. I'm not sure if anyone else can see that. Maybe my mom, but she's delusional. What does that say about me, if the only person who thinks I'm a good guy is a delusional middle-aged woman?

It's pretty cool up here, even if I am all alone. I used to spend a lot of time in the mountains, when I was younger. My dad used to take us up here a lot. There was this really cool place where we'd hike along a river until it came to a huge waterfall. We'd usually sit right there and eat our lunch, just watching the water come over that cliff. Afterwards, we'd have to scale up the side of a mountain. I remember my legs just burning like hell, no matter how many times I did it. Once we'd get up top, and wade across the river, that's where we'd camp. The fishing was incredible. Old Steve would usually spend the entire day out there catching trout. My dad and I would fish a little, but then we'd hang around camp, playing cards, reading books, that sort of thing. Tell you the truth, that's the only time I ever really felt connected with him. Alone in the mountains. Now I never see the old guy. I never see either of them. I guess that's what happens in life. But I have my memories.

Right now my memories are all fucked up. I'm thinking about this dude who I thought was my friend. I'd tell you his name, but since you have him in class, I don't want to get him in trouble. I'm not a snitch. But this dude, man, I thought I knew him. You know, I had nothing but empathy for the guy, and then he double-crossed me. I still can't believe it. Friends. Has there ever been another word more misleading?

The truth is, I don't even want to be so damn cynical. But when I look at things, and I see something happen, like, hypothetically, some kid you thought was your friend who waits until you're out of town and then robs you, and I really start to think about that, and I realize it's a fundamental component to our society that has probably been around since the old cave man days, then I start to get really depressed. So I came up here alone in the mountains to smoke some weed. What else am I going to do?

Man, I'm feeling really super stoned right now. Must be the mountain air, lower oxygen and everything. Usually I can smoke all day and be cool. Right now though, my head is spinning. I'm telling you, if I tried to stand up, I'd probably just fall down and drown in this river. They wouldn't find me for about a year. By then I'd be all eaten up by bears and cougars, and then the trout would eat up my guts that drifted down into the water. I'm just gonna lean here on the rock and shut my eyes for a little bit. I've got a few hours until I need to head home.

PAUSE.

Fuck. It's dark out. And I mean really dark. The stars are so powerful, they make me tremble. I'm telling you, their power up here is intimidating, looking small and close but knowing they are large and far away. The great deception of our universe. I can even see a planet off to the south, about halfway up the sky. I had to watch it for a while, to make sure the flickering red and blue wasn't a plane. I am completely alone with the giant stars and a deceptive universe. It's not so bad, really.

The only other lights I see are the yellow city lights far away. Tell you the truth, those lights look even more intimidating than the stars. There's something entirely out of place about them. It's like I'm looking at an x-ray, and this big old basin is the person's body, all dark and peaceful, but now there's this big bright glowing thing right in the middle. I'm no doctor, but if I saw this x-ray, I'd know something was wrong. Other than that, it's so dark out here I can hardly see my own hands, just from the starlight. I can hear the river, and the water reflects a little of the starlight, so I'll follow it downstream to my Rover.

Alright, I've been walking a little ways. My eyes are starting to adjust. Enough that I can make out shapes of trees and the bigger rocks. Suddenly it seems really loud out, and not just the river. I can hear all kinds of twigs snapping and the wings of bats. I've never been alone in a dark mountain. It's kind of crazy, tell you the truth. I mean, I can't be more than a mile away from my car, but it feels like I'm trapped in some isolated wilderness. I'm just gonna keep walking slowly, and I'll be there soon.

Holy shit. What the fuck is that? Alright, I'm running into the river now. Shit it's cold. The current is strong. But what the fuck was that? I'm standing in the middle of the stream now. I probably shouldn't get so worked up, since

I am carrying a machine gun, but I just saw something that spooked me. It had a long body and tail, and it walked low to the ground, with a pure white coat. It had the shape of a cougar, I mean a really big one. But cougars aren't white. It had to have been a mountain goat or a ram. Whatever it was, I spooked it up out of these shrubs along the stream. Well, to be honest, I didn't really spook it. More like it spooked me. Then the animal just kind of crept away, up the hill to my right. Fuck, it was low to the ground and silent. There's no way it was a mountain goat or ram. But cougars aren't white.

Fuck. Fuck. I can see two red eyes only about a hundred feet away. So bright in the darkness. They're looking right at me. I'm aiming my gun at it, just in case. I'll keep walking down this stream, right in the middle of the channel. It's only about thigh deep, but fuck, the water is cold. Ice cold.

Alright, there's the Rover. I walked all the way here in the water with my finger on the trigger. Haven't seen the animal or its eyes in a while. I'm cold as hell. Seriously, I bet you can hear my teeth chattering. I don't think that's ever happened before. I swear, you can hear the blood in my legs turning into ice. What a fucking night. What a fucking week. What a fucking life.

STOP.

MAY 1999

SUN	MON	TUE	WED	THU	FRI	SAT
~~25~~	~~26~~	~~27~~	~~28~~	~~29~~	~~30~~	~~1~~
~~2~~	3	4	5	6	7	8
9	10	11	12	13	14	15
16	17	18	19	20	21	22
23	24	25	26	27	28	29
30	31					

They say you can tell a lot about a person by what books are beside their bed. On the nightstand beside Eddie's bed was: *Infinite Jest*, by David Foster Wallace, *The Outsiders*, by S. E. Hinton, and *Hunger*, by Knut Hamsun. He had never told his friends about his affinity for books. Street rebels didn't read books. Books were for geeks and intellectuals, both connotations directly implied you were weak, at least among the crowd Eddie ran with. So books were his secret.

He picked up *Hunger*, and opened to a page he had earmarked. He read the words aloud: "The animals that have all their terror and original wildness are the ones that are valuable."

He set the book on his lap and wondered what Knut had known about animals. Mostly, he wondered how the word *valuable* would have been defined. Certainly not a monetary value. There was a deeper value that he was beginning to realize. But it was more than realizing, it was remembering. He paused and replayed moments in his life when he had been in proximity to truly wild animals. There was a sensation that covered his body every time. It was a sensation he could feel in his blood and his breath. The sensation was difficult to define, but calmness came close. As he was replaying these events through his mind, a smile crept across his face. It was then that he realized he felt happy. These experiences with wild animals created happiness, and happiness was certainly valuable.

. . .

It was Monday, and Eddie decided to attend all of his classes. His experience the previous night, seeing red eyes in the dark, and walking through the frigid river, held his focus and it was difficult to concentrate on anything else. He wished he knew someone to discuss the experience with, mostly to ask what animal it could have been. White fur, long and low body, with red eyes. At lunch break he went into the library where they had two computers hooked up to the internet, and he did a search for *White Mountain Lion* which resulted in an article titled *The American Cougar*, and after reading it he learned that there had never been a confirmed sighting of an albino mountain lion in North America.

When the final bell rang, Eddie waited for Alex outside the classroom. He needed some details. Alex was one of the few kids he trusted, one of the small selection he considered a friend. That was gone now.

"Alex, get the fuck over here."

"Eddie, chill man, okay."

"Just follow me god damn it."

"Alright, alright, but be cool man."

"Are you gonna tell me what the fuck happened? How'd you get my stereo? And no bull shit or I'll fuck you up."

"Just relax Eddie, fuck, I'm sorry. I didn't think about it, you know."

"Didn't think about what, jacking me?"

"Shit, you know we've always been cool."

"It's too late for that. I need to know who was with you."

"Damn Eddie, I'll get it back for you, alright. It's not a big deal, you can get another one."

"Alex, you need to tell me who the fuck was with you that night."

"Nobody, man, it was just me."

"Are you sure? You better not be lying to me."

"Yes, Eddie, it was just me. It's no big deal, you know. I just thought it was cool. Darnell said if I jacked you then his cousin's gang would have my back. You know how hard it is for me Eddie."

"Fuck that. You get no empathy from me. Have you told anybody where I live?"

"Why would I do that?"

"Just answer me you little fucker. Did you tell anybody where I live?"

"No, of course not, what do you take me for?"

"I take you for nothing. I'm done with you."

"What are you gonna do? I can get your stereo back man, I promise."

"I don't give a shit about the stereo. I trusted you."

"Fuck Eddie, I just wanted to be like you man, you know, fucking cool."

"You don't want to be like me."

The principal's door opened, and out stepped Ms. Camuto. "What's happening out here boys?"

"Nothing, it's cool," replied Eddie.

"Alex, what's happening out here?"

"It's nothing Miss Camuto."

"Okay, it better be nothing."

"Sure thing," said Eddie. Then to Alex, "This better be finished."

Eddie popped in his Rover and started to drive. He spent the next hour driving aimlessly, cutting through the gridlock, watching the strangers come and go. He pulled up to a red light and dug into his pocket for the mobile phone, then retrieved Vanya's number from the glovebox.

A woman's voice answered, "Hello."

"Yes hello, miss ..." Eddie realized he didn't know their last name. "I was calling for Vanya. This is Eddie. From school."

"Just a moment, I think she just got home. Hang on, I'll see if she's available." The phone went silent.

"This is Vanya."

"Hey, it's me, Eddie."

"Eddie. Oh, hi. I wasn't sure when you would call."

"Well I'm calling now, if that's alright."

"Where are you calling from? It sounds loud."

"Hang on, I'll roll up the window. I was just driving around. Thought I'd see if you wanted to have dinner tonight."

"Driving around? Like you have one of those mobile phones?"

"Yeah, it's no big deal. I just got it because my job sometimes likes to call me in."

"Okay."

"So . . . Dinner?"

"I don't know, Eddie. It's pretty short notice. Let me see if mom will give me a ride into town. I just got home. Dad's already out with the animals. Hang on."

"Sure." Eddie pulled into a gas station and parked. He recognized this place. It reminded him of his friend Brian. Brian's dad was a preacher at the Lutheran Church. Brian had gotten into the heavy drugs, mostly crank. Crank dealers and junkies were the most dangerous, in Eddie's estimation. Brian had met his dealer here in this parking lot one night last summer. He must have been suspicious of this dealer because he brought a pistol with him. His dad's pistol. The preacher's gun. One of Brian's junky friends was sitting shotgun, and the dealer was in the backseat. The junky friend gave a withness account of what happened. There had been an argument between Brian and the dealer about money Brian owed. The dealer found the pistol under Brian's seat. He shot Brian in the back of the head. Dead on site. Killed by his father's gun. The preacher's pistol.

Vanya's voice came back on the line. "Eddie, my mom said she can bring me into town, but only if you can give me a ride home. Is that alright?"

"Yes," Eddie exhaled, clearing his mind from the memory of Brian. "I can do that. How's six o'clock?"

"That works. Where should we go?"

"How about she drops you off at the library? Since you know where that is. Then we can decide where to eat."

"Okay. I'll see you there at six. Please don't be late, they close at six."

"I'll be there."

Eddie clapped the mobile shut and drove to his motel room where he checked on his stash and cash. Business had been so good it was getting tricky to fit all his weed and money above the fan, especially with the machine gun tucked up there now. For the first time, he considered this wasn't enough. Sure, he always wanted more, that was part of the game, but pacing around this motel room, smoking a joint alone, he felt a hollowness creep up on him. This was a prison he had built for himself. Confined and confused, he lay on the floor beneath the window which faced the mountains. In his hands was a copy of *The Wild Within*, by Paul Rezendes. He held the book up towards the ceiling, saw the afternoon sun cutting around the window curtain, and was asleep before finishing the first chapter.

A loud bang, and when he opened his eyes, it seemed like he had imagined it. Something had gone wrong, perhaps an explosion in the motel kitchen. Somebody might be hurt, so he began to stand, thinking he could help. Smoke was filling the room up front, and the door flung open. He heard someone yell, "This is the police, we're coming in." Fuck.

He jumped to his feet and looked around. No place to hide. No place to go. Six men in urban camo rushed through the door with assault rifles. Their laser sights cut through the smoke, and it reminded Eddie of laser light shows they used to watch on the fourth of July.

"Get down. Get the fuck down!"

He laid down face-first on the floor and felt the barrel of a rifle jam into his side. They quickly bound his hands behind his back with heavy-duty zip ties, and then walked him outside. The SWAT team stayed in his room for about two minutes, and then came out and gave a hand signal that must have meant all clear. A second team of four people dressed in lab coats and nylon gloves went into his room, presumably to search the place. Eddie sat on the curb with a uniformed cop looking over him. There was a fire truck and ambulance waiting in the parking lot. What a scene, he thought. Then he wondered what the fuck they knew and who had talked.

A member of the SWAT team passed in front of him, and Eddie said, "I like your piece. Is that the MPX?" The man didn't even look his direction, just hopped in the back of their combat van with the rest of his crew. Eddie then asked the uniformed cop for the time.

"It's time for you to enjoy your last couple minutes of freedom."

"Duly noted. But seriously, what time is it?"

"Quarter to six. Why, you got someplace important to be?"

"I've got a big date with your wife."

"Good luck with that. You should be thinking about which lawyer to call."

The Drug Task Force team had been in his room about ten minutes, and when they finally emerged, Eddie watched closely. This could go down a number of ways and he imagined himself running through the city with hands zip-tied behind his back and a mob of law enforcement hot on his tail. He could ditch them in a Bad Town alley or get shot in the green grass of a middle-class family's house. Either of those options sounded alright to him. Either of those were better than boredom. He watched closely as the four of them walked out of his motel room. They were empty handed.

The leader of the Drug Task Force approached a woman who appeared to be in charge of the scene. "We found nothing inside. Can we search his vehicle?"

The woman looked at the sheet of paper attached to her clipboard. "The warrant is only good for the physical premises, not the vehicle. Shit." She walked over to Eddie and looked at the officer guarding him.

"We can search his person. Stand him up," said the woman in charge. "Where's the drugs, Eddie?"

"Have you checked the pharmacy?"

"Don't fuck with me. If you come clean now I can work with you." The other officer was patting Eddie down, got to his pants pocket, reached in and removed the mobile. He handed it to the officer in charge, and she said, "What's this? Huh. Only people I know your age with mobile phones are drug dealers."

Eddie could tell she was frustrated. Probably nervous as hell, too. They spent a shit load of money bringing all these people here, for nothing. Her boss wouldn't be happy about this. "I am clean. You want to go have another look?"

"We found this," she held up his glass piece, the one Lynch gave him.

"Yeah? Fine, you got me. I occasionally smoke some weed. Who doesn't?"

"Uncuff him," she said to the uniformed cop, who proceeded to snip the zip ties behind his back. "We'll be watching you, Eddie Young."

"You aren't the only ones."

He watched them load up and pull away, a convoy of disappointment. There were people outside of the other motel rooms now, and some had formed circles where they talked and pointed at Eddie. He smiled, and gave a red-carpet style wave. Then the motel manager walked over, hands in his pockets, but serious business written all over his face.

"We're not going to be able to keep you here after this."

"You can't kick me out. I'm innocent. Go ask the cops. They didn't find anything."

"Be that as it may, we run a respectable business here. I can't have customers getting scared away. I need you gone tomorrow."

Inside his room the ceiling fan was in its natural position, so he popped it off. Everything was in place. He'd pack up his shit in the morning. Maybe find a new safe house. Truth was, he'd actually miss this place. Seeing the mountains out the window meant something to him. His mobile started to ring, so he flipped it open.

"Eddie, are you still coming?" asked Vanya.

Fuck. He looked at the clock and it was 6:12. "I'm enroute. Stick tight. I'll be right there."

"Okay. I'll be sitting outside the library. They let me use the phone inside, but they are closing and she is wanting to leave."

Eddie looked into the mirror, squeezed a big gob of mousse into his hand, and massaged it through his hair.

. . .

Despite what his friends might think, or the stories he told, or the ex-girlfriends who would say differently, Eddie believed in the idea of one love. There was a great attraction to the idea of an old-fashioned monogamous relationship. He knew he was too fucked up now for that to happen, but he could change. For the right girl, he would change. With a deep sense of sentimentality, he believed that only a woman could save a man. It was only through the love of her arms and her eyes and understanding that any man could become whole. Each young man had an affinity for romanticism, regardless of how latent or misguided its ideological vision might be, there was a poet inside all of their hearts, waiting for inspiration.

Eddie pulled up to the library and saw her sitting on the cement steps in front of the red brick building and tinted glass doorway. He beeped the horn and she looked up from a book. It was a scene from a postcard, the girl from the country all innocent and curious who sits in front of old-fashioned library in the big city. Damn, if he had the power, he would immortalize her in that pose for the rest of his life. He would carry her around like a snow globe he could peer into whenever he needed a dose of happiness. He watched the sun hit her as she stepped out of the shadow from the building and walked towards the car. Other kids at school thought she was awkward, but he saw her differently, the way she carried herself. It was graceful. Hers was an angle that could only be seen in a specific light.

She popped into the passenger door, smelled like sage brush and wild flowers, like the raw earth itself had morphed into something elegant with long hair and brown eyes. "What happened to your stereo? I thought I'd hear you coming from a mile away." She looked at the wires dangling from the dash, and then back to Eddie. "Let me guess, hazards of stardom." She smiled and Eddie looked away.

"Something like that," he replied.

"Okay, you don't have to tell me all your secrets on our first date.

But the least you can do is give me an excuse for why you were late. I was this close to calling my dad to come get me." She held her fingers up with barely a hairs-width between them.

"I do apologize, it was unavoidable. I guess you could say I got tied up." It was vague, but absolutely true.

"You are a mysterious one, aren't you?"

"It takes two to tango."

"What's that supposed to mean?"

Here he goes, climbing a mountain, push forward or fall back. Perhaps he was distracted by all the other shit in his head, and forgot that he was supposed to be masculine, hide his emotions, but whatever reasons controlled the moment, he replied, "You have an absolutely unique spectrum of reflectivity. A mystery like I have never seen."

She turned her head and looked forward. He noticed from the corner of his eye that she was smiling. He put the Rover in gear and started to drive. "What kind of food do you like?"

"I eat just about anything."

"Okay, let me rephrase that. What kind of food would you like for dinner tonight while sitting across a table from me the man who is going to sweep you away?"

"Well, since you put it like that. I could honestly go for a big old greasy cheese burger. I know, it sounds horrible."

"Not at all. I've got just the spot."

At a red light, he reached into the center console. May as well show his true self. Show it for her now so it doesn't come as a surprise later. He removed a joint and held it in his palm for her to see. "Do you smoke?"

"Is that weed? No, honestly I never have."

"Really? Never? Wow."

"What? What's wrong with that?"

"Absolutely nothing. I just don't think I've ever met someone who's never smoked. Don't worry, I'm not going to try and force it on you." He put the narrow end in his lip and lit it. He felt her eyes on him, inquisitive more than judgmental. He turned his head, rolled down the window, and exhaled.

"What's it taste like?" she asked.

He took a pull and blew out a deep breath of smoke. "If a bunch of angels got together and all shed a little bit of their beauty into a mortar and pestle and ground it all down into something you could sprinkle over your favorite cake, this would be it."

"No kidding? So you're smoking angels. You must be a real devout atheist."

He dismissed the question by pulling another hit. "Okay, pretend that I still had my stereo in here. What would you want to listen to?"

"I like George Straight, Matchbox Twenty or Chris Ledoux if I'm in the mood for something classic."

"Yeah? So you only listen to male singers?"

"What can I say, I'm a bit of a Tom boy, although I've always hated that term. I guess I've just not found any chicks whose songs I like. The thing with dudes is, they've always got something to prove, which is usually about love, or some form of it, and I think that makes good music."

"Hmm. Well, I know Ledoux. My dad used to listen to him. Don't really ever listen to the other two."

"Maybe I'll play them for you sometime."

"You ever eaten here?" he asked as they pulled into the Long Shadow Saloon. It was a relatively new establishment, but by the looks of it, you could've believed it had been here since dirt was invented. They even used old worn-out barn wood as a façade near the entrance.

"They've got one of those mechanical bulls inside." He smiled at her and pulled into a parking spot.

"Never heard of it, but looks pretty cool. Do they make good burgers?"

"The best." Truth was, he'd never been here either, but he'd heard about it. One of his clients worked in the kitchen, and when he was short on cash one day, Eddie accepted a gift card as a form of payment. The client went on to explain that they gave all the employees a twenty-five dollar gift card after completing their first two weeks of training. Eddie's employer, if he could call Lynch that, fronted him pounds of weed and hooked him up with a machine gun. It was basically the same thing.

They were seated at a table with log benches and a beer bucket full of peanuts. The waitress was bleach-blond, wearing daisy dukes with her knee-high boots. "What are ya'll having today?" She was truly horrible at faking a dialect, but Eddie went with it.

"Well ma'am, I'd like me one of those Juicy Lucy burgers ya'll are so famous for. And the little lady here, I believe she'll have the finest bison burger on the menu. Double up on the bacon, she needs some meat on those there scrawny little legs."

"We'll get that right up for ya folks."

"I like this place," said Vanya, eyes searching the room.

"I thought you might, being from a ranch and all."

"Yeah. Truth is, I'm not really from there. We just moved out a few years ago."

"That's right, I remember. But you never told me where you moved from." He noticed the shape of her face change again as if afflicted by something only internal eyes could see. He tried to change the subject. "Do you want to ride the bull before or after dinner?"

She looked back at him with steadfast and serious eyes. He knew she was about to tell him something important. It took her a moment to figure out the words, but he stayed calm, and watched her as she worked on the puzzle.

"Well I used to live in the city, grew up here on the east side. You know where Horizon Boulevard meets Thirty-Fourth Street? This was when that part of this city was still nice, you know, with parks and sidewalks and families riding bikes."

"Yep." He knew the place, it was where the highrises tapered off into neighborhoods. There was a famous meat market there, known for their prime ribs and German style brats. "Over near the Schwiebert Butchery?"

"Exactly. We lived just a block away. It was my mom, dad, sister, and me. Lived in the house my mom grew up in, had been in her family for two generations." She paused a moment and looked at her fingers with worn down nails but soft skin. "My mom cried almost as much the day we sold it as she did at my sister's funeral."

This hit Eddie hard, and his face showed it. He wanted to comfort her, speak some magic phrase that stole away her pain. There was no such phrase in the English language, and he knew it. He knew it as well as she did. It always bothered him when some new acquaintance learned about Steve. They always got a big sad look on their face, said they were sorry, how it wasn't fair, always the same predictable shit. It never served any purpose other than making him realize they had no idea what it felt like. He was ready to tell her about Steve, but then changed his mind. It wouldn't do any good, and would only steal this moment away from her.

"How did it happen?" he asked.

Her eyes filled with tears now as she leaned back in the bench. In the past thirty minutes he had seen her studious, happy, curious, annoyed, and now sad. It was difficult to determine which one made him want to hold her the most. He wondered how many more of her faces he would see tonight, or how many of his he would show to her.

"Oh it was bull shit Eddie." She unrolled the silverware from the plaid napkin on the table and wiped her face. "Sorry, I don't usually swear. It's just, I miss her, you know, every day. And the worst part is, it was just some really horrible accident. Myra was so beautiful, everybody just loved her. We were walking home from school one day, she was two years older than me, so I guess she'd be twenty now. We were just walking on the sidewalk over near Hillview Park, and we stopped on the bridge to look at the ducks in the pond. It was a really hot spring day, and we joked about jumping in to go swimming with them." Tears dripped down her cheek again, and she wiped her face.

"We don't have to talk about this, if you don't want to." He unraveled his silverware and gave her another napkin.

"It's okay. You should know this. You should know I'm damaged. I don't want there to be any surprises. All I remember next was hearing a loud screech, you know, from a car slamming on its brakes. We both turned around and saw a big blue pickup truck coming right at us. It was only a few feet away, and I remember looking directly into the driver's eyes. I saw the shock and horror and the mobile phone in his hand. Myra didn't even hesitate, she pushed me with the strength of a bull over the railing into the pond. She saved my life."

"Shit."

Then Vanya looked away and continued, "I think about those ducks a lot. It's really ridiculous. But I just think about how spooked and upset they were. Swimming around all peacefully one minute, waiting for some kid to come along and throw them some bread, and then splash. Their big shock of the day was me, a random human falling into the pond. It's weird."

He took a moment to soak it in. "What happened to the driver?"

"He tried to plead Involuntary Manslaughter. But they pulled his phone records and were able to prove he had just sent a pager message at that exact moment. I always wanted to know what that message said, or who it was to. What was so important or urgent that he had to kill my sister? But we never got that information." She paused as the waitress set their food on the table. "They convicted him for Vehicular Manslaughter. He's serving ten years at the prison, seven with good behavior. That means he could be out in just a couple years. I can't believe that. He'll be out here driving the streets again."

"Fuck. Well, at least they caught him." Shit, did he really just say that out loud? He really could be an asshole sometimes. But part of him was jealous that she at least had some form of closure. At least she had a face to imagine at night when the rage struck. A picture to pummel inside of her mind.

"Ugh, I know, that's what everyone says. But it doesn't help me any." She forced a smile, and Eddie noticed an enormous strength in that pretty face.

They picked at their food without talking for several minutes. Eddie thought about how unlikely it was for him to meet her, of all the girls in this city. Another young soul who truly understood loss. He was beginning to feel closer to her, as if a serendipitous bolt of lightning had reached down from the sky and struck them both simultaneously. It was one hell of a malevolent bolt. He looked across the table, she wouldn't raise up her eyes. He realized she couldn't be thinking the same thing, without the knowledge of his loss. There'd be a time to tell her, but not tonight.

"So, that note you wrote me, said you were into books. What are you reading?"

She looked up to him, a faint smile across her face. "I'm currently rereading the Willa Cather collection."

"I like Cather. *Shadows on the Rock* especially. Her characters were so fully recognizable. I remember feeling after I had read that book like I had just lived Cecile's life. The space which separated the fact of my existence and the fiction of hers was imperceptible. I was Cecile. Which, I'll admit, is a bit odd. For me to have been a young woman, I mean."

"You are an odd one." She smiled at him. "So, what have you been reading? Or do I need to wait for your next episode in Bonnell's class for those details?"

"Man, truthfully I haven't been reading much lately. Not as much as I used to. Though I did just start a new book. And I do mean a *new* book, as in recently published. It's called *The Wild Within.* I'm only about halfway into it, so I'm not prepared for one of Bonnell's full-length synopsis, but I will tell you it is good. It's about this guy who tracks animals in the wilderness. But what's really interesting is that he has a criminal background. Hardcore stuff. True stories of his wilderness transformation."

"It does sound interesting. Are you into the wilderness?"

"I used to be," he looked away, not wanting to follow that topic where it would take him.

"Ha. I can't tell if you're being humble and are really this great woodsman, or if you actually don't know a thing about the wild."

"Probably somewhere between the two," he smiled at her. "Are you ready to get out of here?"

"If you are."

"Alright, let's go." Eddie paid the tab and they walked towards the exit. Clyde, Eddie's customer from the kitchen, the one who paid for weed with a gift card from this restaurant, hustled up to them and pulled Eddie aside.

"Hey bro, are you holding?"

"Now's not a good time man."

"Shit bro, just a quick dime bag. That's all."

"All right, all right. Just meet me in the bathroom in five."

"What was that about?" asked Vanya.

"It was nothing. Just some dude I know." They walked outside into the brisk evening. Vanya was walking close, her shoulder almost touching his elbow. Eddie reached down and held her hand. He heard her sigh, but it was more than just an audible noise. It was an entire body movement which expressed a level of great comfort and relief. He opened the door for her, and as she sat down, he said, "Crap, I think I forgot to leave a tip. I'll be right back." He popped the trunk and pulled out his backpack. He sighed and realized how close he came to the cops finding this. He could be sitting in a jail cell right now instead of with this girl. He threw the backpack over his shoulder and said, "I keep extra cash in here, just so I don't spend it all."

"That's clever," he heard her say as he shut the trunk.

Five minutes later he returned and fired up the engine. "What took you so long?" she asked.

"Restroom break." He smiled at her and pulled out of the parking lot. "So, what do you want to do next? Cruise the streets looking for trouble?"

"Sounds like something you'd be good at. Unfortunately, my dad said I have to be home by eight. I know, he's really strict. But you understand, he's already lost one daughter." Eddie imagined pulling up and seeing her old man rocking in a chair on the front porch. He'd have a glass of whiskey in one hand, with the ice mostly melted, and his face would be illuminated by the fat cigar he was puffing. By his side, leaning up against the plank wall, with the wooden handle easily in reach, would be a bronze-forged axe gleaming in the starlight.

"All right, well, guess we better head that way." They moved slowly through the traffic underneath the yellow lights. When they got out of the city, Eddie lit up another joint and rolled down the window.

"Think I could try some of that?" asked Vanya.

"You sure? I mean, just because I like it, doesn't mean you have to."

"Just let me try it." She pinched it between her fingernails, and then pulled a puff and held the smoke in her mouth. He saw her cheeks swell up like a chipmunk. She blew it out slowly and with deliberate elaboration.

"You have to inhale, if you want to get the full affect," he told her.

"Inhale?"

"Yeah, watch me." He pulled a deep hit and the fire-burning cherry illuminated his face. "Like that, really suck it in like you're taking a deep breath after a long run. Think about drinking a milkshake through a straw."

"Okay," she gave it another try, and instantly coughed. She coughed for about thirty seconds.

"Don't worry, everyone coughs their first time."

"Can I have another?"

"That's probably enough for someone with zero tolerance. This is the best stuff on the market."

"I don't really feel anything."

"Just wait." They drove through the hills beneath the starlight and gibbous moon. About a mile from her ranch, he reached into the glove box for some Visine. "Here, put this in your eyes."

"Wow, look at all those stars. I've been living out here for many many years and never noticed how many stars there were. I bet Myra's one of those stars. Don't you think she could be?"

Eddie laughed, "It's certainly possible. About as possible as anything else. Just put this Visine in before we get to your place."

"This is really fun Eddie, I had such a great time talking to you. I bet you're a really great kisser. Are you a really great kisser?"

"You'll have to find out."

She reached over and put her mouth on his. It was dry and awkward, and she held it there without movement for longer than she should. "That was amazing. Let's never take me home, okay."

"Maybe someday. But I want to get you home on time tonight." He continued to drive until he saw her ranch. The mountains were so close, and he wanted to continue on and take her up there. Disappear for a while. Reappear both as people new. People other people didn't know. Invisible people free to live their own way. He pulled into the driveway which was narrow, no manmade surface, loose dirt with a mohawk of tall grass in the middle where the wheels never touched. He pulled in looking for her dad on the porch. All the front lights were on, but nobody in sight.

As he parked the car, he saw a figure emerge from the door and wave them in. Vanya was laughing about how beautiful the stars were. Eddie composed himself the best he could.

"Looks like you two had a fun time," said her dad.

"Oh daddy, we had the greatest time. Eddie knows all the finest restaurants in town."

"Good. You deserve the best. Eddie, thanks for getting her back home on time. That means a lot to me. Why don't you come on up so we can talk a moment."

Eddie walked up the creaking steps and stood close enough to see her father's brown eyes in the pale light. "I'm Yuvan," he reached out a hand. "Vanya, would you mind giving us a moment?"

"Sure daddy," she smiled from the doorway, and before disappearing inside she said, "Thanks for dinner Eddie. See you at school tomorrow."

"Have a good night."

"So Vanya tells me you're a big reader. Maybe sometime you can come by for dinner, and I'll show you our library."

"I'd like that." He was cautious, waiting for accusations.

"She's a really special girl Eddie. I'm sure you're smart enough to see that."

Eddie turned his head and looked up the mountains. "I know that."

Yuvan followed his eyes. "Have you visited those mountains?"

"Used to go up there a bit when I was younger. Think I might go camping this weekend."

"Camping?" Yuvan scratched at his chin. It was bald, and the freshly shaved skin caught a reflection from the porchlight. "Be careful, young man. It doesn't take much time in the mountains before they start to feel like home."

"I believe it."

"Alright. I better let you get going. School day tomorrow."

"Okay, it was nice to meet you." Eddie reached out his hand. Yuvan gripped it firmly, didn't release it while he spoke.

"Ed. I'm going to be straight with you. We will be friends until the day you fuck with my daughter. You don't want to learn what the opposite of friends is to me."

"I got it. You don't have to worry." He turned and walked away. At the Rover he saw Yuvan still watching him. "Hey Yuvan, just out of curiosity, you ever hear of an albino mountain lion?"

Yuvan rubbed his bald chin, shook his head, and continued to watch him. Eddie pulled down the driveway and turned towards the city. He continued alone down the dark country road winding around the river and over the hills.

On his way home, Eddie thought about Vanya's sister, how they each lost the person closest to them, and he believed he had found a timeless sort of romance, the type that happens in novels and movies, and sometimes in reality.

MAY 1999

SUN	MON	TUE	WED	THU	FRI	SAT
~~25~~	~~26~~	~~27~~	~~28~~	~~29~~	~~30~~	~~1~~
~~2~~	~~3~~	~~4~~	~~5~~	~~6~~	~~7~~	8
9	10	11	12	13	14	15
16	17	18	19	20	21	22
23	24	25	26	27	28	29
30	31					

Eddie woke early and rushed to get ready. He wanted to leave before seeing his mom or Cole. Too much going on to have time to explain anything to them. He snuck upstairs and wrote a note for his mom. "Mom, I'm leaving early to go fishing. Then I'm working the overnight shift. They asked me if I could do that because they were short-handed, plus it pays more. I won't be home until tomorrow."

He got in the Rover and rolled out the driveway. In the glovebox was the glass piece from Lynch and it still had a couple hits loaded. As he reached over, he noticed something on the dashboard. It was one of Vanya's hairs, long, dark and thin. He thought about her tears at the dinner table and he admired her for being able to express so much to someone she barely knew. He would tell her his story one day, when it was time, but he wasn't ready. He didn't like to think about the past too much. So he retrieved the glass piece and puffed on it as he drove out of the neighborhood.

He stopped at the corner convenience store, saw the payphone outside, thought about all the times he stood there to make a call, the people who he talked to in code, and the deals he made. He flipped open his mobile and thought of calling Vanya. He could invite her to the mountains, spend time watching her hair in the natural air. If they were in the freedom of wilderness he would tell her everything. Open it all up for display. Let her be the judge.

He clicked his mobile phone shut and walked inside. Another day and another time, he will bring her there. For now he wanted to be alone, unknown and with some space. At the register, the kid working said, "You're Eddie Young, right?"

Eddie did not recognize the kid, glanced him over again, avoided eye contact and replied, "Never heard of him."

"Shit, I remember you. Cassie's party last summer. You brought all that killer weed."

Eddie thought through the faces in his memory from previous parties at Cassie's place, but he still didn't recognize this kid. "How much do I owe you?"

"How about you pay me in weed?"

He thought about the brick in his trunk, how close he was to having the cops find it earlier this week. He laid a ten dollar bill on the counter and said, "That should cover it," then walked outside.

At the payphone now were several kids his age, baggy blue clothes, hats cocked to the right, talking loud and with exaggerated body movements. It would be so easy for him to sell this stash, move on to the next, the bigger score. Instead he returned to the Rover and started to drive.

Abstract and indifferent. These youth lived unlike others before. In appearance this was obvious; attire too loose and hats crooked. Even more obvious was the attitude. It could be heard any distance within fifty feet. Minimum of three curse words required per sentence if they wanted to be respected by their peers. Speak highly only of themself and their crew, everyone else was dirt, mud, or horse shit on the bottom of their shoe. Fantasize about idolatry, of those on the movie screen or CD covers, but act as though they were better than that. Even if you couldn't hear them, the body language said enough. Sign language to the rhythm of music was gang signs only understood by others like them. Movements so powerful you could almost believe they had enough experiences to understand what the fuck they were doing. Loose backs hunched over and squinty eyes. Shoulders seemed double-jointed as they swayed their arms in walk.

It was not uncommon to hear an adult yell towards them, "Pull up your pants!" or "Go get a job!" But this only amplified their sense of rebellion. If ever a generation of youth has made sense to their elders, it certainly wasn't this one. This was a spectacular achievement only capable by the truly young and free. Only an original ability for indifference and abstracting from the norm could create a person this strong. This weak. This certain. This confused. Time and culture had created a hybrid of human behavior. The other people talked, as they always had.

Eddie heard the rumors, but they weren't good enough for his ego. He thought of his peers and wondered why they all seemed so comfortable in designated roles, specific slots like a block puzzle, but he knew they were immeasurable, and could not be contained. Whatever other people said, that he was a rebel, a never-do-well, or bound only for prison, he knew better. He knew about the secret force of hope and ambition which ruled his mind. It was only for them that he hid this. It was an inherent sense of empathy and altruism which allowed himself to be misinterpreted. Misinterpreted because he revealed false information. They couldn't know who he was, because then he would have to be who he was. That was the most difficult idea of all.

He hadn't forgotten. He remembered how it once was. He was even younger then. If he traveled backwards through time his innocence was restored. Time travel wasn't possible in real life, only in his imagination. Whenever his imagination traveled back in time, he stopped it by pulling deep on a joint, or bong, or one-hitter, whatever medium was available. It was better to move forward, to ignore his conscience, and to simply say *fuck it* whenever he felt emotions. The world respected a man who was stoic, and he was old enough to have learned this. He was old enough to have learned many things, but most of them he ignored. The greatest feeling was immediacy, and to react to each situation as though it were the first. This method allowed him not to think about how things got fucked up before. It would be inevitable for things to get fucked up again, but for now, at this juncture, his future was irrelevant because his present was so damn powerful.

Voice Recording #5

Alright, I'm back. Back in the mountains. I came more prepared this time. This morning I stopped over at a sporting goods store, but I had to make it quick. That place was pretty depressing. Which seems odd, since it's filled with so many cool things. But when I'm in there, it doesn't really seem like enjoying the natural world is the purpose. It feels more like a place to get a bunch of competitive things to look cool so you can brag about dominating the natural world. So I made it quick. Got some good stuff though. I picked up this nice little one-man tent, a sleeping bag rated to negative twenty, a nylon tarp, and this camp saw. I bought this really awesome canvas backpack to carry all my stuff in. Plus this little isobutane burning camp stove, a frying pan, and a couple of barbecue utensils. I found this bad ass camp knife, seven-inch blade, smooth and angled on the back side, with a solid wood handle, full tang with bronze accents. Had to buy some new fishing waders, I found my old ones in the garage, but they were way too small for me now. I also bought a water filter, plus some food and a flashlight. I brought my machine gun again, in case I see that red eyed animal. Just so I could defend myself, if needed. Everything in the natural world has to defend itself from just about everything else. Pine trees make the soil around them acidic so it is difficult for other plants to grow and steal their nutrients. I remember Steve flipping stones in a trout stream and showing me how caddisflies made little cabins out of super small rocks so that fish couldn't eat them. Speaking of fish, I'm using my fly rod tube as a walking stick, probably use it to catch a bunch of trout for dinner. Man, this is a lot of weight to carry up this steep incline at high elevation. Think I'll stop off and take a break to twist one up.

I'm at about the same place where I stopped last weekend, right near this river. It's truly beautiful here. I'm sure that sounds generic, doesn't really give this place the expression it deserves, but it's true. Absolutely beautiful.

I want to think radical thoughts. I want to see the world unique and new. I want to see through different eyes. I want to learn how to not hate the things that fucked my life up. Is that why you gave me this assignment, Mister Bonnell?

On the way up here I drove past the old ranch house where this girl I know lives. I dropped a book she asked me about in her mailbox. We've been seeing each other a lot this week. Yesterday she told me about how she was homeschooled the past few years ever since they moved into the country. I thought that sounded kind of nice. She said her parents decided to send her back to public schools for the final semester of her senior year so that she could redevelop social skills before going off to college. Her family's been through a lot, to tell you the truth. Almost as much as mine. I think they've got the right idea though, get out of that city. A proactive pursuit of happiness rather than living amongst the demons. A person could separate themselves from the past and start fresh in the country.

Okay, I'm going to walk up a little farther.

PAUSE.

This is a nice spot. I didn't go far, maybe another half mile or so. Think I'll set up camp here, not have to lug all this gear around anymore. I've never camped alone in the mountains. There's still a few patches of snow scattered in the shady areas, so it's not going to be super warm tonight. I'm in this big valley that the river cuts through, with all these pine trees and big boulders. To the south is this smaller mountain that blocks my view, nearly enough to hide the city from me. Directly to my north is this giant peak that is as high as the clouds. Maybe I'll bring a map next time, I'm sure somebody's named that peak by now. Seems to me that by giving something natural like a mountain peak a name, you're stealing something from it, making it sound manmade and generic. Maybe I won't bring a map. I'll just know it as the largest peak I can see.

Think I'll assemble Steve's old fly rod and put on my waders. The river's right there with this nice-looking bend that I'm sure is full of trout. I'll probably just catch a couple and eat them for dinner. Should be pretty easy. I haven't eaten a fresh trout in a long time.

Okay, I'm standing in the river, balancing my feet on two slippery cobblestones. I'm about thirty feet downstream from this nice bend where the water cuts around a sharp cliff. The water enters the bend as a riffle, and then gets real deep around the outer edge. I remember a few of the tricks Steve taught me, and that's where the big trout will be. I've got this stonefly nymph tied on. I don't remember what this exact pattern is called, but it's yellow and black with a copper bead head.

Shit. Hooked one of those shrubs that hangs over the water with my backcast. That's alright. Steve used to tell me if you aren't getting the occasional snag, you aren't fishing the right spots. Alright, try this again. There we go, I hit the deep pool. Sort of at the bottom end, but it's in there. Whoa, I got something. Nope, snagged on a rock where the deep pool pours out into a shallower riffle. Damn thing's stuck really good, I'll have to walk up there and get it. Holy shit. This is slippery. I almost just face planted in the water. Fuck, I spooked up two really nice trout. Guess I better give this hole a little rest.

Steve used to say that fly fishing rewarded two things, patience and humility. He said that you could only fully appreciate the game by being patient, and that it took humility to know that you would never know it all. There would always be another lesson to learn, scenario to experience. Competition, ego, arrogance, bragging, these only reduced your ability to be fully immersed in what it meant to be a fly angler. Not sure if I believe any of that, so I tried to remember how peaceful he looked standing in a river.

Okay, so I laid Steve's rod on the shore and I'm sitting on this big boulder in the middle of the river reading a book. It's called *The River Why,* by David James Duncan. It's a fly fishing book, so I wouldn't be surprised if you haven't heard of it. It's really quite peaceful just sitting here with water rushing all around me reading a book. I bet if everyone spent one afternoon a week doing this, there'd be a lot more happy people in the world.

Think I'm going to walk back to camp and grab a little snack. I brought these gourmet chocolates made with real pieces of oranges in them. Shit. Fuck. I just fell in the river. Is this thing still recording? Looks alright. Damn it, I'm soaked. The water went completely down my waders. I was carrying my book, which went down in the river with me. I wish they made books waterproof, so that I could read them in the shower, or in the rain, or while standing in a stream fishing and fumbling like a fool.

PAUSE.

The fire's going pretty good. This new saw of mine cut up the wood without a sweat. I brought this big slab of prime rib from that butcher's place near where Vanya used to live. Truth is, I just wanted to go see her old neighborhood, try and understand her a little better. It's a nice neighborhood. I mean, there's lots of old buildings that sort of look like shit, but people take care of their yards and all of that. Most of the houses have driveways, and there's usually a nice looking newer car parked in them. It's not the kind of place where you'd imagine your teenage daughter dying on a walk home from school.

Fresh meat over a campfire, that's about as good as a meal can get. Smoky and bloody, with some charred edges. Still a little left I'm going to save for breakfast. I wrapped it tight in my canvas bag and hung from a tree about fifty feet from camp. It's starting to get dark and looks like it might rain tonight, so I'm gonna set up my tent quick.

Yep, it's raining real good now. So I'm sitting in my tent with the flash-light reading my book. It's still a little wet, but if I'm careful, I don't tear the pages. I just hot boxed this tent with a fat joint. The smoke hung out in here like a cloud, apparently nylon is impermeable to the stuff. Truth is, I was a little nervous being up here all alone, but now it's cool. It is a little bit lonely though, but not in a bad way. Just seems like it would be better if I had someone to share it with. Maybe I'll bring Vanya next time. For now I've got my book and this recorder.

The rain's still going pretty good and it sounds like someone's throwing pebbles at my tent. Just for the hell of it, I opened up the fly to have a look. I'm telling you, there's nothing as dark as a night storm in the mountains. It's almost as dark as closing your eyes. And the thunder, man, it's about as loud as some thug firing a pistol at you from close range. Trust me, I would know. The clouds are real low, or rather, they're close to me, since I'm actually pretty high right now. I can see lightning cutting through the sky. Reminds me a little bit of watching a pin ball bounce around its machine.

This girl Vanya, you know, I think she really understands me. I mean, I haven't told her about Steve yet, but we've got a lot in common, and that's something a person can sense regardless of what information they have. Mostly it means that being together is easy, you know, there's not all those subtext or assumptions, we're just being ourselves. It doesn't happen too often that way, at least not in my experience.

I'm sure this will sound cheesy as hell, but man, being up here in the mountains, I can't stop thinking about the old times with Steve. I was still pretty young the last time we came up here, it was the weekend before we moved to the city. I remember the three of us were camping above the waterfall I already told you about. My dad was feeling really sick, looking back on it now, he was probably hung over. I remember him staying up alone by the campfire real late the night before. So that next day Steve and I went off alone. We hiked up the river, and then followed one of its tributaries all the way up until it was just a five foot wide trickle coming through a meadow. There were about a hundred elk there. Seriously, the most either of us had ever seen. It was pretty late in the season, some of the aspen trees were turning yellow, and there were a few of the elk bucking each other with their antlers. The rest of that trip me and Steve kept pretending we were elk, holding our hands above our heads, bugling, and fighting around. I thought Steve was crazy when he said he was going to fish right there, with the elk all around, in this tiny piece of water. But that's what he did, stepped into the river, it wasn't deeper than his calves, but he stood there and started casting. The elk knew we were there, but only a couple of them seemed worried. On his third cast the line went tight and his rod bent forward. A trout leapt from the water thirty feet in front of him, and I can still see that picture clearly, as if it's a painting that's been hanging on my wall for the past ten years, something I've looked at every day and memorized each color and shape. The way the elk were paused behind the trout, scattered around this high meadow with the pine trees and aspen. I swear, from the time we moved to the city, until the time he died, I don't remember a single thing. But I remember that day as clear as if it were this morning. That was the last time the three of us went camping together. None of us knew then that would be the last trout Steve caught in his life. It sure was beautiful.

Whenever I start to think about the past, it creates a nervous feeling in my body, like there's this energy pulsing through me trying to push it out. So I got up to pace around and think. Only lost photographs that were never taken know what my mind speaks of when we are alone together. And Steve is still there, framed in that memory, standing in a small pristine stream in a high mountain meadow, surrounded by elk, with a wild trout leaping on the end of his line.

I remember his funeral too, and the way people talked. It was a big mystery and a giant tragedy. All kinds of people showed up, people I had never seen or would have guessed even knew him. His funeral was a place to be seen, to be known, to have been a participant in something few people experience, that type of tragedy. Knowing him meant you were something great. He had that affect. They gathered at the funeral to show that they were somebody great, great because they knew him. It was a status symbol of sorts, to be one of the mourners. That was the thing about him, if he ever gave you all his attention, then you understood why people thought he was special. He had this ability to look directly into you and see something, and by simply seeing it, he was showing it to you. People always liked that, seeing something new about themselves, in a favorable light.

Ever since then, I've gotten the impression that some people wish a death would happen close to them, so they may pronounce their understanding for this most mysterious tragedy. Like they're walking around with the idea that it could be real, but don't really know, and they want to know. People need to understand things. But when I see somebody who has actually experienced it, who has felt it closely, there is only the wish that it hadn't happened to them, and that this part of life had remained a mystery.

STOP.

Eddie woke in the morning before the sunrise. He emerged from his tent and put a flame to the half-joint from last night. He walked barefoot in the dark and noticed the verdant aroma of a mountain morning after the rain. In the springtime it was musky, rich with masculine pheromones from the angiosperms and pollinators. It smelled a little bit like sweat, but the good kind, the type that dripped from his back after a long hike in the mountains. It was the smell of being awake and alive. It reminded him of a memory from his youth, drinking water from his hands that were dipped in the stream. It was synesthetic the way this growing green foliage transported him through time and place. A smell became a taste which created a sight that brought a touch he could hear. It was forever and yet simultaneously whittled down to single moments. He watched them pass as he breathed them in. The glowing green and lush aromas he could see. He closed his eyes again and knew this was home, that he was a part of the glowing green, a pollinator, a walking aroma, a member of this symbiosis. A morning owl was hooting nearby.

Then a fox passed in the light of the rising sun. It was following its nose, searching for the source of a scent. Guided by the purpose of its existence, permeating the dim light with a single focus. The visual of it was brief, as Eddie watched the animal dissapear around a tree, but he retained a sense of it and knew it was still there walking through the mystery, the darkness, the aromas which filled this air. And Eddie was here with them. Equally invisible and yet perceptible. No better or worse, that's the only way he could exist. Harmonious and gracious, the gift of a conscience. So he closed his eyes again. He breathed in through his nose. He could smell it, this teeming conglomeration of life. It was beneath his feet and between my fingers. It was inside of his lungs and behind his eyes. He breathed in, and knew this was being alive.

Voice Recording #6

Sunday morning and I am immersed in the open air asylum. The smell of mountains after a rain is a song to my senses. Whoever coined the term, a breath of fresh air, this is what they meant. There's all these water droplets hanging on to pine needles, and the rocks glisten as the sun hits them. The river, well, it just keeps flowing. There's some mist floating above it, and the sunbeams sort of cling to it, as if they've got no place else to go.

I finished reading that book last night. It was about a young dude trying to catch the best fish of his life. It became his singular focus. Probably a metaphor for trying to give his life meaning. His family life wasn't the greatest, especially the relationship with his dad. Until Gus, that's the main character's name, finally forgave his old man. I should tell my dad about that. I wonder if he's been catching any more of those redfish. Think I'll get myself some breakfast, and then try fishing again.

Son of a bitch. Looks like something got into my pack. I had it tied about ten feet up on this pine tree branch. The bag's on the ground now all tore up. Yep, the rest of my prime rib is gone. Must've been raccoons. Those little fuckers. Or maybe not. What the fuck is that? Shit. Sure enough, it's a mountain lion track, perfectly formed in the soft mud. I knew that's what I'd seen the other day. Now that I'm looking for them, I can see tracks all over the place. They're fucking huge. Larger than my hand.

I'll admit, it's a little spooky, knowing the thing was creeping around here while I slept. I'm actually surprised that it went for that little chunk of prime rib rather than coming after me. The part that bothers me the most though, is that it completely destroyed my new pack. Not that I can't buy another one, but how the hell am I going to carry all this gear out?

Since you wanted me to study my feelings and everything, I'm going to tell you that I'm pretty pissed off right now. I'm just sitting here smoking a joint and thinking about how I'll carry all my gear out. I probably shouldn't be so pissed off. I mean, mountain lions gotta eat too. If I were a mountain lion who spent all its time stalking prey and hunting, and sometimes going days without food, I'd take advantage of the fact some dumb human left a prime rib out right where I could reach it. It's really my fault, if I think about it. Tell you the truth, most things are my fault, if I really start to think about them.

Here's something completely random. Out of nowhere I just wondered what my hair looks like. I know, ridiculous, nobody's going to see me out here. I can feel it sticking up all over the place, and crisp from the mousse I put in yesterday. I probably look like a madman. Sounds vain as hell, I'm sure, thinking about what my hair looks like while I'm up here in the mountains. Suppose it's built into my mechanics, the routine of every morning, spending time to get my hair just right. What can I say, I like to keep up appearances.

Doesn't matter. Most of the shit I think is super important probably doesn't matter too much. It's tricky though, when I get used to something, to imagine it any other way. Take my stereo for instance. Man, I loved bumping that thing through town. People could hear it a mile away and knew Eddie

Young was coming. For about the first week after the thing got jacked, I kept reaching for the knobs to crank it up. Past few days though, I couldn't have cared less. I even started rolling my windows down just to hear what was happening on the streets. I'm not too sure, but it seems to me that we can change anything, as long as there's something new to replace it.

It's a really pretty day up here, and not a stir of wind. I used to be good at casting the old fly rod. Good for a little kid anyway. Think I'll go give it another shot.

PAUSE.

I just got back from the river. After the spill I took last time, decided to wise up and keep my voice recorder safe and dry on shore. So here's what happened. I started to remember how to cast a fly rod. Took a little while, and I won't lie, several trees were hooked in the process. It's really a spectacular feeling though, when I get that perfect arc of line shooting in front of me. I decided to go with a dry fly this time, since there were all these little bugs on the water. I found one in the box of flies Steve tied that my dad gave me. I swear, it looked exactly like the real ones floating around that the trout were getting excited about. They ignored every single cast, even the ones that looked really good. And, just to prove the mind of a fish is better than the mind of a man, they continued to eat every real insect that drifted over them, even if it was right next to my fly. Cocky little shits, I swear. But, truth be told, that makes me respect them a little more.

Broke down my tent and gathered up all of my gear. No way I'm going to carry it all the way to the Rover without my bag. I plan to spend as many weekends here as possible. So I'll stash it someplace safe up here. I climbed up the hill a little ways to this spot with some juniper shrubs. I tucked all of my stuff in there, including my machine gun. Felt a little weird not bringing that with me, considering that Blunt and his gang are probably looking for me. But with the heat I've been getting from the police, I'd rather take my chances avoiding Blunt than them. So I wrapped the tarp over everything and secured the corners with rocks. The only thing I'm carrying out with me is my mobile phone and hunting knife. That cougar could still be around here, and I'm not walking through the mountains entirely unarmed.

Truth is, I'm going to miss this place for the next week. I've got a lot of shit to deal with down in that city. Ever since I got kicked out of the motel, business has been a little tricky. I don't really like driving around with all that weed on me. It used to be fun, the rush of it, but it's getting old. Seeing the same people every day who always want something from me. It can wear on a guy. But I'll be back soon. I'm going to catch a trout next time.

STOP.

MAY 1999

SUN	MON	TUE	WED	THU	FRI	SAT
~~25~~	~~26~~	~~27~~	~~28~~	~~29~~	~~30~~	~~1~~
~~2~~	~~3~~	~~4~~	~~5~~	~~6~~	~~7~~	~~8~~
~~9~~	~~10~~	~~11~~	~~12~~	~~13~~	~~14~~	~~15~~
~~16~~	~~17~~	~~18~~	~~19~~	~~20~~	~~21~~	22
23	24	25	26	27	28	29
30	31					

There were more thoughts in his head than he could ever explain or give proper attention. His mind was foggy as he sat in his bedroom and passed a joint to Vanya. The images in his mind ran fast like flashes of lightning and he wanted to hold them all, pause them, suspended in midair, and touch them with his fingers. If he could grasp them in a comprehensible format, then, and only then, could he share his thoughts with her.

"Isn't your mom going to smell this?" asked Vanya as she passed him the joint and looked to the bedroom door.

"Who knows. She's never said anything about it."

"Doesn't your mom do your laundry?" she asked, after exhaling a cloud of smoke into his pillowcase, and watching him dump a basket of clothes on the bed.

He pulled up his back straight and made a serious face, "That's the best men are bred for in our generation, to be stoic servants who can fold their own laundry."

"You are an odd one," she laughed. "But your mom does seem pretty cool. Don't you think?"

"Yeah, she's alright."

"My mom's alright, too." Vanya stood up and started pacing around the room with the joint in her fingers. "We've kind of grown apart the past couple years. I remember how it happened. We had only been living at the ranch for a little while. Her and my dad were still pretty messed up from losing Myra, we all were. But it was nice being at the ranch, and every once in a while, we were all happy. There was this one day all three of us were drinking tea on the front porch, and the mailman came all the way down the driveway. I thought that was kind of weird, since the mailbox was at the end, but I guess he wanted to introduce himself. My dad got up and shook his hand, and all of that guy stuff. Then Mark, that was the mailman's name, he turned to my mom and me. We all introduced ourselves, and he told us what a beautiful house we had. That made my mom real happy, for a minute or two. Then he tipped his hat and said it was nice meeting you ladies. I remember that clearly, he said you *ladies*. It was the first time anybody had ever called us that, and those simple words elevated me up to being an equal with my mom. I was no longer her little girl, and even strangers could see it. I think my mom noticed it too. It made her kind of sad. She probably missed me being her little girl."

"You are unbelievable," he smiled. "Think I could get another hit of that joint, before you let the entire thing burn out?"

She ignored his request and paced around the room, seeming to investigate every object. "Why do you have so many books next to your bed? I never hear you talk about reading any of these books. You only talk about books in Bonnell's class. When you go."

He looked at her, sat on the bed, and reached his hand out, making a pinching movement with his fingers, as if to request the joint.

"No way," she said, "not until you share more with me."

"Okay, so you asked about these books," he leaned back and looked up at the ceiling.

"Have you read all these? Tell me something about them. Which is your favorite?"

Eddie turned his head the opposite direction from her and the books. "I remember the first time I read a Hermann Hesse book. It was one of those real small paperbacks, had found it at a thrift store. Pages all falling out. It was one of his lesser known books, called *Rosshalde*. But I tell you, I was absolutely enthralled by the introspective qualities of those words. 'The kings of art are nature's brothers and friends, they play with her, they create where we can only imitate.' So I've read every book he's written. German poet, philosopher, novelist."

Eddie stayed seated on the bed, turned his head to the stack of books. "Every book shelf or stack I've had since first reading *Rosshalde*, has held at least one Hesse book. Sometimes more. Never less." He looked now at Vanya, "Is that enough sharing to get me at least one puff?"

She was standing by the door now, and put the joint into her lips. Then she got down on the floor and started crawling towards him. Eddie sat on the edge of the bed and watched her feline body movements. Her hair was wrapped tight with a single band at the base of her neck, and a long ponytail hung over her shoulders. She handed him the joint, and he leaned back and pulled in a deep cloud of smoke. Just as she placed her hands upon his knees the mobile phone went off in his cargo pocket. Fuck.

"Scott, what's up man?"

"Eddie, I need to see you."

"Can't it wait bro? This isn't a good time. It's about the worst possible time."

"This is fucking important Eddie." Scott wasn't one to lose his cool, in fact, he was one of the best Eddie knew at keeping it, but he sounded out of breath. Plus, the fact that he called him instead of a simple page, got Eddie concerned. "Just meet me over at the Bodega on Ninth Street."

"Shit man, when?"

"Right now Eddie. Please."

Eddie clicked his mobile shut and looked at Vanya. "Shit, I gotta go. I'm sorry."

"Now?" she looked up at him with her brown eyes.

"I know, it fucking sucks. You can wait here if you want."

She stood up and snatched the joint from his fingers. "I'm not just going to sit here and wait for you. What do you take me for?"

"It won't be long. Just stick tight and I'll be back in no time. You can even go upstairs and pick out a book from the shelf."

"I'd rather not. Why don't you take me over to Kathy's, if you don't want to hang out with me."

"It's not that I don't want to hang out with you. Wait, Kathy's? How do you know her?"

"Everybody knows her. I went over to her house and had a couple beers the other night. She's a pretty cool chick."

"Really?" He was surprised, but not that much. The gateway had opened, and you never knew who or what would pass through it. "Fine. Let's go."

. . .

Eddie pulled up to the *Twisted Top Bodega.* This was the kind of place where everyone from grunge kids, to jocks, to stoners, to middle-class families, and even uniformed cops could be seen popping in and out on any given day. It was designed like an old soda fountain café with a bar and swiveling stools. They served espresso shots and lattes, wine and beer, sandwiches and salads, plus a little market which specialized in imported foods. They were notorious for not carding people, and Eddie was pretty sure the cops who came around knew it.

Scott was sitting alone on the front patio at a blue metal table. Eddie never saw Scott alone. He was a hockey player, a team player, and was always with people. Scott held a green bottle of beer in his hands and was fumbling with the label, oblivious that Eddie had arrived.

Eddie carried his bag in and ordered a light beer. There was a young dude working the counter, he had a greased black mohawk and rings in each of his nostrils. He was a jittery dude, and Eddie figured he drank free espressos all day. Then the kid said to him, "Are you holding?"

"Excuse me?" Eddie had never seen the guy before.

"You're Eddie Young, right?"

"No, you got the wrong guy. Can I just get my beer?" He looked out towards Scott, "Actually, make it two."

He carried the beers outside and pulled up a seat next to Scott. Scott was still looking sulky as hell, so he handed him a beer and said, "Cheer up buddy, this one's on me."

"I don't want your beer Eddie. I don't deserve anything from you."

"Now what's gotten into you? Did you lose your game last night or something?"

"Fuck, Eddie, I wish it was that simple."

"Nothing ever is. So talk to me bro, what's up? Because this better be important. If you knew what was about to happen when you called…"

"Shit Eddie, stop joking around. This is serious shit." For the first time since Eddie sat down, he saw Scott's eyes. They looked confused, scared, and far away.

"Lay it on me bro."

Scott looked back to his empty beer bottle and the label peeling off. "You remember that night I got arrested at the park? I didn't tell you the whole story."

"What happened man? Please don't tell me the scouts lost interest. Because that would be absolute bull shit."

"It's not that man." He looked away towards the busy street and the sidewalk full of people. "I talked, alright. I fucking talked. I told them everything I knew about you and your operation. I had to man, that's the only way they'd drop the charges. And my parents were right there. Fuck, I'm sorry Eddie."

Eddie stood up in a fury and paced around the table. He took a deep swallow of his beer before responding, "Fuck Scott, you realize you could have got me thrown in prison?"

"You could have gotten yourself thrown in prison."

Shit. He was right. This was all his fault. Everything, all of it. The burden lay heavy on his shoulders. "Is that how they knew I was staying in the motel?" He was thinking out loud now, not really expecting Scott to know the answer.

"I don't know man, I just told them everything."

"Wait a sec, how the fuck did you know I was staying in the motel? I didn't tell anybody."

"Shit Eddie, it's not like you're a big secret. Everyone knows about you."

Eddie sat back down and pulled another slug from his beer. Scott could have talked to him sooner. He didn't have to snitch. Eddie would have listened to the concerns of a friend. Then he looked over at Scott who somehow seemed larger now. At least he came clean and was being honest. Honesty was about the most uncommon attribute amongst friends. At least the friends Eddie knew. Among those friends, the punishment for honesty was infinitely worse than the punishment for dishonesty. They encapsulated themselves in a sphere of fiction.

"Shit!" yelled Scott as he jumped up and knocked his chair to the ground.

Eddie saw a crowbar swing across the table and catch Scott on the chin. This quick movement made Eddie fall back to the concrete, still in his chair. He looked up and saw Blunt, but what he saw most was the boot coming down on his chest. It caught him in the ribs and sent all the breath from his lungs. Then he rolled out of the chair and saw Gunner sitting atop Scott sending blows to his face. He started to get up, and yelled, "Get the fuck off him!" but was quickly hit with another kick to the back.

Eddie made it to his knees and caught the next kick with his arms, but Blunt was a heavy dude, and he couldn't pull him down. Now a fist hit him in the back of the neck, and his face crashed down to cement. He kept thinking that this sort of thing doesn't happen in broad daylight, and tried to take his mind away from it. For a moment, the pain of his body finally expressed the pain he felt inside. It started to make sense. He started to feel stronger.

On his feet now, he grabbed the chair from the ground and threw it at Gunner. This sent him toppling off of Scott. But now the two of them were coming at Eddie. He could run. He was in pain, but he wouldn't feel it if he ran. There was no running. This was all his doing, and it was time to finish it. Win or lose. He made a step towards his bag. The hunting knife with seven-inch blade was still in there. Pull it out and make a clean kill. Eliminate both these fuckers from his list of problems. When he looked at them again, he saw the fierceness of caged lions in their eyes. These were people who only knew pain and anger, that was all their life had taught them. They were experts in the ways of giving and receiving hurt. It was the only language they knew to be true. Eddie grabbed the shoulder strap and started to pull on the zipper.

The sirens were loud as a squad car pulled up on the sidewalk. It was the first time Eddie could remember ever being happy to see the police. It occurred to him in that brief moment that he had a lot in common with the cops. Sure they operated on opposite sides of the law, but they both worked jobs that made them simultaneously hated and appreciated by the people they served. Blunt and Gunner scattered, and Eddie leaned over to Scott. "You're gonna be alright man. The cops are here, they'll take care of you. I've gotta bolt." He stood up and wrapped his bag over his shoulders. It had blood – Scott's blood – soaked into the tag end of straps. He caught his breath as his heart skipped a beat, and then ran into the alley. Two cops popped out of the cruiser. One went to Scott, the other pursued Eddie. It was easy to ditch him through the busy streets and narrow alleys.

. . .

Outside of Kathy's house he gathered himself for a moment while smoking a joint in the Rover. It was dark now with several other cars parked in her driveway. Hide the pain deep inside, he thought. Keep it in a place where nobody could see it. The lessons of a young man in an old city. He walked around back and entered the basement through the sliding glass door.

"Eddie!" the room erupted. Vanya ran up to him and flung her arms around his neck. He cringed slightly, but tried to hide it. "What's wrong?" she asked.

"Nothing. What's happening here?" Mostly he was surprised that she was happy to see him. When he dropped her off earlier this evening she seemed like a person who would prefer he didn't exist.

"The usual." She was holding a silver can of cheap beer, the brand Kathy's dad drank. Then she noticed the red welt on the back of his neck. "What's that?"

"It's nothing. Don't worry about it."

"It doesn't look like nothing."

"I was just in the right place at the wrong time. Can we move on now?"

"Whatever you say Eddie. Mysterious Eddie. If you would've just stayed with me, that never would've happened."

"Well if you're so tough, can you at least get me a beer?"

"Here you go," said Kathy, walking up and cracking open a can. "Got any weed? We just smoked the last bong." She looked at Vanya and they broke out with laughter.

"Of course I do." He sat on the couch and opened his bag on the table. The couch was packed full of others his age, and not a single one sober. He looked around the room at the familiar faces, and those of strangers. He believed himself the strangest one here.

"Have you heard about Cassie's big party?" asked Vanya, as she hopped onto his lap.

"I have," he replied, peering around her and trying to roll a joint above her lap.

"Well you just missed her. That chick is so cool. She's gonna let me try shrooms. Said I could have some for free, since I've never done them before."

"Shrooms, huh? Weed's not good enough for you anymore?"

"Oh stop it. Everyone's at least tried them."

"I haven't, but if that's what you need." He licked the sticky end of the joint paper and sealed it shut.

"Be careful Eddie, you're almost about to offend me."

"You can only be offended by something if you believe it."

"Why are you dragging me down?" She started to rise off his lap. "I was having so much fun before you showed up."

"Just hold on there," he replied with the joint in his mouth. He placed a hand on each of her hips and pulled her down. The last thing he needed tonight was another fight, another scene. All he wanted was to relax and be normal for a little while. "I didn't mean anything by it. Here, I'll let you do the honors." He handed her the joint and put a flame to it.

"I want to dance," she said with big eyes. "Won't you dance with me?"

"Here? Now?"

She rose up with the joint in her lips and grabbed him by the hands. Why the fuck not? He stood up and in a swift motion she was spinning beneath his arms. Feather-light on her feet, she jumped up and down. A smile formed on his face and he forgot where he was or what had happened today. He started kicking his feet, never releasing her hand. It was easy to let it all out with the music loud and a pretty girl in his arms. They were shaking and vibrating and nothing else mattered. Then she slid in close and lay her head upon his shoulders. When she looked up, her irises appeared purple in this light. Purple and giant, consuming her entire eye. Lizard-like, or a goddess. He blinked several times, but they didn't change. He decided this was an apparition of something deep within her. Some supernatural sensation broadcasted now as if to remind him that there was color in the world. Life in the spectrum. It could be contagious, if he let it.

He pinched the joint from her lips and swayed to the music. Her breath was heavy upon his chest, and he closed his eyes. He thought about seeing her in the front row of Bonnell's class, wearing a long dress with braids in her hair. She loved books more than people that day. Then another day came, and another. That's what days always did, they changed. They changed the time, and the people wearing the time. He remembered how he felt when he thought she was someone different. Everyone else was the same and that was a boring scene. He looked at her now and she seemed like the rest. This feeling had changed, and it changed fast. He held her close, but could already feel her slipping away.

"Ooh, share that with me," said Kathy rushing up to them.

Eddie sat back on the couch and watched the joint make its way around the room. Vanya continued to dance, and pretty soon the entire room vibrated. He rolled another joint, and another one, and another one. They could smoke his entire bag tonight, for all he cared. He could disappear into the mountains and never be seen again. Nobody would care.

"Let's go for a drive," suggested a young dude named Quinn who Eddie just met tonight.

"That sounds perfect," replied Kathy. The room then developed into a sort of *who's got the shortest straw* game. Except this one was designed to determine who was the most sober and eligible to drive. They performed all kinds of crazy stunts, like who could balance this lighter on their nose the longest, who could recite the most lyrics from Snoop Dogg's song *Gin and Juice*, and who could close their eyes and count how many people were in the room. Eddie sat on the couch and watched. Not a single one of them passed a single test. So it was decided that since this was Quinn's great idea, he would be the one to drive. This upset him greatly because the driver would be the only one not allowed to drink. Not allowed to drink any more, that was.

"Alright, I'll bring the bottle of Schnapps," said Kathy as they headed for the back door. "Eddie, you bring the weed."

They smoked several more joints and the bottle of Schnapps was dry and rolling on the passenger floor. It didn't matter if they were more drunk or more stoned. This made them feel better. They didn't understand this anger, this rage, this ultimate uncertainty, for they were all young but had lived long enough to know something wasn't right. There was injustice and defeat for even the bravest and most successful, and though their experiences were limited, they had seen enough in the people around them to understand that the truth was something they didn't want to understand, and getting fucked up made that easier. They should've known better, but they didn't. There was nothing better and that was good enough for now. The wheels were spinning fast and the bends were sharp and difficult to manage. Being young was the gift they were given, but they didn't see it yet. They were taking it by the breath, consuming it like death, but this was being alive. Life was the bends in the road and the blurry vision and the certainty that they were immortal and could not be defeated like all those who came before. That was perfect. Confusion. Magic. Unconcerned. Full of hope but so doubtful. Inimitable. It was dark and dreary but their minds were so full and creative that nothing could stop them unless they said so. That was the power and the glory. This would last forever, until forever ended and something new came along. Don't stop now, this was the best part so keep it in gear. Hug the corners tight and accelerate through the straightaways. Put your brights on in the dark and roll down the windows in the light. Play that fucking music loud and ignore what the rest might think.

This was all true and happening around him, but he was still there, in the mountains. This world had more than one truth. In his head he was pacing around a tree thinking about tonight, what was happening now, as if it were the past, and it still didn't make any damn sense. He wasn't going to sleep tonight. There were too many thoughts to figure out, too many places to understand, too many people to wonder about. He wasn't going to tell a single person where he went when he left the city. That was his place, and they didn't need to know. He was a pioneer, an explorer, a wanderer, a woodsman. He was young but free. He knew even though he was young, someday he would be old, and perhaps this would make sense then, the way a tree in winter knows that it will spring new leaves after the snow has gone. A sense of predestination, but more true than a prediction or the roulette wheel. It was dark in the backseat and Vanya put her hand on his lap.

He thought about how much she had changed. Only a short time ago, she never would have put herself in this place. He missed that about her. Now they were riding in the backseat with a driver drunk and stoned. Didn't care. Life was too powerful, and they were insects floating on the river. She seemed at peace and he wondered which was better, the before, or the after. He imagined she had just read a really good book, which influenced this dramatic change in her life. It convinced her to live radically and unreserved for at least a brief duration of her youth. And he pictured her turning the very last page, with the smile of epiphany on her face, and realizing that she could do whatever she wanted. The choice was entirely hers. There was no blame in his heart for her now, as she laid her head on his lap.

They were so young and drunk and the world spun together as they spun together to the enchanting lyrics and invigorating melodies. There was no way to know then that this moment they wouldn't remember tomorrow, would be a moment of longing and goosebumps stretching into the future. Elasticity and music. It was the way they had danced. It was the softness of her neck and the confidence of his shoulders. It was the world that didn't exist outside of this circle. It was now, it was strong, and it was disappearing. But the past remembers and replays and recycles the old into the new. Tomorrow, it begins again.

MAY 1999

SUN	MON	TUE	WED	THU	FRI	SAT
~~25~~	~~26~~	~~27~~	~~28~~	~~29~~	~~30~~	~~1~~
~~2~~	~~3~~	~~4~~	~~5~~	~~6~~	~~7~~	~~8~~
~~9~~	~~10~~	~~11~~	~~12~~	~~13~~	~~14~~	~~15~~
~~16~~	~~17~~	~~18~~	~~19~~	~~20~~	~~21~~	~~22~~
~~23~~	~~24~~	~~25~~	26	27	28	29
30	31					

Morning came late but still too soon. As he rolled over in bed he felt the pain in his ribs and the throbbing at the back of his neck. Eddie rose up from his room and upstairs found the house empty. Cole at work and his mom and Carl someplace other than here, which was rare for weekdays. A note on the counter that read, "You must've worked late last night so I decided to let you sleep. Please don't miss any more classes, you're so close to finishing. Me and Carl walked to the community garden to plant some vegetables. Let's talk after school. Love, Mom."

He flipped the piece of paper over and wrote a note, "Mom, I'm rushing off to school because I don't want to miss any more classes. Thanks for letting me sleep in. Don't expect me home early tonight, I will be working late again."

He pulled into the school parking lot and waited with his windows down. Lunch hour was coming soon, and it felt like any other lunch hour. This was something he didn't enjoy, the idea it was all repetitive. Repetition of a cycle that needed to be destroyed. Destruction was not always destructive because it could create something good. He hadn't even thought about smoking weed until he saw Alex walking out and towards him. He lit up a joint, stepped out of the Rover, and walked towards Alex. Pulled a hit from between his fingers and blew a cloud of smoke into the calm air. No longer a care for who would see or what they thought they could do to him. Inconsequential were the consequences.

Alex walked in zig zags, as he usually did when the allergies were bad. He sneezed, scratched at his eyes, and then noticed Eddie coming at him. He turned and walked faster, but Eddie caught up.

"Alex, you need to stop and talk to me."

"Fuck you Eddie," he held a gang sign up over his shoulder. It was the same gang sign Eddie had seen Blunt and his thugs flashing.

"What are you doing kid?" asked Eddie, as he grabbed Alex by the shoulder. "Just stop and talk to me."

"Don't fuck with me Eddie. My boys got my back. You mess with me and you mess with all of them."

"Do you really believe that? You've been hanging with Darnell and Blunt too much kid. They don't give a fuck about you."

"You don't know shit Eddie. They put me on the set last week. I stood in the circle of six and stayed on my feet. Nothing but respect from my boys now. I make one call and ten cars full will come and erase you. I suggest you back the fuck up."

"Alex, don't take this the wrong way, but you're a scrawny white kid with allergies who's a sappy poet. Get your fucking head right."

"You get your head right. Now back the fuck up Eddie, or I'll make the call." Alex pulled a mobile phone from his front pocket and held it up.

"Alright, you want to play it like that. Make the call. Since you're a big timer now. Call him. Call them all. I don't give a fuck. Tell Blunt I want to meet him. Tell him the alley. He'll know the place."

"You must be suicidal Eddie. Meeting Blunt in an alley. Go and dig your own grave first."

"What the fuck happened to you Alex?"

"Already told you. I'm on the set now. Fools like you can't fuck with me anymore."

"I hope you wise up, Alex. But either way. Make the call. Tell him I'll be there at six tonight."

Eddie popped back in the Rover and drove away feeling sad. The things Alex said should've pissed him off, and not so long ago that would've been the effect, but now it made him worried about a kid who used to be a friend. Nothing he could do to help though, people blazed their own trail. He thought about Alex when they were freshmen. He was the most awkward kid in school that year, but he didn't care. He hadn't yet come to terms with the fact that he was different. He lived in a separate peace which allowed him happiness in oblivion. An imagined life most likely created by all the chaos he had experienced. The imagination was happier for him. Eddie missed that kid. He missed himself, too. The person he used to be. But that was some sappy bullshit he set aside. There were new issues to deal with.

He drove to the hospital, and in the parking lot he called Lynch. As the phone rang, he took a deep breath. This had to be done. If not now, it never would. The phone continued to ring until Lynch's voicemail came on. Eddie began to hang up his mobile, but then decided no, he had to do this now. "Lynch. It's Eddie. You need to know. I'm done with this. Tomorrow I will pay you what I owe, and then we're finished."

He walked inside and asked the receptionist for Scott's room number. On the third floor he paused and sat on a chair near the elevator. The last time he was in a hospital was the day Steve died. That event had left such a scar on him that he refused to visit his mom in the hospital the day Carl was born. Hospitals were haunted and he swore to never return. This was different. It was all his doing that Scott was here. There was nothing he could do to make this right. Certainly a visit wouldn't change anything. The most likely scenario was that Scott would get upset, tell Eddie to fuck off, and then he would leave feeling even worse. As he sat in the chair imagining the possible outcomes, all of them negative, he knew this was something that needed to be done. Put a cap on it. Show his face in all its wounded glory. Let Scott have the final word if for no other reason than to give a friend some peace. Some closure. As he stood up and walked towards Scott's room, he knew this would be the last time they ever talked.

This was an alien. A body mutated. A figure other than Scott's lay in the bed with bandages, casts, and tubes. Eddie found himself struggling to locate Scott's eyes. Swollen and bruised, yet focused directly at him. Scott's mouth tightened as Eddie approached the bed and said, "You ready to get out of here?"

"What do you want, Eddie?" Scott was struggling for breath as he talked.

"Scott, you're looking good. Seriously, this is an improvement. It looks good on you."

"Stop fucking around Eddie. Who were those guys?" He was talking slow and deliberate.

"Which ones? Oh, you mean the dudes in white coats who were walking out of here a minute ago? Shit, they looked like a bunch of fake doctors to me. We should get you checked out on the up and up. Seriously, let me have a look." Eddie leaned over Scott with a playful smile on his face.

"Enough bullshit Eddie. You know who I'm talking about. Who were those fuckers that jumped us?"

"Shit man, I wish I knew. Seriously, I've been asking around, trying to figure the same thing out. Everyone's all hush hush about it. But as soon as I find out, believe me, they'll regret it." Damn. Was he really lying? Now. He couldn't focus his eyes anywhere near the direction of Scott's face. The window curtain was open, so he walked over. "Damn, the least they could've done was give you a room with a view. Don't they know who you are? I mean seriously, the state's best hockey player deserves better than this."

"There's no hockey player in this room."

"What's that supposed to mean?"

"I mean look at me Eddie. I'm all fucked up and we're one game away from the state finals. The scouts don't draft anyone unless you play in the finals. I'm done. Finished. A fucking memory already forgotten."

"Don't talk like that. With your record. You'll be back in full health before next season. Any team in this country would be lucky to have you."

"Shit, the doctor says I may never see out of my left eye again. I'll be lucky to get a desk job that pays the bills. You need to tell me who those fucking guys were."

"Even if I knew, what good would a name do you?"

"I need to know, Eddie. There may be nothing I can do about it, but I still need to know."

Eddie turned from the window and walked to the door. He put his hand on the silver knob and paused. The past held him hostage and this was his ransom. Paying in full was the only way to leave this room without hatred for himself. More hatred. The past and the future converged in this moment. He turned back around and sat on the bed beside Scott's feet. He looked up at the ceiling and saw white panels in gridlock suspended by gravity. Gravity was powerful but had nothing on him. A force much stronger than anything physical was the only way he could come clean.

"Get the fuck away from me Eddie," said Scott as he turned his head and looked at the opposite wall.

Eddie stayed on the bed and said, "This is my fault, Scott. All of it. Those fuckers were coming for me. Nothing to do with you. This is all a god damn mess. It shouldn't have happened."

"You don't need to tell me it shouldn't have happened."

"What can I do Scott? What can I do to make this right?"

"There's nothing to make this right. It's too late for that."

"I'm going to get those fuckers. Believe me. I'm going to make them regret this. I will teach them a lesson for good."

"You need to teach yourself a lesson, Eddie. Now get out of here."

"Scott…"

"I'm done with you Eddie. I may end up hating you forever, but I never want to see you again."

Eddie got up, and at the door he paused. "If I deserve anything, it is your hate." Then he walked out of the room.

. . .

In the Rover he checked his mobile. Three new voice messages. The first was from Lynch. "Nobody quits on me," was all he said. The second was from his mom. "If you get a break tonight please call. We need to talk." The third was from Alex. "Blunt will meet you in the alley. He says you better not puss out." He ignored them all and thought about Vanya. He barely recognized her the last time he saw her at Kathy's house. He sensed that her metamorphosis was his fault. If he could change her one direction, then perhaps he could change her back the other direction. Tonight he would drive out to her house and leave a book in her mailbox. Maybe inscribe it with a note. Something intelligent and playful. Invite her away from the chaos.

He decided to give her a call first. If she was home, he could tell her that he would pick her up, take a drive through the mountains. He knew a place where the flowers were blooming and they could be alone. Her hair would be down and it would flutter slightly with the natural breeze. He would tell her about Steve, about his damages, so she could understand they were the same. They could change together and escape this mess. He pulled out his mobile and dialed her home number.

"Hello."

"Vanya, hey. It's Eddie. I wasn't sure if you'd be home yet."

"Yep. Just got home. Not gonna be here long. What's up?"

"Not much. You know, it's a nice night. Thought I'd come pick you up in about an hour. Let's go for a drive. I know a cool spot I want to show you."

"Can't Eddie. I'm doing shrooms tonight. Cassie is hooking us up. Kathy wants us to be alone for my first time."

He paused. Damn, maybe it was too late. "You sure? I mean, that sounds fun and all, but they'll be there next time. Have you ever seen anyone on shrooms?"

"Gotta go, Eddie. Dad just said dinner is ready. Kathy is picking me up after I eat." She hung up the phone.

Eddie put the wheels into motion and watched the city pass around him. Hypercolor and psychedelic in its disorientation. There was a steady pulse that he couldn't control. He was a spectator and it moved too fast. The best he could hope for was to be lost, forgotten, pushed aside and removed from the cycle. The cycle was not that kind. To be removed required escape, and escape required a plan. He drove into Bad Town and parked a block away from the alley. He tucked the brass knuckles in the back pocket of his pants and walked.

They were already here, all five of them. Blunt, Gunner, Darnell, Alex, plus one skittish fucker Eddie didn't recognize. He walked down the alley towards them. Houses on both sides but no one else around. The sight of them standing in the alley made him uneasy. It was anger he felt more than anything. That had to be pushed aside. Anger wouldn't solve this problem. They had to be erased from his existence. This wasn't going to be easy.

"Fool, you better have something good for me," said Blunt as Eddie was ten feet away.

Eddie stopped and looked at them all. Each of them seemed smaller to him now. They were starting not to matter, and this made them begin to disappear. With a smile on his face he said, "This is your lucky day. I have something exceptional for you, and you don't even need to jack me this time."

"I'll jack a punk like you any time I want," replied Blunt.

"Here's the thing," said Eddie, "I'm not even going to be mad at you. In fact, I'm going to completely forget everything that happened. But only if you accept my offer."

"Stop fucking around Eddie," said Alex. Then Blunt looked at Alex, and Alex took a couple steps backwards.

"This is what's up," said Blunt. "You don't make the offer. I tell you what's gonna happen."

Eddie laughed and took a few paces forward. "I think you will want to hear this. I'm done. Finished. But the thing is, I've still got a duffel bag full of primo weed that I need to unload. So I was thinking to myself, what am I going to do with all this primo shit? And you know what? I think you'll like this part. I figured the best thing to do would be to give it to you. Just to show I've got no hard feelings. But here's the catch. I give you my full stash, and I forget about you. That means you also forget about me. Make sense?"

"Here's my offer," replied Blunt, taking a step towards Eddie. "You give me your shit now and maybe we don't fuck you up. Maybe you get right with me and I allow you not to be afraid any more. Sissy little fuck."

Eddie took a step closer to Blunt. Gunner, who was standing to the right of Blunt, lifted his shirt to reveal a pistol tucked into his belt. Eddie looked at the gun, but what he was thinking about was the white mountain lion. The proximity of a foreign species that could kill him without a sound. How it chose to eat his scraps while he slept instead of making a fight. It was a powerful and dangerous animal, no doubt, but had chosen to avoid contact. Eddie then looked directly into Blunt's eyes. Dark, dangerous, and focused only on this immediate moment. Eddie exhaled, and replied, "You don't deserve my fear. That's not what this is about. I'm done. Done with designing my life around the likes of you. After this is finished, I'll have forgotten you ever existed. It's really that simple."

"That so?" said Blunt. "I will make it so you never forget me. Shit fool, you're just a little whiteboy wannabe, like your brother was. Nothing but a punk."

Eddie's heart pounded fast, and he felt the speed of his thoughts jump. "Fuck you. You didn't know my brother. Steve would never associate with scum like you."

"Think again fool. That little punk ass you call a brother used to come around Bad Town. Thought he was tough shit. We all know how that turned out. Same for you, if you don't watch yourself."

Eddie lunged at Blunt with a right hook that made contact with jawbone. The brass knuckles caused pain in his hand, and this pain felt good. Felt like redemption. He saw Blunt topple over with speckles of blood on his forehead. Before Eddie could regain balance from the swing, Gunner had the pistol removed and cracked Eddie hard in the back of the head with the butt of the handle. This sent Eddie to the ground. Blunt bent low over him, grabbed him by the hair, lifted his head and slammed his face into the loose gravel. Eddie lifted his head and watched them walk away with his bag. He felt tears in his eyes. Tears not from the pain. He didn't believe what they said about Steve. Only said it to get a rise out of him. That much he believed. The tears made his fury escalate. The fury made his focus clear.

After a moment he got to his feet. They were out of sight now around the bend. He got up and ran, found them walking down the sidewalk along the busy street with cars moving slowly. They had their backs to him. Blunt was in the middle. Easy target. He gripped the brass knuckles tightly, wrapped around his fingers, clenched his fist, and ran at them. Three feet behind them, he jumped in the air and came down with a blow on the back of Blunt's head. Blood splattered and Blunt fell to the ground. Gunner turned towards him and started to remove the pistol. Eddie caught his balance and swung an upper cut that made contact with Gunner's neck. Solid brass on flesh and windpipe. Gunner went limp and fell to the ground gasping for breath. This wasn't what he wanted, but they gave him no choice.

Alex and Darnell turned to run, but the fifth, whom Eddie didn't know, was prepared to fight. He removed a telescoping baton from his belt, whipped it into extension, and swung at Eddie. Eddie dodged the first swing, and made an attempt with the brass knuckles, but missed. The second swing of the baton caught Eddie where his neck met his spine. He fell to the ground and felt a kick to the back of his head, which made his face hit the concrete. His head lay turned on the sidewalk, blood dripping around him, and he watched the cars crawling past. None stopped. All too scared or too wrapped up in their own shit. He heard the footsteps of Blunt, Gunner and the skittish dude running away from him. Couldn't turn his head from the pain in his neck. He thought about Carl now, and wanted more than anything to show his younger half-brother how to drift a stonefly nymph through a deep bend in a mountain stream.

Then he heard the sirens. Loud and close, clearly from more than one squad car. He stood up but was dizzy from the loss of blood on concrete. Took a turn but lost his bearings so went down on one knee. The police swarmed in around him but he didn't hear what they said. His thoughts were someplace else and he smiled. He was thinking about the time Steve took him quail hunting. It was autumn and the prairie grass was dry. Skies blue and wide open above rolling hills. Steve shot the first two birds, and then handed the twelve-gauge shotgun to Eddie. The gun was almost as long as Eddie, but Steve instructed him how to hold it tight and follow the target. He missed the first three birds, but hit the fourth in the wing which sent it circling to the ground. When they found it in thick brush it was flapping its good wing and spinning frantically. Steve picked up a rock the size of his fist and handed it to Eddie. "This is how we live, by taking life. It's part of survival. It's the only way we survive."

Eddie felt the steel cuffs tighten around his wrists behind his back. The officer was saying something, but he still wasn't listening. The other officer held a bandage up to his head and compressed it tightly. There was a smile on Eddie's face as they shoved him in the backseat of the squad car. At the station under a bright light they asked for his statement. "This is how we live," he said.

"Alright, if that's how you want to play this," replied the officer. "You can live the night in a jail cell."

They opened the thick steel door and shoved him in. He landed in a room ten foot by eight, with two cots on the floor. There was an older man lying on one cot. Grey beard, dark eyes and grizzly skin. Looked like a ranch hand or mountain man. Someone who didn't spend much time around people. Spent his time in the elements. He looked up at Eddie, smiled and said, "Welcome home young man."

Eddie stumbled in and fell on the empty cot. He looked at the man again who had a giant grin on his face. The grin seemed friendly and sincere, which struck Eddie as being out of place here. He looked closer and saw the man had one front tooth that was much brighter than the rest. The man caught his look, reached in and in a single motion pulled out the tooth, held it up to Eddie and said, "It's a conch shell. I whittled it myself during my time on the islands."

Eddie looked away and shuffled into his cot. "Don't talk to me," he said.

"You must think you're pretty tough, with your face looking like that. I've seen worse, kid." The old man crawled to Eddie's cot, leaned over him. Eddie's eyes were closed, still feeling dizzy. "A kid your age looking like this. They should take you to the hospital, not here."

"I'm old enough to take care of myself," said Eddie, without opening his eyes. "This is only a temporary problem."

"True," said the old man, "and that's a wise way to look at any problem. Makes you feel strong. But be careful, kid. The weakness of a man is the knowledge of his strength."

Eddie heard the old man lean closer and felt his breath. He felt the wrinkled fingers pick pebbles from his forehead. He tried to think about something else, but then the man spoke.

"Open your eyes man. I know it's difficult to see the world around you when you're a young dude, because so much exists internal, but open your eyes. What surrounds you today will be your only chance to see it as it is, because it will change. And so will you. Open your eyes."

Eddie turned his head away and kept his eyes closed. "Why are you in here?" he asked.

"Same reason as you. Same reason as anyone comes in here. I was doing what felt right in the moment. Got trapped up in all that fury of spontaneity. Forgot to think about what would happen next."

"That's not why I'm here."

"I suppose you don't think so. Tell me about it then. Secret is safe with me."

"Just some street shit. You wouldn't understand. Simple difference of opinions."

"Opinions," the old man's voice rose and trailed off. "Opinion is a simple word for a person's entire belief system, the programming of their life through every experience of their five senses. Opinions are the attempt at making our belief systems simple and expressible. It's never easy, to take the internal and make it external. To consider not only our personal belief system, but how that weaves together into the greater narrative of our species and environment. This takes focus and practice. Opinions are a dagger and expression is the stone that sharpens them."

The old man reached down and wrapped his fingers around Eddie's right hand. Fingers bent and crooked from making contact with brass knuckles. "Was it a good fight? What I mean is, which side of the odds were you on?"

"It was just some shit I had to do old man. Now can you leave me alone?" Eddie pulled his hand away and tucked it under his leg.

"Here's the thing, something that took me a while to understand. You can learn as much from not getting in fights as you can from getting in fights, they're just different lessons."

"Are you always so full of shit?"

"Have been. But here's the thing, I know it."

"Doesn't change the fact that you're full of shit."

"Nope."

Eddie turned and opened his eyes. The man was kneeling close to him. Something struck him as calming about the man. He was like a hybrid of John Wayne and Carl Jung. Peaceful and wise, but could probably hit the eye of a crow at two-hundred yards with a rusty old six-shooter. This observation came from a sense other than sight. Something intangible. Sublime. A sensation reserved for the poetry in nature. How a bird knows a storm is coming. A tree knows of winter and water returns to the sea. Interpretations without consciousness, without the requirement of thought, but simply, truly, understood.

"Okay," replied Eddie, as he rolled his head towards the man.

The man pulled the sleeve of his flannel shirt over his left hand, and compressed it firmly to the wound on Eddie's forehead. "The funny thing about wounds like this," he started, "is that they don't hurt so much now. The hurt comes later. Much later. And it isn't physical hurt when it comes. It comes as pain much more powerful. It will return over and over again in your waking dreams. Every moment that you could have lived differently. This is the most valuable type of pain, but only if it is used effectively."

"How am I supposed to use pain?"

"Pain will make you better. It's an unfortunate flaw in our design that we must do what is wrong first, before we know what is right. The real struggle comes after we learn what is right. It is then we must decide to repeat what is right, which is typically the more difficult choice. It is more difficult to be good. Because goodness is not inherent in people. It is chosen by the individual to be made, and then remade, every day. If you skip it even for one day, all the previous days of goodness will be forgotten."

"Why should I listen to you? For all I know you could be some crazy old child molester."

"That is a good point. You don't know. The great thing is we get to decide what we believe. But we must also understand that everyone else has this same power of choice. What we believe becomes our reality. Because of this, no single person will ever see us in our entirety. Except ourselves. But even this is selective. The fragments we see of others is not who they are, but only a sneak peak of who we believe them to be. Of who we are, broadcasted on the faces of others. What we know is so little. What we hide is so deep."

Eddie closed his eyes, and felt the mans' sleeve, now sticky with his own blood, still firmly pressed against his forehead. He pictured Steve's smiling face while standing in a trout stream. No other image of his brother was this vivid. Perhaps his memory had been selective. Of all the others that happened after that day and before his death, this was the one he chose to remember. This was the idol of his brother created by his own intentions. He understood this now, but still didn't believe what Blunt had said.

MAY 1999

SUN	MON	TUE	WED	THU	FRI	SAT
~~25~~	~~26~~	~~27~~	~~28~~	~~29~~	~~30~~	~~1~~
~~2~~	~~3~~	~~4~~	~~5~~	~~6~~	~~7~~	~~8~~
~~9~~	~~10~~	~~11~~	~~12~~	~~13~~	~~14~~	~~15~~
~~16~~	~~17~~	~~18~~	~~19~~	~~20~~	~~21~~	~~22~~
~~23~~	~~24~~	~~25~~	~~26~~	27	28	29
30	31					

Morning came but it wasn't sunlight or alarm clock that woke him. Cold, stiff, with sore bones and blood scabs on face. Too young to feel like this, yet there was no other age that deserved to feel like this. The steel door swung open with loud squeaks and clang against concrete wall. Eddie rolled over and saw the old man asleep on the cot near him. Arm's length away and both on ground level. Something primitive and personal, sharing a holding cell with a stranger. Made him feel a little better. Feeling good about himself made him also feel good about this stranger. They must be equals to share this predicament.

The guard stood in the door, broadcasting shadow across the small room. "Eddie Young, get your ass up. We're taking you out of here."

This voice woke up the old man. He rolled towards Eddie,

scratched at his beard, and said, "Looks like the age of youth has prevailed today." Then he sat up, leaned towards Eddie, something far off and pensive in his eyes, "Just know this. Things in this life change fast, and they change every day."

Eddie looked at him and felt something new. Perhaps it was the proximity that could only be known in a small concrete room, or maybe it was simply the fact that he was leaving and knew he'd never see this man again. Either way, for a moment he was relieved of stubbornness. He felt young and vulnerable and knew this was a sensation that wouldn't last. "What's your name old man?"

"That's not important. It is good to know people and try to understand them. It is better to know yourself. Neither is easy, but the latter is more difficult. We can make excuses for ourselves when other people are doing the same thing. This makes it seem okay to do what we know is wrong. Ultimately it comes down to what you are capable of doing alone. When we are alone there is no one else to blame and only ourselves to judge."

Eddie stood up and walked to the door. The guard grabbed him firmly by the right forearm. He turned and looked at the man who was leaning on one elbow in his cot. Nothing he could say, this was a brief understanding between strangers. The guard walked him out of the room and down the hall.

When Eddie exited the front door, the clouds were low and threatening to rain. He looked towards the mountains but only saw grey. He pulled the mobile phone from his pocket and thought about who to call for a ride. His Rover was still parked in Bad Town. That was a long walk. As he scrolled through his contacts list, he heard a car horn blare three times fast. Looking up he saw the rusty beige Honda Accord he knew to be Kathy's. It was a surprise when the car stopped in front of him and he saw Vanya riding shotgun.

"Eddie Eddie, fresh from prison," said Kathy from the driver's seat.

"I think that's sexy," said Vanya. She had a giant smile on her face with eyes unfocused.

"What are you girls doing here?" he asked.

"We heard about your stunt with Blunt," said Vanya. "Don't you need a ride?"

The back window rolled down and Cassie held up a bag of shrooms. "Let's get you feeling right," she said.

Eddie glanced behind him, and then back at the car. He reached out and pushed Cassie's hand down. "Keep that shit away from me. Are you trying to get all of us arrested?"

"Damn, kid," said Vanya, "we're just trying to show you a good time. Can't we just have some fun?"

"Come on Eddie," said Cassie, "this girl's wild on shrooms."

"Eddie Eddie, my teddy, come ride with me. This is the greatest." Vanya's head was swiveling, seemingly disconnected from her neck. Eddie leaned in and looked closer. She wore a low cut V-neck tank top and tight cutoff shorts. Fingernails painted pink to match her lipstick. The only thing that hadn't changed was her cowboy boots, except they were no longer caked with mud.

He leaned back and felt the raindrops start to fall. The thing about storms around here was they never lasted too long. There was already blue sky on the western horizon. "I think I'm going to walk," he said.

"Oh fuck that Eddie. We never hang out any more. Don't you want to hang with me?"

"I'd still like to talk to you about that book I finished reading. But you look busy now."

"A book? Ha!" She leaned forward and started laughing. She laughed longer and louder than any sober person would be capable. When she finished, she looked up at him with happy tears in her eyes. "I don't have time for books any more Eddie. This is real life now. It's so much more fun."

Eddie turned his head and held back a sigh. "Will I see you at school tomorrow?"

"Oh Eddie, my youth would be a terrible thing to waste on something so ordinary as an education." She turned towards Kathy and said, "Let's get out of here. This kid's gotten lame."

As they pulled away, Cassie yelled out the window, "You can still come to my party."

The dizziness came and he wasn't sure if it was from the physical pain or the knowledge he had destroyed her. It was a rapid transformation, and he was the catalyst. Perhaps this is how she was born to be, he thought. You cannot mold somebody into a form which did not already exist, however hidden or latent, at the very core of their being. She had been born in the city, trained on these streets, didn't matter that she had found a semblance of happiness in the country. That happiness was only a surrogate for the pain she felt. That life was not for her. Anybody could learn to ride a horse or talk romantically about the mountains. No matter how many influences you threw at a person, the interior could not be changed. It existed the way a mountain exists, designed in angles and curves that could never be duplicated. Hidden and mysterious by its very nature. He admired the wildness of it all, and knew he could never love her again.

So he walked. Rain on shoulders and feet dragging concrete sidewalks. One foot then the other, keeping pace with the rhythm of his thoughts. Thinking about her more than his own pain and struggle. Loud cars passing but no concern. Wind on his back and he pushed forward. Dried blood on face and crooked knuckles. Nothing broken on the outside could make him feel like this.

She could've been great with a smile that perfect. He couldn't change her without changing himself. Lovely was her face when the sun broke over mountain peaks. That was the image he chose. That was the picture he carried as his feet moved farther from home. Time didn't matter now, it was less powerful than these conditions. He could make all of this right, somehow. He could take her away from this place and temptations. They would change together and find happiness in the mountains. He could see her smiling in a sundew meadow. A waking dream overtook him.

When he returned from the daydream, his feet were on gravel road. He looked behind and saw the city burning yellow beneath a retreating storm cloud. Grey and blue met in the sky above him. This was the place he knew best. The periphery of grey and blue. Beneath the grey was the city, its memories, his pain and his home. Underneath the blue were mountains with meadows and canyons and streams. He looked at them stretching across the horizon, etched in sharp lines towards the sky. He saw the crests and the folds, the peaks and canyons, the trees and the rocks. Passages unknown yet calling to him with a familiar voice. He walked until sunset cut purple lines over the prairie, then he laid his head down on a pillow of sagebrush and fell asleep.

. . .

Morning came with the songs of meadowlark and coyote jabber. He stretched in the cool morning air and saw golden light hit prairie grass. The mountains were close to the north and looked pink in the morning. The city was not much farther to the south and looked grey as steel. He knew which direction was home, but could not travel that way. Not yet. Home could only be entered with a happy heart and a clear conscience. There was something he had to do first.

After a long walk he entered school as the bell rang to end third period class. He stood in the hallway and watched the students pass. It hadn't occurred to him that his hair was a mess and he had blood scabs on his face, until he saw a group of junior girls laughing at him. He decided to let it be. Wild hair was only another way he was different. Differences were visible in more than the physical. He wondered which of these girls had ever known the sunrise on mountains. Too busy with their friends and imaginary lives. If he had the power, his first task would be to take it all away and return them to a natural life. Strip them of their name brand clothing. Erase their ideas of self-importance. Free them from the constricts of imaginary lives. Take each one alone into the mountains and let them be happy.

When Eddie entered English class he saw Mister Bonnell sitting at his desk. Bonnell looked up and caught Eddie's eyes, but didn't say a word. Eddie sat down and looked out the window. Students were shuffling in and talking quietly to each other, looking at Eddie, his blood scarred face and crooked fingers, with hair still a mess. He was known but wanted to be invisible. He looked back at Bonnell and realized it had been a couple weeks since his previous journal entry.

There was only one reason he came to class today. He wanted to see Vanya. To study her long brown hair as she sat in front of him. To say something intriguing enough for her to turn her head and look at him. To pass her a note and see her smile. When the bell rang for class her seat was empty.

Eddie attended the rest of his classes that day without speaking a word. After the final bell rang, he left the school building and walked towards Bad Town where he hopped in his Rover and drove home. He knew there would be a scene waiting for him.

"Eddie, where have you been?" asked his mom when he entered.

"Sorry mom, I had to work late last night, so decided to just sleep in my car at the school parking lot. Seemed better than waking you all up."

"I tried to call. Why did you give me your mobile number if you aren't going to answer it?"

"My phone died and I didn't have the charger."

Eddie stepped in closer under the kitchen lights.

"Oh my!" exclaimed his mom. "What happened to your face?"

"It's nothing mom. Don't worry. Just a little accident at work."

"You'll have to do better than that, Eddie," said Cole, as he stood up from the dining room table. "How can loading packages result in that kind of injury?"

"It was stupid really. I mean, me and a couple guys were just horsing around." Eddie was improvising rapidly. "We were having a contest to see who could raise the forklift all the way and balance on the forks the longest. I was doing really good until Jim threw an empty box at me and knocked me off."

"Oh Eddie," cried his mom, "why would you do something like that?"

"It was just for fun mom. Work gets boring sometimes."

"Forgive my language Samantha," said Cole, "but that sounds like absolute bull shit to me."

Eddie's immediate reaction was to feel angry and defensive. Then he looked at his mom. She was sitting at the table with Carl on her lap. Carl had apple sauce all over his chin, but still smiling. Carl looked like a stranger and he wanted to hug him. He wanted to take him into a separate room and tell him all his experiences. He needed to share this pain and let it all out. These people were strangers and would continue as such unless he told them the truth. He took a deep breath and leaned into the counter.

"You're right, that's not the truth. I got in a fight, okay. I wasn't actually working last night."

"Eddie!" cried his mom. "What happened?"

"It's not a big deal mom. Someone offended Steve, and I had to do something." Wasn't the whole truth, but wasn't a lie either.

"Eddie," Samantha looked away and wiped a tear from her face. "That was brave of you. You shouldn't get in fights though. There's other ways to handle things."

"I know mom. It just really upset me and I had to do something."

"Young men get in fights sometimes, it's natural," said Cole. "You just have to be smart enough to choose your fights wisely, don't let anger make decisions for you."

"I know. Listen, I just came to get some text books so I can study on my break at work. They've got me on the overnight shift again this weekend. I'm almost finished with school, and there's going to be lots of tests I need to study for."

"Okay, I understand," said Samantha. "But before you go, can I give you an ice pack for your face?"

"It's going to be okay mom. Don't worry."

Eddie went to his room and packed a bag. He removed the last bit of weed from his pocket and stashed it in the nightstand drawer. Before leaving, he gave his mom a hug and kissed Carl on the forehead. "I'll miss you, little dinosaur," he said, and then walked out the door.

He drove through the city and parked outside of Kathy's house. The windows were dark upstairs, but lights were bright in the basement and he saw the shadows of a dozen people. Surely Vanya was one of them. He played the scenario through his head, how he would convince her to leave with him. He could lure her with books and a camping bag. They would talk about music and their dearly departed. Laughter and tears and a long caress. They would be alone in the mountains and this would make sense. He put the car in gear and drove out of the city.

The clear yet unstable future which encompassed this horizon, spoke furtively about happiness and serenity, displayed multiple layers of confusion and uncertainty about what had already passed. This dark and jagged horizon lay before him now as an infinite maze, and he wanted to wander every corner and crevice, seek out the very heart of his existence, and explore forever until he gained a sense of recognition. The angles were obscure and there were too many paths to follow, so he would have to rely on instinct. The gears in the city would always turn, constantly grinding strangers and friends in and out of his life, but only the mountains knew his potential.

Voice Recording #7

Another beautiful morning in the mountains to wake up in a tent. I guess it's Saturday. Difficult to say for sure. I didn't go to school much last week. It's been a wild ride lately. Not sure how much I can tell you. So much exists on the inside.

Here I go again. Singing into this voice journal again. Walking in circles again. Confounded by the paradigm of my own design again. Lost again, but I know where I am. I will be found, but by nobody other than myself. A specter I exist in the crowds. Immortal, but only in rumors, and rumors run the world. I will never be still or stagnant, too much possibility for that. I will climb, I will read, I will think, and I will fish. This will be a voice journey, not a voice journal.

So follow me, if you dare. Lose me, if you know what is good for yourself. I will lead you astray and cause you pain. There are many in that yellow city who can testify to this. But they may not even realize it. They may have found comfort in their pain just like me. They may see nothing past the immediate because they live in an artificial land where the horizon is an illusion. The curvature of earth bends farther away the closer I get. Sunshine seeps over the mountains in a multitude of colors but it has no pull like that of money, of greed, of belonging, of owning and dominating and…

Fuck.

It's been a hell of a time lately, Mister Bonnell. If you knew all the shit that's been going on, man, you either wouldn't believe me, or you'd try to lock me away. I wish I could explain it all, but the truth is, it's a mystery even to me. That seems funny to say, since I'm the one dealing with it. I'd tell you all about it if I could, but it's trapped someplace else. The past knows, and most of it will stay there.

I'm not even sure if I should be pissed or remorseful. If I should push forward and see this thing through, or if I should change. It seems like everything else has changed around me. It really didn't take that long, either.

I'm sitting here on this boulder watching the river. Got my camp all set up again when I came up here last night. I told my mom that I'm working the overnight shift and then sleeping days at a coworkers so we could carpool together. The truth is I just didn't want to see anyone for a while. The river continues to flow as it always does, and there's about a million trout rising. I watch them up and down this sparkling water, this meadow light glowing on the surface, the ripples shifting and returning. I see them puncture the top to purchase an insect, and two separate worlds are trading energy. This scene is so simple, yet foreign and complex, like a faraway land I thought was imaginary. I cannot live my life as a bystander, I lack that ability. It is time to wet a line.

PAUSE.

It occurred to me that I haven't smoked any weed since yesterday. The strange part is, I haven't even thought about it. For the past several hours I've only been thinking about trout, or rather, the gentle rhythm of my fly line pulling back and pushing forward, unfurl and fall softly to the water. I'm starting to get the hang of this. It's probably the simplest pleasure I know.

Not that I caught any fish. They were elusive as any worthy achievement should be. I was thigh deep in the water and all the distractions in my head were pulled into the river and dragged downstream. As I walked on the slimy stones and knelt behind boulders to hide my shadow, I had completely forgotten what brought me here in the first place. If a trout jumped out of the water and shouted Blunt's name at me in perfect English I wouldn't have understood. In fact, I would have been euphoric that a trout was willing to communicate, since all the others of its kind have completely ignored me.

What a beautiful struggle it is to be an angler. To kneel in the pulse of life which is flowing water and fling a wand with nothing more than hope. It is the best kind of hope because even if it is unfulfilled, if its potential isn't realized by the manifestation of a catch, it only creates more hope, never loss or a sense of failure. It is a perpetual pursuit with no end in sight because there is no such thing as the perfect catch. There is always the chance for a better fish, or scene, or river, or cast, or retrospection. To be an angler is to be trapped infinitely in a mystery, and to be okay with that. More than okay, but to devour it, bask in its perpetual current, and know this is home.

Or at least that's what I suspect. It's what I believed while in the river and engaged with its flow. It's what I knew to be true because there was no one to say different. I'll let you know if it's still my opinion after I catch a fish. The difference between believing something, and having somebody else believe you, is a simple matter of proof. Of tangible evidence to validate what I've already told you. But don't worry, it'll happen, and then you'll believe everything that I've said, and you'll wonder what's hiding in everything I haven't said.

PAUSE.

It is dark out now and my vision is clear. There are no distractions in my view to mislead my mind. Darkness is the only place where I can actually see anything. The light interferes and gives birth to illusions. What happens around me is less important than what I see on the inside. I've been thinking about all of the shit that's been happening lately. I tried to ignore it, but that won't help anything. Despite what I know to be true, that I am better than these problems, and there are people who love me, I am still filled with rage. I remove my machine gun from the camp bag and load the clip. It would feel so damn good to release all of these rounds and hear it echo down the mountain. Echoes go so much farther in the dark.

I think about it now, getting jacked by some thugs, robbed by a friend, betrayed by another, and seeing a girl I admire changing beyond my control. Of losing my brother and being disconnected from my family. I know it is my fault, that it is myself who causes this anger and frustration. I place both hands on my gun, there is only one thing I can do. I chuck the fucker as far as I can. I hear it clang against a rock in the night. That isn't good enough.

With flashlight in hand I seek it out. I find where it lays, and remove my knife from its sheath. I see visions behind my eyes of people who betrayed me and of those I've betrayed, and their faces are so clear I could touch them with the sharp tip of this blade. There is another face, foggy, distorted, shapeless. It is the face of unknown murders and injustice, of a relentless weight that pounds on my spine, clogs up my head, and shuffles me around like silt in this river. The handle of my knife is cold as I pound this blade into the earth, into this rocky soil, into the organ which gives life to my memories. I am searching for the heart of it all so that I may stab it a thousand times. Digging and digging, it is my only hope. Entomb this weapon deep beneath the surface, proximal to the place where I hide my pain. Let them shoot it out for a while. When the hole is deep enough I bury the gun inside. It will die here along with my anger.

I returned to camp feeling something accomplished. I watched the dark night sky and the stars in the distance, but I didn't wonder about my mortality or finite existence. I wondered what I have done wrong and why I have lacked any further understanding of my place, not in this unfathomable universe, but in this proximal atmosphere. I've been living and watching and feeling since I was born, but comprehension has eluded me. I am walking as a hollow man in concrete shoes. I want to fill myself with knowledge and something complete, but those streets and people and reasons confound me. I am a fool of simple motions but my mind is full of complicated notions. I walk like any other but so different, still I wonder if they think like me. Are they as confounded by their course as I? Wouldn't it be great if we could speak on a level below but above these superfluous topics that make us feel comfortable. I'm going somewhere, but right now the darkness is too consuming, and I have been blinded by thought.

I started to think about this girl I know. I guess that's what being alone does, makes me romantic. I was one day away from saying I loved her. I really was. Then some shit happened. Now here I am alone and thinking about her. She has a big heart but I know I will lose her. I have lost others, but they never left me, at least not intentional. They remain by my side when the night gets cold. My memory is the danger that makes me stronger to survive it. I see the past through multiple angles but none of them make the present any easier. The people I pursue with my time use me and I use them. It's fair, but so unfortunate. Don't you want to know me? I want to know you, but only if it makes sense. The flame crackles and I am alone on this mountain. I see the yellow city lights far away in the sky beyond the prairie, but they look so strange, and I never have been there. Where I have been is lost, and no place can contain that.

PAUSE.

Sunday morning and I awoke fresh and alive. I don't mean *alive* as in simply breathing. I mean alive as in being happy, as in seeing the world around me in its heart pounding glory, hearing the river pass over the stones, the wind parting through needles on the trees, and the sun so full of colors I couldn't count them with all my days. I laced on my boots and hiked up until there were patches of snow in the shade, still hiding from the spring sun, waiting as long as possible, clinging to this moment they were given, before returning to what they have always been. A river that flows from sky to earth to sea and back again.

As the sun burned and pushed the shadows away, I watched the patches of snow slowly melt and trickle down the landscape towards the river. I watched the cold water converge and grow, become something new, different, but born of the same material. I witnessed something solid transform into liquid, but it didn't surprise me. Everything I know changes. That's simple enough, but this was beautiful. I saw something original, and though this river may bend and crash and break, it started here, and I have seen it.

I'm taking the long way back to camp, switch-backing down this mountain. The joy of walking without a trail, and the idea my feet could be the first human feet to ever touch this place. To place a step in this exact spot. I could be the only man alive. I could live forever without ever knowing the date or time. I could reach my arms wide, inhale deeply, and know this is home.

I just crossed a narrow animal path, and I will follow it a while. It would be gratifying to see some wildlife. Skirting along the side of this mountain on loose rocks, and the river is deep below me. The air is tangible up here, full without the presence of manmade objects. It is a landscape that is both young and old. There is history and future in these rocks and trees. These trees and even the wind that is born here knows nothing of the rules in a city, or the ideas of men. We are the aliens who live in a distant land, and this is the earth. It's concerning to me that nature, in its purest form, has become almost like science fiction to our civilized minds.

And there it is. Holy fuck. Less than fifty feet away. It sensed me, but didn't shy off. Bright white as I remember. Red eyes and as big as me, only wilder. An apparition, perhaps, but materialized in animate form. He's standing there in the trail with his shoulders down and looking directly at me. I am completely at its mercy. If I turn, it may take me as prey. If I advance, it may see me as a threat. So here I stand, alone. This cougar is alone, and doesn't seem concerned. Nothing about its body language expresses any fear. It has not been introduced to the danger inherent in men. As I knelt down, the animal also went into the prone position.

Okay, we've been sitting here staring at each other for about five minutes. I'm talking really quiet and trying not to move. I don't have any idea what I'm supposed to do in a situation like this. Every time I start talking, it perks up its ears, seemingly more curious than anything else. It's possible this animal has never seen a human. Even more possible that no other human has ever seen it.

Okay, shit, it just stood up, still looking right at me. I've removed my knife from the sheath. Truth is, I hope it doesn't attack. Not because I'm afraid of it, even though if we went to battle right now, it would likely win. More than win, it would tear me to shreds, treat my carcass like a buffet, until my bones had been picked, and even then continue, drag my bones one by one to its lair, crack them open late at night, and drink the marrow dry. But there's a thought stronger than not wanting to become cougar food, the core of my being doesn't want this animal to see me as a threat. I want it to accept me. I want this animal to forgive me. I know that sounds strange, at least it does to me, because I've never asked forgiveness from another person and meant it. I know that people remember, and because we remember, we don't forgive, even though we may pretend that we do to make things easier. I want this bright white animal to look deep into me with its crimson red eyes and forgive. To understand that I am flawed and selfish but to recognize that was part of another world, and this is my home. I may be inexplicable to others of my kind, but if I could be understood by something wild and natural, then I'd make sense.

Okay, he's apparently bored, and has leisurely turned and continued down the trail. Wow, that was intense. Only now did I just realize my heart is pounding in my chest. I'm going to get off this trail and take the shortcut back to camp. I can't believe what just happened. An albino mountain lion exists in this mountain, and I have seen it. More than seen it, I have made eye contact and won in a staring contest. I am the luckiest man alive.

I have returned to camp and stashed my gear in the same place beneath the tarp. I will now fish my way down to the Rover. The only items I am carrying out are my fly rod, knife and pack of weed. I didn't smoke a single time this trip. The battery on my voice recorder is getting low, so I'll have to end this recording here. But one final note. If I should die or end up in prison before I return to this place, let it be known that the serenity I found here has changed me deeply, and there will never be a home more revered in this young man's mind than the side of a mountain, in proximity to trout, and in the eyes of an albino cougar.

STOP.

MAY 1999

SUN	MON	TUE	WED	THU	FRI	SAT
~~25~~	~~26~~	~~27~~	~~28~~	~~29~~	~~30~~	~~1~~
~~2~~	~~3~~	~~4~~	~~5~~	~~6~~	~~7~~	~~8~~
~~9~~	~~10~~	~~11~~	~~12~~	~~13~~	~~14~~	~~15~~
~~16~~	~~17~~	~~18~~	~~19~~	~~20~~	~~21~~	~~22~~
~~23~~	~~24~~	~~25~~	~~26~~	~~27~~	~~28~~	~~29~~
~~30~~	31					

He heard them pass around the trees, voices of old ghosts, mountain men screaming at a tragic death lost and alone in the wilderness, or worse still, the cries and helpless murmurs unheard in the city of rape and murder and fallen angels who will never touch earth the way it was meant to be known, or see the sun rise above the hilltops without a streetlight in sight, and the deep burning glow of a million stars pasted upon a dark flowing river. He felt the loss of their ideals, of people he would never be but only divided by simple twists of fate, interwoven connections that bound them all together yet separated like fabric at every scratch and nail, and he watched them pass in the moonlight, so lost and lonely, so downtrodden but full of hope, and he wished for them nothing more than what he knew now, that it was all possible, the pain was worth the reward if he followed it through the bends and hills and met his demons square in the jaw with a smile upon his face.

. . .

Eddie woke in his bedroom but he kept his head on the pillow, eyes open. Daylight crept under the window shade and cast shadows across the floor. He watched the shadows of the window shade sway back and forth and thought of the pine boughs near camp, the way they created movement on the forest floor. He closed his eyes again and pulled his arms out of the blanket, stretched wide and flat on the bed. It was almost tangible, how the mountain air felt fresh yesterday morning. Cool, calm, and full of song. He listened to the river pulse, gurgle, and crash against boulders. Birds chirped from treetops and between their chirps he heard it, the silence. Then he opened his eyes and heard traffic rushing through the neighborhood, to all the busy places, blind and congested. People too busy to ever breathe. This world was not for him, but then again, it wasn't meant for anyone. They were all trespassers, foreigners, tourists faking their way through happiness. A masquerade and he was counting the days. This was the final week of high school, and he could change. Purge this blood from his veins and fill it with something new. The idea of something new gave him ambition and he jumped from bed.

After the shower he dressed and pulled a ball cap onto his head. He was unconcerned with his hair today. The cap seemed a better fit. It was an old one, he had to dig it out from the bottom of his closet. It had been Steve's. Brown bill, six panels, the back half were mesh. The front was waxed green canvas with an embroidered patch of a fly reel, no words. Just this antique looking reel. He pulled it low, down to his eyebrows. It was better if no one saw his face today. It was better yet if he didn't have to look at theirs.

In the kitchen his mom was doing what she did every morning. Coffee for Cole, and breakfast for Carl. The three of them were at the dining table when Eddie entered the room. He could walk right past, a specter in this family. He was eighteen and a week away from graduating – maybe. He figured they'd be better off after he left. It would be easier for them to go about their routine without another person to distract them from this new family. He paused a moment at the edge of the room and watched them. Samantha was spoon feeding Carl his morning applesauce. Cole was sipping coffee from a ceramic cup and held a newspaper in his other hand. It was a peaceful scene, and he imagined himself as part of it. He'd be sitting next to Carl, holding the bowl of apple sauce up so his mom could scoop it out and feed his baby brother. Cole would read a passage from the paper, something relevant and important, and he would have something valuable to say on the subject. Maybe even make a joke, and they'd all laugh a little. This alienation wouldn't exist. They'd all be happy.

Cole peeked over the paper, and without turning his head he said, "Isn't this your final week of school?"

Eddie pulled his hands out of his pockets and walked to the kitchen counter. "Last full week. There's two short days next week."

"It happened so fast," said Samantha. "Seems like only yesterday I was feeding *you* apple sauce. Except it wasn't this organic kind."

"He turned out alright," said Cole. "Are you going to graduate?" he asked Eddie.

Eddie rummaged through the cabinet, not really hungry, but trying to look busy. Graduating hadn't been high on his list of priorities lately. Did it really matter? He wasn't sure. He wasn't sure about much anymore. But it seemed to matter to the adults in his life, so he replied, "Yep, all I have to do is turn in my final assignment for Bonnell's class, and I'll have all the credits I need."

"I'm so proud of you Eddie," said his mom. "I'm so proud of all my boys," she added as she shoveled another spoonful of apple sauce into Carl's mouth and smiled at Cole.

"Thanks for including me, Samantha," said Cole.

"Of course honey. You know I am proud of what you're accomplishing. You are on the verge of being a part of this country's history. And to think that my hubby is going to be responsible for one of the most memorable laws in our age. That makes me so happy."

"Well, it hasn't happened yet. I meet with the committee later this week at the capitol. Our governor will be there. Ultimately it will be up to them to pass. But I think it makes sense and has been a long time coming."

Eddie wasn't sure what they were talking about, but he also didn't want to waste the time figuring it out. "I'd better get going. Only five days of class left, don't want to be late."

"Ok baby," said his mom, "I remember my last week of high school. It really wasn't that long ago. It's funny what we remember and what we don't. Anyway, I'm sure you're going to have fun and make a lot of memories. Don't take this time for granted."

"I won't be home tonight. Staying at a friend's house to study for finals." He left the room and hopped in the Rover. He had a small portable CD player in the passenger seat, and inserted his *Pan Flutes* disc. The music was quiet, barely audible, but it provided enough background sound to help him ignore the sounds of the city.

When he pulled into the school parking lot he saw a crowd of people off to the corner. That was his corner, and it was his crowd. He parked and walked over to see Alex standing in the center, passing out bags of weed to his clients. Alex looked like somebody new – new pants, new shirt, even a new hat. Eddie stood back and watched it all happen. He watched Alex in performance, a young man reborn in costume. A costume Eddie used to wear, now recycled. It seemed to fit Alex better, the way he wore it lightly over the shoulders. The way the pain of his life seemed to fit with this rebellion. Eddie waited until the crowd thinned and then approached.

"Alex, what are you working with?"

"Eddie, what the fuck are you doing here?"

"Just looking for some dank. What are you holding?"

"I'm not supposed to be working with you. Lynch said you're eighty-sixed."

"That's what Lynch said? Well fuck that, I just need a bag."

"Can't do it Eddie. Lynch said you owe him big scratch. I'm the new dealer here and you're on the do-not-serve list."

"What the fuck are you doing, kid? Why you getting messed up with Lynch?"

"My boys need a hookup for the good shit. You lost your cool so I stepped up. Don't blame me for you getting a bad rep."

"Alex, seriously, this isn't you man."

"You don't know me. I got the hookup now. You better clear the fuck out. This isn't your business anymore."

Eddie tilted his hat up a half inch to look Alex in the eyes. A car horn blared on the street nearby and he turned his head. Traffic rolled like a river in front of the highrises, and beyond them on the horizon he saw the mountains. They were blue and grey, round and sharp, distant yet familiar. He looked back towards Alex whose eyes were red and swollen, nose dripping snot and throat full of slobber. Alex deserved this. He deserved a moment of being noticed for something else. Somebody different than his ailments – both the physical and the conditional. This was the easy way to acceptance, and Eddie understood. He knew the reasons for this behavior, and even though Alex had made himself an enemy, he still felt empathy. This kid was struggling in a world alone and selling weed made him known for something different. Everyone deserved to be known even if the person they were known for was a character in fiction. So he smiled and said, "I don't want to get you a bad rap. I'll find my weed someplace else."

Truth was, he still had a large stash from his last hookup, and hadn't even smoked in days. He still owed Lynch a lot of money but wasn't too interested in selling anything. He shoved his hands back into his pockets and said, "I wish you luck old friend." This was difficult to say because when he looked at Alex he mostly saw the deceit. But he accepted this as something natural, like the way the moon seemed so large and close when he was up on the mountain, bright and powerful, but always out of reach.

He decided to skip class today, hopped in the Rover and drove. He cut through the grids around the highrises, over Lost Horse River bridge, and pulled into the cemetery. Sunny skies and vernal grass made the tombstones seem bright as he walked through the phalanx of the dead and found his brother's resting place. Steve would need to know what's been happening. The truth couldn't be true, and he was drowning in confusion. His eyes watched the toes of his shoes move across the bright green grass. He knew the way blind, had been here a hundred times, days and nights when he felt alone. The dead had that power. An ability the living lacked, to give life meaning and perspective. These gravestones were inspiration and each had its own voice. He heard them as he passed beneath the sunlight. Voices of the past saying nothing much had changed. They told him their lessons were learned in vain because people continued to do the same. The same only worse, and he was in the mix. He felt their lives beneath the soil and the past filled the blood in his veins and pushed hard against his idea that he was unique. His story was nothing new, only a new way to tell it. His feet were dragging through the green grass when he looked up and saw James leaning against Steve's tombstone.

He stopped in his tracks, surprised, not only by seeing James here, but because of how happy he appeared. Eddie stood still a moment and watched. James was pacing around the tombstone, telling a story and gesturing with his hands. He even broke out in laughter so convulsive it forced him to go down on one knee. Eddie couldn't stand it anymore, he had to know what was going on, so he approached.

"James, what are you doing here?"

James turned his head and stood up with a big smile on his face. "Oh man, I'm just visiting with your bro. This dude is hilarious. I sometimes forget what a riot he is."

At first, Eddie figured James was on shrooms again. Had to be, acting like this. But as he approached, he saw the clearness and lucidity in his eyes. Stone sober, a condition he hadn't seen James in for a long time. "What the hell's gotten into you? Figured you were tripping hard when I saw you laughing to yourself."

"I wasn't laughing to myself, man. I'm right here with Steve. I was talking about that time at the carnival. You remember how they used to have a carnival on the North Side every summer? There was always live music every night. I was just talking about that year when the three of us went together, we were jamming out to some hard rock band that flew in from back east. They were pretty good, right? If you remember. Maybe you don't. I don't know."

"I remember," said Eddie. This fact surprised him, that he did remember. It was the funny thing about memory, how it could hide things away, assumed to be forgotten because it was never thought about. Then it could rise right up to the surface when the occasion demanded.

"I knew you would," replied James. "That was hilarious shit. When I dared old Steve here to do it, I didn't think he would. But you fooled me didn't you?" He rubbed his hand across the top of the tombstone, a motion similar to petting a dog. "You ran right up and grabbed that giant speaker, lifted it above your head. I swear, the crowd was going absolute ape shit, cheering you on as you pumped it up and down over your head. And then you started running back and forth with it, man, that was fucking cool."

Eddie, now with a glaze over his eyes and a faint smile on his face, started nodding his head. "That's right, he was running back and forth with it. The singer was so confused and astounded he missed a few words."

"Sure did, but that didn't stop the jam from going. Those boys were loving it. The crowd was loving it." James broke out in laughter again, bent at the waste with hands on his knees. "That was a riot man, when you ran too far with the speaker and the cord came undone. I remember the loud ZAP it made." He was having a difficult time even finishing the story between his gasps of laughter. "But that look on your face when it happened. I thought you were just gonna throw the speaker and run from embarrassment. Hell, that's what I would've done. But old Steve here," James now calmed himself and collected a more serious tone. "Stevie boy just calmly turned around and plugged the damn thing back in, and continued pumping it up and down until the song was finished. You should've been a rock star man. Cool as that."

Eddie wasn't laughing, but he was smiling. The power of a memory to bring a wave of happiness. It's the first time he felt this way while visiting the grave. "He was a rock star. If you ever went fishing with him, you would agree."

"No doubt man. No fucking doubt." James put his arm around Eddie's shoulder. "He was a good dude." Then he turned and looked Eddie in the face. "What brings you here today?"

"Man, just been dealing with some heavy shit. Thought I could forget it for a little while if I was here."

"Yeah, I've heard about it. I saw Cassie yesterday, for some of these," he revealed a bag of shrooms from his cargo pocket. "Anyway, we got to talking about her big party coming up and she told me to tell you not to go. She said she'd miss you and all, but that Lynch was pissed as hell. Plus there's always a chance that Blunt and his crew might show. I don't know what you did, but those are some dudes I wouldn't want to piss off."

"They're not so tough."

"Easy for you to say, with a face looking like that. But I'm serious, promise me you won't go. I want you to say it right here in front of Steve. You're going to stay away from that party. Stay away from Lynch and everyone from Bad Town."

Eddie looked away. He looked at the rows of gravestones and knew that any one of these could be him. It was a mystery that one already wasn't, with all the shit he's been doing. Truth was, he no longer cared about Lynch, or for that matter, Blunt and Darnell, or even Alex. "I have to go," he said, now looking down at Steve. "She needs me."

"She?" said James. "Now I get it, that's why you haven't been coming around my pad as much lately. Eddie got a girl. You hear that Steve, your little bro finally got a girl. Must be a troubled one though, if she's hanging around with you."

"I'm the only trouble she's had."

"Tell me about it. If this girl's someone you need to save by risking an encounter with Lynch or Blunt, then tell me. Give me a reason."

"I can't. You just have to trust me."

"If you go, I go."

"Don't even think about it James. You stay away from there, this isn't your problem."

"Don't fucking say that to me. You know what I tell Steve every time I visit here? I tell him I'm going to watch out for you. I tell him I miss him and I swear, whatever you may think about it, I can hear him say he misses you. So I promise him, every fucking time I come here, that I will look out for you, like I'm your big brother." James looked away to hide a tear in his eye. "I haven't been doing a very good job, clearly, but there's no fucking way I'm letting you walk into an ambush alone."

Eddie's insides were churning. Emotions he hadn't felt in a long time, didn't know he was capable of feeling again. A bond of brotherly love that made his heart feel so large and full it was difficult to breathe, let alone speak. He forced himself to sputter out these words, "You stay the fuck away from there," and then he turned and rushed away before James could see him cry.

Voice Recording #8

The forest never looks the same twice. I've walked this route a half dozen times in the past couple months, and each day is different. Today I have yet to see a patch of snow, and the flowers that were blooming on my previous visit are gone. New flowers have bloomed in orange and yellow. The parts of the forest that were bare on my first visit have been filled with green growing foliage, which means I can't see as far. In fact, for most of the walk I can't even see the river, even though I can hear it gurgling less than fifty feet to my right. Occasionally I'll pop over through the thickets and sneak a peek at the water. It is flowing fast and clear, and I wonder what kind of underwater acrobatics trout are capable of performing to live in such a turbulent environment. Although, if I'm being fair, people live in a turbulent environment also. Hopefully trout have adapted better to theirs.

I'm about halfway to camp. I won't be in class tomorrow, even though it's the final week. I need a day alone to prepare. The hike is going easy since I don't have much to carry, now that I've gotten in the routine of leaving my gear stashed up there.

Right now I'm walking through this really thick patch of small trees and shrubs. It's amazing that I can still see the trail made on my previous visit. I never would have thought that occasionally walking through the forest would leave a trail. I mean it's not super wide and obvious like some city sidewalk, but it's there, and it's enough for me to follow. It's kinda spooky in here, actually. I mean, if you knew the type of shit I've been doing, you'd probably think I was fearless, but man, walking through a thick mountain forest alone is something different. I just keep imagining a bear lunging out from any of these million hiding places and shredding me apart with its claws and fangs. People get killed by bears every year in these mountains. Maybe that's why not many people come here. I guess, in that case, I should be happy for the bears. I should see them as allies. I mean fuck, now that I'm thinking about it, a lot more people get killed in the city every year for no damn reason at all. I should probably be more afraid of that wicked place. So here I am.

This is the most beautiful home a young man could ever want. The foliage clears out to sparse pines. Large boulders are strewn about, but the ground is soft and covered with needles. Long shadows come down from the trees and spread across the river. The water moves a bit more slowly here and it is so clear that the colorful cobblestones three feet deep appear to be part of the surface. That's an interesting practice, I think, to take what is deep and wear it on the surface. To take the stones and bones of your being and broadcast them clearly. There's a lot of courage in this river.

PAUSE.

In the silence of this mountain night I know it is true. What has happened so far is not the only way. I can live courageous like this river, quiet like this mountain, and that will be peace. If I listen closely in this silence, I can hear words almost audible. I can hear the rhythm and the pulse flowing around me. I'm telling you, as crazy as it fucking sounds, this mountain forest is a guru from which I can learn how to be better.

The fire is burning and there's only a faint light in the sky. While I was cutting the wood I started thinking about Blunt, and Alex, and Lynch, and that caused anger. What a wonderful mess I have made. As I was working my saw front to back, cutting and cutting, all the while imagining the log was Blunt's neck. Slicing through him as if that would erase my pain and anger. But eliminating one enemy will not solve my problems. This I know. I know that if I took him out and continued my same life, a new enemy would come along. New challenges and pain and anger. There is no resolution in retribution. I must realign with my *self*, my ways, my focus, and even my pleasure. I must change myself to change my condition. I will not forget or forgive, because what happened was real and that cannot be ignored. Instead, I will accept it. I will decide not to hate myself for the mess that I made. I will move on. I will move here, to the mountains.

But, Mister Bonnell, I have no fucking clue how to make that happen. Every way I envision myself leaving, starting new, moving into the mountains, each of those avenues involves me first settling the score with Blunt, getting right with Lynch, and correcting the destruction I have caused in Vanya. I don't know if I can move on without finishing what I started.

PAUSE.

If I think about it, and I mean actually stop doing anything else and just think about this one thing, I realize that the best part of being alone in these mountains, for me, is that it calms my nerves. When I'm around people my nerves are a damn wreck. I mean I feel them boiling in my blood, pounding through my entire system, creating confusion and discomfort. This system is designed to make me feel out of place. They call it the Central Nervous System. And you know what the central word is in *Central Nervous System*? It's *nervous*. I don't know if anyone else feels like this. If they do, they sure hide it well. Maybe because they're usually drunk or stoned, or going on about some menial and malignant topic just to distract themselves from how damn nervous they are. I wonder if they think I hide it well? Shit, when I would get stoned I was a damn stone. Solid. But you know what the funny thing is? When I'm up here in the mountains, and all I see are these trees and rock croppings and blue sky with thin white clouds, and all I hear is the gentle breeze pulsating through the pine needles, and the stream pulsing around the river stones, and occasionally a bird chirps. When that's all my senses are focused on, and when I'm alone with no one to impress or to wonder about, here I don't even need to be stoned to be calm. I feel those nerves empty out of my system, drain from me like snow melt rushing off a mountain. Calm like the rocks that haven't moved in a million years. Here there is only a single pulse, and it flows constantly in a slow steady beat. It is teaching me to be free. Free from the burden of worry, free from the necessity of acceptance, free from the rush of the city. In a word, it is relief. The mountains are my relief and this is the place where peace lives. And I can breathe. That may be my favorite part – the deep breaths that fill my lungs with cool clean air. Crisp and virgin. Unlimited in their volume. I could live forever and be the only man alive on this mountain.

But then I think of her. It's a god damn curse really – love. If that's even the right word for it. I mean, I barely know this girl. Hell, maybe we never really know anybody. But what I do know is that she gives me a sense similar to how I feel here in this mountain. Serenity perhaps is a better word for it. The root of serenity is serene. The mountains are certainly serene. Perhaps she is also. The sight of her. At least, she used to be. Then I ruined her with my alternate personality. That person I am in the city. That person I never thought I would be, but now it's how everyone in my life sees me. Makes me wonder which is more powerful and accurate. The person we are inside, or the one others see. She saw me as somebody else, somebody worthy of changing her. Perhaps she even thought I had something figured out, and I deserved to be followed. As if my bad ways and tendency of rebellion were really just a manifestation of being free. And I suppose they were, in a sense. But not like the freedom I have here. She'll have to figure that out for herself. You can't really teach anybody anything. It all comes around in the end, one way or another.

PAUSE.

Random thought, I know, but they say arches are the strongest form in architecture. In fact, arches and architecture share the same root word, which I never realized until just now. Arches put together make circles. Circles bring the beginning around to the end, but the funny thing about them is that there's no beginning or end. No single waypoint to distinguish the start from the finish. Like the concentric circles that form on the surface of this river after a trout plucks a mayfly. The place just below the bend where the water is slow and placid. And so I try to think about that. I think about the trout resting parallel to the flow of the river, hiding out near the bottom where the smaller debris and insects are churning. Even though the water is crystalline, the trout hides. It survives in harmony with the eons that taught it to be invisible. Then it rises. It makes contact with the world above and sucks a mayfly from the periphery that separates water from air and land. If I could rise up through the atmosphere and pluck something from space, I wonder what shape that would make. It would have to be a circle. A circle that repeats itself and flows. I watch it happen again in the slow part of the river and my hand is automatically drawn to the cork handle of this fly rod.

I pulled on the wing feathers of a dry fly to pry it from the foam pad. It was a small pattern that looked like these bugs I see buzzing around with erratic movements. Pale green and grey. I could see the hook was a little rusty, like it had been here a long time. It was stuck in there pretty good and managed to pull the foam sheet right out of the fly box when I tugged on it. I was almost upset until I saw what was under the foam. It was a picture, printed wallet size. Looked like it had been in there a long time, had been weathered by the heat and river water. Creased and wrinkled, with faded colors around the edges. It was me and Steve. Shit, I was just a little kid then. We were standing next to that river where dad used to take us up in these mountains. The waterfall was in the background and Steve was holding his fly rod, the fly rod that's with me now and lying on the cobblestones near my feet. It's pretty fucking surreal, kneeling here next to a river with his old rod, looking at this picture of us as if it were yesterday, but man, so much shit has happened and changed. Wonder what old Steve would say if he were here with me now. He probably wouldn't say much, to tell you the truth. He'd probably just want to get his feet wet in the river as soon as possible. Wouldn't have to talk much if he was fishing. He'd stand there in the water waving this rod over his head trying to communicate with the trout. The trout were always honest with him. At least that's how I see it now. Sometimes they were agreeable, sometimes not, but never faked it. I understand now that there was never any false expectations for him if he was fishing. He knew what he was getting into every time. Nothing more complicated than simply passing the time. Passing the time in no hurry engaged in an activity that was simultaneously simple and creative.

I really wasn't prepared to see a picture like this. Hell, I thought I'd be left alone and not have to think much about anything. Now this picture has me remembering the old days with Steve and dad. Must've been really hard on old Steve when we left the country, when we were no longer in proximity to trout streams. That was his life, it's where he could be calm. Everyone should have a place where they can be calm and left alone to their own pursuits. Sure as hell doesn't happen in the city. That busy mystery. That place so large but also so confined. I bet if we never moved to the city he'd be here now, somewhere deep in the mountains, alone in a river with this old fly rod. That's not the way it worked out. Turns out I'm the one alone in the mountains with this old fly rod. Funny how it all happens, unpredictable. Old Steve never got to be old. I wonder if the river remembers him. If the water still bends around the places his feet used to stand. If there's trout still alive and swimming here who have felt his hook in their lip and are now skeptical of any insect floating through their feeding zone.

PAUSE.

It is early evening now and I feel happy. It's amazing how a simple accomplishment can wash all the detritus away and leave me feeling fresh. A full stomach helps, too. So here's what happened.

I stepped into the cold river, fly rod in hand, and cast forward. My bare feet wet in the flowing water. The cold flow mingled with my body heat. This transfer of energy and I felt alive. My casts were tight and gentle. All I could hear was the river pounding around me. All I saw was the glare of the sun off the surface, and the particolored cobblestones resting beneath. My fly – Steve's fly, the Luminous – was attached to a long fine tippet. It landed softly on the water and I watched it drift and bounce. The palmered hackle was buoyant and kept the hook from drowning. I admired its colors pasted upon the clear water, and then a shape rose up from beneath. It didn't look large at that distance and through the refraction of water, but it had the shape of a trout and its colors glistened. My fly disappeared into a mouth and I set the hook. The tug came fast and strong and I thought I wasn't ready. I balanced my feet and pulled the line tight. The rod tip flexed as the fish pulled forward.

Ahead of me was a bend where the water formed a deep pool. The water rested there and gained latent energy. River water is heavier when it's deep, but stronger when it's shallow. Upstream of the bend was a riffle where a fallen tree hung across. The trout pulled that direction as if it knew my weakness. It knew I could not fight the weight of deep water nor maneuver under the fallen tree. So we fought there, where the pool emptied into a riffle.

I shuffled my feet into some slack water near the edge. The trout had pulled out enough line to be resting at the bottom of the pool. I held the line tight with my left hand, and pulled the rod tip up with my right. The trout rose from the bottom and I saw its tail beating against the current. It was alive and strong and I felt its energy pulsing through me. As I stripped in the line it came closer, but not willingly. I wondered if it felt my energy also. Breath by breath, my lungs filled and emptied as its gills opened and closed. Slowly it came nearer to my reach as I retrieved the line. I took two steps backwards and felt dry land beneath my left foot. The line was retrieved to the edge of the leader, and I swung the rod tip towards shore.

The trout leapt from the shallow water, I saw its rainbow-colored sides and the orange under its gills. It landed with a splash and was momentarily stunned. I took this opportunity to pull it up on shore as I ran towards it. The fish laid on the soft sand along the river's edge and flopped frantically. I picked it up and felt its slimy skin making contact with my fingers. It was as long as my forearm and I held it up towards the sun. I could not help but smile and yell: STEVE! I GOT ONE! I looked around and felt foolish like a child, but then I thought that being a foolish child felt pretty good.

I lay the beautiful trout on the shore and admired its colors. The small fly released effortlessly from its upper lip. A trout this size took years to grow in a small mountain stream. I looked back towards the water where it hid unnoticed. It knew that river, every cobblestone, bend, riffle, and crease in flow where the water slows. That was its home. The multitude of insects it had killed and devoured for its own survival. I knew this was being alive. I knew this was life pounding in my hands, and I picked up a stone.

I pressed the trout pinched between the soil and my left palm. The trout squirmed, almost slithered as a snake would. It was more beautiful than any snake I'd ever seen. I raised up the stone in my right hand and slammed it into the trout's head. It went limp and I could feel its body warming instantly. Something changed in my own body. A relief in my chest as if a great opening had been carved. I inhaled, and what I felt most was a greater connection to this place. As if I had become a part of it. That thick wall which separated me from the living land had been breached. I reeled up my line and carried the dead trout across the river to camp.

I retrieved my knife and sliced the trout from beneath its gills to anus. I had never cleaned a trout, but watched my father and brother do it many times. That was years ago. It's also been a long time since I rode a bike, but still remember how to do that. I removed the guts with my fingertips. They were brown and orange and purple. A cloud of stench passed across me, and then I smelled the flesh. The flesh smelled clean like a handful of river water and freshly mowed grass.

I set the trout aside, wrapped in green leaves, and I started a fire. After the orange flames burned off and turned white and blue at the tips, I set the trout on a hot stone and listened to it sizzle. I realized this caused the scent of fresh flesh to release into the mountain air, and that any predator within a reasonable distance would smell it. I was okay with that. I am also a predator in this mountain. This was my kill.

I ate the fresh flesh of a wild trout and now feel light and powerful. I imagined the trout as a living breathing and thinking animal, and this made it more delicious. I consumed its powers and now that's a part of me. I thought about the fast food cheeseburgers I've eaten and how they made me feel heavy and unnourished. I thought about the lines of people waiting at the drive thru to fill themselves with that junk, and they are still trapped in that city. As much as I enjoy my solitude here, the empathy of being a human makes me wish there was space for each of them to experience this simple pleasure of feasting on a naturally harvested meal. The enjoyment I feel while being out of mobile phone reception and listening to the river flow beside a crackling campfire. How much more peace would be in the world if each of those people experienced a part of this?

As it is now, in my present and selected condition, I am the only human here. But I am not alone. The trout is providing me life through the life it lived. I can offer the same. So I take what is left of the fish, its head, tail, scales, and entrails, and I carry it away from camp. I hike it uphill to a large boulder with a flat top. I lay the remains scattered across where the flow of air will carry its scent over the land. Surely an animal will smell it tonight while I sleep in my tent. After it is dark and the stars burn above there will be food available for whomever comes first.

It is getting dark so I add fresh cut wood to the hot coals and blow on the fire. In the silence and darkness my first feeling is fear. I allow that feeling to pass through me, and then I picture Steve's face. He is sitting across the campfire from me. Campfires were best when my brother was here. We didn't have to say too much. The flames did most of the talking. I sat here imagining his presence across the fire from me, and then I looked up and saw his face through the orange flames. He was smiling when he said only two words: Nice trout.

STOP.

JUNE 1999

SUN	MON	TUE	WED	THU	FRI	SAT
		~~1~~	~~2~~	~~3~~	4	5
6	7	8	9	10	11	12
13	14	15	16	17	18	19
20	21	22	23	24	25	26
27	28	29	30			

Eddie woke up in his bed and was about to fall back asleep until he remembered it was Friday. This morning there was no sunlight spreading through his window curtains. He looked over at the clock, and it was early, twenty minutes before his alarm was set. He never woke up before the alarm. With his head still on the pillow, he stretched out wide and inhaled deeply. Mountain air had the ability to stay with him, filling his pores and blood, for a long time after he'd left the mountains. And he could feel it, that freshness and certainty, even though it had been several days behind him. This week had been spent in the city, going to school – most of his classes, but laying low after the final bell. He wanted to enjoy this feeling of carrying the mountains with him, fill his mind and body with a sensation that would help it linger, something he could inhale and feel permeate. An elixir that could transport his senses back to the river and his campsite. So he rolled over and reached for the nightstand. He shuffled through the pile and retrieved a book, *Indian Creek Chronicles*, by Pete Fromm, and opened to page one.

When his alarm clock beeped beside him, he reached over and pressed snooze, then continued reading. He continued to read until there was no longer enough time to shower before class. That was okay, it was Friday, the last Friday of high school, and he figured there wouldn't be much happening, certainly not enough to look clean and candid for. This coming Monday was the official last day of school, the day he would sit through one more round of classes, the day he would see most of those people for the final time, and then graduation the day after – if he graduated.

He made it to school just as the first bell rang, and passed Scott in the hall. Scott had most of the bandages off except for the one around his right eye, and he walked with a limp and crutches. Scott refused to look at him in passing, not even with his one good eye.

After the final bell, Eddie exited the building, alone. He walked towards the crowd in the far corner. Crowds were like wheels, always focused on a central hub. He had been the hub, but no more. He wasn't sure yet if he missed it or not, but he did know that something else was going to happen for him, something new. In passing the crowd he spotted Vanya, and started to approach her. Ten feet away Kathy turned to face him, and she took several aggressive steps his direction.

"Don't bother her Eddie, she doesn't want to see you."

"This is none of your business Kathy."

"Just get the fuck out of here, we're all so done with you."

"Fine." Eddie started to walk away, but still had his eyes on Vanya. She watched him, he could tell she was, even though she wouldn't look directly at him. Maybe there was still hope, he thought.

During his drive home he didn't notice the traffic, or highrises, or neighborhoods. His thoughts were focused someplace deeper. A place never real but his imagination gave it more power than most of the real places he had been. A vision of a mountain stream, pine trees, and a large boulder, these were all familiar, but there beside him was Vanya, in a purple dress. Her hair flowed long down her back and lifted slightly with the gentle breeze. Her eyes were bright and a smile on her face. Eddie watched her in that imaginary place until she began to disappear. This vision was replaced by the sight of his house as he pulled in the driveway, and he thought about the look on her face when he left the school. Her expression had changed and he felt like a stranger in her eyes. He was in pain because she did not understand him, and he felt lost because nobody ever would.

. . .

In his room getting ready, he started to feel nervous. This was the time when he would usually kick back on the bed, tuft up the pillows, roll a nice fat joint of the finest dank around, and leisurely inhale and exhale the smoke. But not tonight. Tonight he wanted a clear head. He wasn't really sure how this would all go down, there was a good chance Blunt's crew would tear him up the second he showed face at the party, but he had to try. This was the last weekend of high school, and it weighed on him with a sense of finality. He couldn't let it end without a fight, without the effort to correct at least one of his wrong-doings. He wasn't too sure, but he guessed that these next few days would be days he remembered for the rest of his life, and he wanted that hindsight to display images he was proud of, whatever the results.

He dressed in creased cargo pants with a blue button up shirt, and pulled Steve's old hat down low across his forehead. When he walked out of the bathroom, his mom was waiting in the hallway. She stood there and stared at him, not saying a word, until he figured one of them was either going to bust out laughing or in tears. Then she nodded her head, forced a half-smile – the type of smile that could either be interpreted as hiding sadness, or as being so full of happiness that it left her speechless – and she walked past him down the hall. He waited until she was at her bedroom door, and then said, "I love you mom. See you in the morning." She didn't reply.

. . .

By the time he arrived at the party, the place was already packed. Driveway lined with cars and youth scattered throughout the yard and into the house. It seemed like Cassie had actually done what she said and *everyone* was here. Faces he recognized, names he knew, memories they shared, and even strangers. Strangers who didn't seem so strange because they were part of this crowd, part of the here and now, part of this microcosm in eternity.

Eddie watched them all through his windshield. For a time he had been known, and thinking about it now, he depended on them for that reason more than any of them depended on him for theirs. He could turn the Rover around and drive out of here. They would be part of his past and he of theirs. But he knew that everything done today would echo, create ripples like the surface of a stream, and follow him, reverberate long after he was gone. So he exited the Rover and joined the party.

In the yard behind the house he saw Cassie, she was prancing one of the giraffes around, leading it by a long leash. A crowd gathered around her and the animal. Tillicum, the male giraffe, had wide open eyes and clenched face. Terrified. The black tuft of fur at the end of his short tail was curled up between his long legs. The people were jumping and cheering, with some reaching out to stroke his fur as the giraffe walked through the grassy yard. Eddie watched in disbelief, and then he saw Lynch.

Lynch was standing in the yard with several other dudes, and his mouth was pressed into a six-foot bong. At the other end of the bong he saw Alex with a lighter in hand. Lynch exhaled an incredible amount of smoke which sent a large cloud hanging over Alex's head. Eddie didn't really want to deal with that scene, but he had to find Vanya.

He walked into the house past the cage of rottweilers barking ferociously. Inside the house was a tall foyer with glistening chandeliers and large paintings with ornate frames hanging high on the wall. He had to give it to Cassie, no matter how crazy she was, this girl had class. Probably a hired decorator who had the class. Either way, Eddie stood in the room a moment admiring the view, then he walked towards the kitchen. He knew the kitchen always became a central hub at these parties. It's where the large coolers of beer and wine lived, the long counters covered with imported cheese, exotic nuts, locally baked pastries, and the table that served as a buffet of coke. It wasn't just coke, there were several large wooden bowls filled with different types of shrooms and sticky buds, each with a label describing their type of high, and then a crystal bowl with gold trim filled with pills – pink, yellow, and blue. Not a single person in this room seemed to notice he was there. But he saw her.

He watched Vanya on the other side of the room near the long table as she held a pink pill between her forefinger and thumb, placed it on her tongue, and then swallowed it down with a drink of wine. He clenched his jaw and shoved his hands into his pockets. He understood she had pain – a type of pain he could relate to better than anyone else in this room – but he wanted to share with her that he had discovered a cure in the mountains, and he could take her there away from this mess. He searched his head for the words to express this to her. He thought about scenes from books he'd read, and tried to imagine a way to pull her back, pull her up and out of this distress. He feared it was too late when he saw Kathy, who was standing next to her, also pop down a pill and swallow it with a glass of wine. Maybe he could get to her before the drugs kicked in.

Eddie pushed through the crowd and stepped right up to her. "Hey there little lady, care for a dance?" He knew this was a weak attempt, but perhaps she would find it humorous, just a little, and it would cut through the shell. Just for a moment, just enough to allow him access, a brief conversation alone and he could convince her. Get her out of here. Undo the mess he had made. But that wasn't his only reason, it was more than just recognizing that he was the catalyst for this behavior. He truly felt that she was the only person he could connect with. She was the one who's hair was blowing in the wind when he imagined his future wife running to him through a prairie. He knew he couldn't reveal that sentiment, it was too soon and she was too far gone. He had to begin with a stealthier approach.

Vanya gave a short snort from her nose, and he couldn't tell if it was an amicable laugh, or if she thought he was ridiculous. Before he could find out, Kathy popped between them and said, "What are you doing here loser? This party's only for fun people. Nobody here even likes you. You're a thing of the past."

Eddie had anticipated this obstacle, and he knew how to deflect it. "Kathy, you're looking hot tonight. Fucking stunning." He reached into his pocket. "I've been laying low lately because the cops were putting heat on me, but damn, seeing you look like this, I'm coming out." He removed a baggie filled with bright green buds, buds that for all financial reasons still belonged to Lynch, since he hadn't paid him for the most recent round. He couldn't pay him, since he stopped selling. He couldn't even sell now since Lynch had passed the reins to Alex. But he'd deal with that later. "Let's run away together and smoke this entire bag while bathing nude in the river." He winked at her and she smiled, eyes already starting to lose focus from the pill.

"Eddie you're a damn fool. But you're also fucking cute. You give me that entire bag and I'll tell everyone here that you're still cool."

"You're a classy lady, Kathy. I see big things in your future." This is what he said out loud, but he imagined that in three years she'd have no teeth and be turning tricks for dime bags of crank. He kept that part quiet, and grabbed Vanya's hand, guiding her to the next room. She didn't come easy, was actually pulling against him, but he pulled back.

"What are you doing Eddie? Trying to ruin my party?"

"Vanya, I just need to talk to you for a minute. It's important. Listen, shit's been going bad lately, for both of us."

"Nothing's been bad for me. I'm finally starting to have some fun. I haven't felt this good since Myra was alive."

"But this isn't real. Kathy's basement. This party. Those pills. That kind of happiness won't last. There's something I haven't told you, haven't told anybody. I've been spending a lot of time alone in the mountains. It got me thinking, you know, really seeing things for how they are. And if you're honest with yourself, you'll see it too."

"You're one to talk," she huffed. "Be honest with myself. That's a load of shit coming from you."

"What do you mean?"

"I was hanging out with Alex …"

"Now you're hanging out with Alex?"

"Yeah, he's a cool kid. Troubled, I mean, like the rest of us. But he's really sweet and a great poet. He told me that you hate him, even though he apologized. You should really learn to give people a second chance, Eddie. We all fuck up sometimes."

"Really, that's what he said?"

"Oh, he told me much more. He tried to explain to me that you haven't trusted anyone since your brother was murdered. I couldn't believe my ears when he said that. After all the time we spent together, after I told you my sad story and even cried in front of you. You never told me about Steve. I was so furious. Alex was trying to defend you, he really is a sweetheart. He said you've just got your own way of dealing with shit. But Jesus Christ Eddie, how am I supposed to ever trust you after you hid something like that from me?"

"Vanya … Listen … I want to tell you all about Steve. I want to tell you the whole story, all of it."

"It's too late for that Eddie. We're all done with you." She started to turn away, but then looked back at him. "Alex gave me this. He said you're supposed to read it later when you're alone. I told him I didn't ever want to see you again but he insisted I at least give this to you." She handed him a folded piece of notebook paper.

Eddie looked at the piece of paper without opening it, shoved it in his back pocket, and said, "You should leave here with me."

"I'm not going anywhere Eddie, especially with you." She looked at him as though about to slap his face, but then realized she didn't care enough about him to slap his face. She turned and walked away while Eddie stood and watched.

He walked outside and saw the sun beginning to dip behind the mountains to the west. It would be dark soon, and that's when the real chaos would begin. He couldn't leave yet, so he paced the yard, and that's when he heard it, a sound like ten-thousand voices cheering in a coliseum. Screams of horror and hatred and fury. The energy of a mob consumed with violence. He rushed around to the backyard.

A large crowd of people moved as one in the shadow of dusk with two giraffe heads rising up from the center. This had turned into a fucking circus, but it wasn't the giraffes who were the animals. The people were sloshing around together, screaming and cheering. Eddie approached, and as he got nearer, he could hear the dogs growling and barking. This crowd had created a ring around the act of violence.

Eddie had seen some crazy shit, and even been the instigator of it, but none of that prepared him for what he saw as he made his way through the crowd. Blunt and his crew were holding the rottweilers by leashes, and the dogs, hungry for the hunt, were pulling hard trying to chomp at the giraffes who had been tied to a large tree. The giraffes were making screaming sounds like a horse startled by a rattlesnake. Rising up on their hind legs and circling the tree to which they were tethered. But like a game of tether ball, this circling only shortened their arena, kept them bound tighter to the tree until there wasn't enough slack for them to rise up on their legs.

The crowd was getting louder and began pushing each other. It had become a giant mosh pit and Eddie forced himself through. Before he made the center, Blunt and his crew released the dogs. These dogs had been trained to kill, to fight, to defend, and they looked hungry as hell. They didn't waste time strategizing like a pack of wolves, but lunged in fangs-first. The immediate screams came loud from the giraffes as the dogs grabbed them by the legs. The crowd of humans momentarily paused, all briefly silent in unison, and then one person yelled "Hell yeah!" and the crowd grew loud again, shifting, swaying and cheering. Eddie was so horror-stricken that he couldn't move. He watched it for a moment as though it weren't real, it couldn't be. This type of shit didn't happen in real life.

When he snapped out of it, he sprang into action, not thinking about anything other than the screams of those baby giraffes. Baby giraffes who were now each on their knees being chewed on by dogs with blood on their legs and faces. He ran in and grabbed the closest dog by the leash and started to pull. These dogs were large, easily over a hundred pounds, and strong. He pulled hard and managed to yank it back, just out of reach as the dog continued to chomp at the air.

Eddie managed to pull the dog two steps before he felt the strong push on his shoulder which knocked him to the ground and forced him to release his grip on the leash. Before he saw his assailant, he watched the ravenous dog immediately return to the giraffe, snarling and biting and clawing. This was certainly a scene from the Serengeti, but he imagined it wasn't the one Cassie had originally planned.

When he looked up over his shoulder, there stood Blunt, looking down on him while pointing his finger and yelling, "Stay the fuck out of this Eddie. I'm going to deal with you later."

Eddie stood up but didn't reply. People were cheering and splashing drinks and wild-eyed all around him. He rushed back towards the dogs and grabbed a leash. Before he could pull, he felt the shove on his shoulder again, this time with more force, more anger. "Stay the fuck down boy." Blunt had fire in his eyes. The fury of this mob and the adrenaline of this scene, it did something to people, brought out something primordial. Primeval.

Eddie stood up again, and again went for the leash. This time Blunt came hard, clearly looking for a punch. From the corner of his eye Eddie saw a movement, a person other than Blunt, a body much smaller. This body lunged at Blunt and together they fell into the swarm of animals. It was Alex. Eddie watched them tussle on the ground until Blunt got on top and started sending blows into Alex's face. Eddie was so surprised by the action, this display of friendship from someone he thought had become an enemy, that he was momentarily frozen, unable to process or move. He got up and began to rush towards Alex, free him from Blunt. Then he felt a solid object make contact with the temple over his left eye, and he fell to the ground. Colorful lights started moving like a twirling planetarium. He heard a loud bang and then shut his eyes.

. . .

He wasn't sure how long he had been unconscious, but when he awoke, there was Vanya, kneeling next to him and holding an ice pack to his forehead. The sky was dark above him and the crowd had disappeared. "What happened to Alex?" he said as he started to lean forward.

"Eddie, you crazy fucker, just stay down."

He leaned up on his elbows and looked around. "Seriously, what the fuck happened to Alex?" Then he saw the grass beside him covered in blood, and smelled the stench of opened flesh. There, not more than ten feet away, were the dead bodies of two giraffes. "Holy shit," he said, "they fucking killed them." His head started to spin, and he worried about Alex. "Vanya, you have to tell me what happened to Alex."

"It's bad Eddie." She started to cry. "They killed him. After Blunt and his thugs started beating on you, Alex jumped in. He knocked Blunt straight in the nose. One of his thugs, some large ass dude, came up from behind and shot Alex in the head." She leaned over and was sobbing.

Eddie was trying to process this. Why the fuck would Alex jump in the middle? It didn't make sense. This couldn't be real. "Where is he?" was all he could say.

Vanya, between sobs, replied. "James showed up. He had a sword. A fucking sword. He sliced the guy across the arm, the one who shot Alex. That made Blunt and his thugs all run off. They scattered in the crowd. Everyone was running and screaming."

"Wait, James was here? Where'd he go?"

"Yes. He drove Alex to the hospital. But it's too late. I just know it."

Eddie stood up, shaky on his feet and dizzy. He looked at the dead giraffes lying on the grass. There was nobody else around, just him and Vanya. Up in the house he saw Cassie standing in a high window, a framed silhouette staring down at them. He watched her for a moment, waiting for some gesture, anything, but she didn't move. Then he looked back at Vanya and said, "They killed Alex?"

Vanya stood next to him and put her head on his shoulder. Tears strong enough to wet his shirt. She looked up at him in the dim light. "He died a hero, Eddie. He saved your life."

"Fuck," said Eddie. "James was right. I shouldn't have come here. Why the fuck did I have to come here? This is all my fault. I just wanted to see you and take you away. None of this should have happened."

"It's not your fault. How would you know that they were going to attack the giraffes? You tried to save them. That was really brave of you, Eddie," said Vanya, reaching out and holding his hand. "I'm sorry I've been such a …" She trailed off. "I'm not really sure what I've been. But we're done with all that now. Can we be done with it?"

Eddie couldn't take his eyes off the bloody carcasses of the giraffes. He remembered how happy Cassie was the day she showed them to him. He thought about Alex, the poet with allergies, the friend turned enemy turned hero. He imagined what Steve would say if he were here now. Probably something nonchalant like, "Here's another reason to go fishing in the mountains." Eddie looked at Vanya but couldn't say another word. He squeezed her hand firmly, then they turned and walked away. Together.

Voice Recording #8

Here I am again. Another Saturday in the mountains again. Except this time I am not alone. Truth is I've never been alone, except when I've chosen to see it that way. But I brought a friend with me this time. Yes, a real animate living breathing female friend.

Hello Mister Bonnell. This is Vanya. You probably know me as the super intelligent and quiet girl who sits in the front row. Eddie here is a pretty great guy, don't let him try to convince you differently.

Be that as it may, I think I figured out why you wanted me to do this voice journal thing. You're not so bad after all. I hope you listen to it all the way through. I'm not even going to bother editing out all the shit I thought I would. You deserve the real story, the full version. Take it as it is, pass or fail.

Eddie, it's starting to rain. Let's go inside the tent.

Go ahead, I'll be right there. I need to finish this first.

But for real Mister Bonnell, I don't think I would've made it through all this shit if I hadn't learned to hear my own voice. Hold on a second, I'm going to walk over to the river so she doesn't hear me. Not that I have anything to hide from her, though she certainly doesn't know the whole story yet. But I'll give it to her, in pieces. I've got to retain some of the mystery and stoicism that draws a young woman's attention. The rain's coming down pretty good, can you hear it? If I stand under the bow of this pine tree I don't get as wet. I can see the lamplight glowing in the tent and her shadow on the wall. This really is a beautiful scene. Has a way to clear my head and give me peace.

By the time you listen to this, you'll probably have heard what happened. So I won't go into details. I'll just tell you that a good friend died. He was so much better to me than I was to him. How can we treat the people we care about better? I fucking miss that kid already. Other kids are already calling him a hero. That much is true. But he was so much more than that. He was a deep thinker, super good at seeing things the rest of us don't. I don't think I ever really knew that when he was alive. He gave me this piece of paper. It's a poem he wrote. He wrote it for me. He wrote it for me even though we were enemies at the time. There's a note at the top of the page, above the poem, where he said he wrote this because he wanted to understand what it was like to be me. He knew things that I hadn't even told him. I'm going to read the poem for you:

In the mountains when I walk there is music on the ground

and all around bells and chimes and trumpets play

and they say to me in a voice anew

the few troubles I have found will wash away

the day will come when I have cleansed this pain

and tomorrow will be fountains filled with gold

filled with glowing trout

filled with the joy of forgetfulness

I will forget what they did to me

what I did to them

but never will I forget what we meant to each other

how we filled the spaces in each other's lives

and how we fed each other with razor knives.

I'm telling you, the guy was super intuitive. He wrote it as if he was inside my brain. But I could never write like that. I hope he aces your class. Even though he can never be there again. You owe him that. I owe him more. That kid deserves the world.

So I've been thinking about Alex, and Vanya, and my mom, and everything else. Mostly I've been thinking that we never really say our true thoughts to the people who we care most about. Why is that, Mister Bonnell? Do you know? It might be this clear mountain air, but I feel like my thoughts are really clean right now. Almost like I can touch them.

STOP.

JUNE 1999

SUN	MON	TUE	WED	THU	FRI	SAT
		~~1~~	~~2~~	~~3~~	~~4~~	~~5~~
~~6~~	~~7~~	8	9	10	11	12
13	14	15	16	17	18	19
20	21	22	23	24	25	26
27	28	29	30			

"Today's the big day," said Samantha as Eddie entered the kitchen. "Are you ready for this?"

Eddie sat down at the table. His temple was still swollen from the blow he took to the head at the party, and when he reached his hand up, he could feel the lump. This had become a trend, and his mom no longer noticed his new bruises. If she did notice, she kept it to herself. He was alright with that. She had enough going on, didn't have to deal with his issues. He was an adult now, and today he might graduate.

Cole walked through the front door with a tie around his neck and a briefcase in his hands. He smiled and said, "Did I miss breakfast? I was driving faster than I should, hoping to make it home in time for your oatmeal and eggs." He walked over and kissed Samantha on the cheek. "Where's Carl?"

"He's still asleep. That poor boy was awake with an upset stomach all night."

"If he was awake all night, then you probably were too." Cole gave her a quick rub of the shoulders and then sat down. "I'll tell you what, right after breakfast, why don't you go lay down, catch a nap. I'll clean up the kitchen, and I'm sure Eddie here is anxious to get out the door for his final day of school."

"That's sweet of you," she said. "But first, I want to hear about your visit to the capitol. How was it yesterday, talking with the committee?"

"Oh it was more than just the committee. There was also the governor and two senators in the room. There were all kinds of important people there. Several mainstream media were there. The real deal."

"And?"

"And they were very receptive to my ideas. Not at first. At first I think they thought I was some hippie stoner just trying to get easier access to my drug of choice. But when I gave them all the data, and the numbers speak clearly. Once they saw the data they were convinced that having pot illegal actually creates more crime than if it was legal."

Eddie's ears perked up. This was the first he'd heard about the real reason for Cole's visit to the capitol. Maybe they had talked about it before, but he wasn't listening. "Wait a second," he calmed his voice so they wouldn't think he was too interested. "Did you just say the government is thinking of legalizing marijuana?"

"Oh they're more than thinking about it. Everyone in the room was in favor by the time I left. It's only a matter of rewriting the policy and passing some votes to make it all official." Cole paused as Samantha placed their breakfast on the table. "Why do you suddenly seem so interested?"

"No reason. Just seems like a pretty big deal. I didn't know you were a part of it."

"Oh I'm more than just a part. Samantha, come sit down for a minute. I have something important to discuss with you."

"Okay," she said, uncertain if she should be nervous or excited.

"The governor himself made me an offer. He said if this new law passes they're going to need an entirely new department of officials to run it, make sure everything is written and enforced correctly. He wants me to be the head of that new department."

"Wow," said Samantha. "That is amazing. I'm so proud of you."

"There's more. This is a high-ranking government job, and since I'll be reporting directly to the governor himself, he wants me there, at the capitol."

"Wait," she was gathering this all in, "so you want us to move? To the capitol?"

"That's right. And with the money they're offering me, we'll be able to afford any house we want. It's a beautiful city Samantha."

She looked at Eddie. "What do you think?"

"I think it sounds like a great opportunity for you, mom." And he did. "But I have other plans."

"What do you mean, other plans?"

Before this conversation started, he had planned to tell her all about his campsite in the mountains, about Vanya, hell, he may have gone so far as to tell her about Alex and the giraffes, but now he couldn't. This was too much new information. If she were here in this city he imagined she'd understand him living in the mountains. Probably wouldn't have been too thrilled about it, but at least she was close if he needed her. He knew there was no way she could make peace with the idea of him living up in the mountains if she was a couple hundred miles away at the capitol. That would cause her too much stress and anxiety. So he chose to redirect. "I'm going to be staying around here, you know, so I can be close to friends."

"What do you say, Samantha?" asked Cole. "We'll only be a short few hours drive away. It will be great. And Eddie's a man now, he can take care of himself."

"The capitol. Wow. Okay, let's do it!"

"Great! We're going to have a good life there, I promise."

Eddie felt a sense of relief pass over him. His greatest concern had been Blunt and his gang seeking retribution and taking it out on his family. After what happened at the party, they probably wanted him even more. But if his mom, Carl and Cole were moving to a new city, they would be safe.

He stood up and said, "Congratulations," and then walked into Carl's room. He leaned over the crib and watched his baby half-brother sleeping in dino pajamas. He wondered if they would ever grow to be close, or if this would be the time that they knew each other best. He patted the boy on his head, felt the soft skin on his scalp, and then gave him a kiss on the cheek. "I love you, little brother." Then he left the room and walked out to the Rover.

. . .

Eddie pulled into the school parking lot for the final time. He stayed in the car for several minutes thinking about the events of the past couple months. He removed the poem Alex wrote for him out of his back pocket, glanced over it, and then slid it into the center console next to the picture of him and Steve he had found in the fly box. He was surprised, not so much by what happened, but by how comfortable he had become with it. He figured he had to get dirty when he was young, otherwise there'd be nothing to think about in twenty years. Alex and Steve would stay with him as long as he lived. This made it easier to manage, a sense that this was all part of his story. A predestined script.

A canyon wren landed on the hood of the Rover, paused there, made eye contact with Eddie, bobbed its head, and then flitted away. Eddie watched it fly and disappear into a tree, and he was reminded of a line from Hermann Hesse: "The bird fights its way out of the egg. The egg is the world. Who would be born must first destroy a world." He nodded his head and began to exit the Rover, but then saw something that made him pause.

Vanya was crossing the parking lot, alone this time. She carried a backpack on both shoulders and wore a long beige dress. Her hair was in a single braid and it stretched down the contour of her back all the way below her waist. Eddie watched as she neared the crowd of kids on the far side of the lot. He recognized all the faces, knew most of their names, had memories of some and barely knew others. He knew what they would be talking about. It was the final day of high school, but that was not the most important topic of the day. They would still be talking about Cassie's party. It had been three days now. The party had grown to legendary status amongst the youth. He imagined that none of them mourned for Alex, even the few who knew him best. It had been three days which was an eternity in the circle of rumors and gossip. Alex's name would still be known, a martyr for this kingdom of rebellion, but for so long as a person is known, they will not be mourned.

Eddie knew something else, too. He knew that despite all the chaos of the party, Cassie would be even more popular now. Her parties would be elevated, and he wondered if this was the new bar set. If this happened now, what would happen at the next?

He shook his head and watched as Vanya continued across the parking lot. She never turned her head to look at the crowd of youth. They, too, seemed to not notice she was there. Invisible again like the days before. He grinned and watched her until she approached the orange and flaking doors. There was a man painting the outside of the door. Halfway finished, a dark navy blue. Eddie saw her smile at the painter as he opened the door, and then she walked inside.

There were no official classes today. The seniors were supposed to check in with their teachers and review their grades. Eddie knew it all hung in the balance of whether or not Mister Bonnell would pass him. He decided not to care, couldn't care, because if he didn't pass then he would be let down. He knew what he had learned, had the scars and memories to prove it. A piece of paper or a teacher's grade wouldn't change that.

He walked fast and caught up to Vanya in the hallway of lockers. As he approached behind her, he said, "Know any good sheep farmers around here?" He immediately thought that was a stupid thing to say.

She turned around and smiled at him. "Looks like your eye is healing. Again." She smirked and put her hand on his face. "Have you turned in your assignment to Bonnell yet?"

"I'm on my way there. Wanted to see you first. You know, I've been thinking about our plan. I know we said we were going to wait a couple weeks, but I'm ready. I think we should leave tomorrow. I had some money stashed away from my previous job. It's not a lot, but it's enough to get us all the gear and food to get started. After last weekend, I can't wait to go spend more time in the mountains with you." He reached down to hold her hand.

Vanya pulled her hand away from him and turned her face. He noticed her entire shape change. She began to walk away, so he walked beside her. "What's going on?" he asked. "We don't have to rush it if you aren't ready. I just figured why wait."

"That's not it, Eddie. I think it sounds great to go live in the mountains with you. Maybe the most romantic thing I can imagine, like it's from a book or something. But I need to be realistic. I'm eighteen years old and about to graduate high school. I can't throw that away to go live in the mountains. What would we eat? How would we survive the winters? What are we supposed to do all day?"

"All of that will work itself out. I know it sounds crazy, but that's why we should do it. Go towards the abnormal and unknown, not away from it."

"Just forget it, Eddie. I've already changed my mind."

"What do you mean? I thought we had this all planned?

"I can't, okay. It sounded great when I was up in the mountains with you. After the party and everything else . . ." She trailed off a moment and stopped in the hallway. She turned and looked at him. "I was accepted to an out of state university several months ago. That's part of why I started coming to school here. My parents thought it would help me prepare to be around lots of students again. I hadn't made up my mind. Especially after meeting you and all the other kids. We had some wild times. I started to think I'd just stay. I could live here and know people. Be known by people. That's got an appeal to it, you know."

"I understand what you're saying." He turned his eyes away from her, couldn't let her see him sad. "I'm happy for you, Vanya. You deserve to be happy, wherever that is." He took a deep breath and figured if he didn't say it now, he never would. "I have this vision of us returning to the woods. Since the first time I met you, I've been able to see you there clearly, in the mountains. I want to take you to a place where you are free to fully be the amazing person you are. Here in the city we are surrounded by so much judgment and so many expectations. It seems like we're never ourselves. I want to take you someplace where you don't have to adjust yourself constantly around people who either don't see, or are threatened by how amazing you are." He turned his face back towards her and saw tears streaming down her cheeks.

"I can't Eddie. That sounds amazing, but I have to keep going. I worked too hard for too long to stop now and not follow where that will take me. I'm sorry, but no."

He reached his hand up and wiped the tears off her cheek with his thumb. "You're the coolest kid I know. You'll do great things. What are you going to study? At the university."

She smiled and her eyes brightened up. "That's the best part, Eddie. I'm going to major in social sciences. After everything that happened to Alex, I want to help other kids. He was so smart and caring. I don't think anyone ever realized that. Honestly, I probably didn't, until it was too late. I want to make sure that other kids who have hard times but good hearts get more chances. You know? I want to help them be successful and happy."

Eddie felt his chest swell up with a sensation that had been unfamiliar to him. It was difficult to breathe, for a moment. He clenched his jaw and blinked his eyes several times so she wouldn't see him cry. He smiled and said, "I admire you more than you will ever know. Those kids will be lucky to have you. I was lucky to have you. We'll see each other again some day." Eddie turned and walked down the opposite hall. His heart was beating fast so he took two long and slow breaths. He was thinking about the purple flowers that were blooming in the mountains on his first visit, how they made him think of her, and he wondered what he would think the next time they bloomed. His heart sank in his chest, a feeling similar to when he heard Alex had died. Same with Steve, longer ago. He realized that murder and love lost were practically the same, when it came down to how the heart felt about them.

He rounded another corner and saw Bonnell's room ahead. In his pocket was the voice recorder and he rubbed his thumb across it. This small mechanical instrument held his thoughts, personal thoughts, things he had never shared with another person. He considered keeping it, telling Bonnell that he had decided not to do the assignment. Wouldn't matter either way. The mountains didn't care if he had a diploma. He could bury it away like none of it had happened.

. . .

Eddie opened the door slowly and heard Mr. Bonnell say, "Enter now or never at all, whoever you are."

Eddie peeked his head around the door, saw Bonnell sitting at his desk, heard the radio playing softly on the other side of the room, and he said, "Good, you're still here. Wasn't sure if you would be."

"Mister Young, come on in. You were the last person I was expecting to see today. Have a seat. Let's talk."

Eddie sat down and made eye contact with Bonnell. The two were silent for several long beats. Then he said, "I thought you were crazy when you gave me that assignment."

Bonnell straightened the glasses on his face. "I probably was."

"Yeah. So I did it, though. Anyway. I wasn't sure if I would. But then after I started, it just sort of happened on its own. I wasn't even sure if I would give it to you."

"What did you decide?"

Eddie reached in his pocket. "Here it is. I didn't type it up, but honestly, it's better this way. More raw, and gives you the full story." He handed the voice recorder to Bonnell.

Bonnell rubbed his bushy eyebrows for a moment. "Was it worth it?"

"You'll have to be the judge of that."

"I'm not sure, Eddie. The assignment specifically stated that you type it out, and now you're giving it to me untyped and on the last day. Which doesn't give me much time to read … I mean, listen to it. This seems like a short cut. I don't pass short cuts."

"Just listen to it. Pass me or fail me, the choice is entirely yours."

"I gave you this assignment because I saw something in you. It's been a long time since I had a student who truly appreciated good literature. That's not very common in our contemporary society, especially among kids your age. I wish someone had told me to keep a journal when I was young. Now all I have are memories. Memories are selective. The older I get, the less I trust them. But that's not my point. As a teacher I need to be fair to all my students . . ."

Eddie's ears tuned in to the song playing on the radio across the room. It was quiet, he could barely hear it above Bonnell's voice. But he recognized the song. It was Louis Armstrong singing "What a Wonderful World." He focused on the words, pulled into a separate place, and no longer heard what Bonnell was saying.

He remembered the last time he heard this song. It was a sunny day, green grass, and a crowd of people dressed in black. They were sitting outside, he was beside his mom who was crying, and his dad had stood up in front of the crowd. The casket was lowering into the ground as the song played. His dad knelt in the grass and put his hand on Steve's casket as it went under. There were tears in his eyes as he tilted his head back and sang loudly the words: "I hear babies cry, I watch them grow, They'll learn much more, Than I'll ever know, And I think to myself, What a wonderful world." It was the only time Eddie could remember seeing his dad cry.

He blinked his eyes several times and heard Bonnell talking. "If I pass you, even though you barely attended class, what message does that give to the rest of my students? Or my students next year."

Eddie couldn't think of an answer. His eyes shifted around the room. It was then he noticed the newspaper laid open on Bonnell's desk. The front page was facing up. He focused his eyes and saw a picture of Alex in black and white. In large letters above it were the words: "Local foster kid murdered. Killers still at large."

He expected there to also be a picture of the dead giraffes, or a stack of drugs. But there wasn't. It was only a picture of Alex, the one from their senior yearbook. His hair was cropped short, a shirt buttoned all the way up his neck, and he was smiling. In that picture you could almost believe he was somebody else.

"I don't know," he replied, realizing Bonnell was waiting for an answer. "Like I said, pass me or fail me. The choice is yours."

"I've had smart kids in my class before, Eddie. Don't think you're the first. I've also had bad kids. Don't think you're the worst. But you are something different . . ."

Eddie lost track of Bonnell's voice as he looked down at the picture of Alex on the front page. He remembered when he met Alex. It was his first day coming to school in the city after they moved here from the country. He didn't know anybody. Dressed different than all the rest. He didn't even understand the things they talked about. From what he could tell, the most important thing in these kid's lives was some television show called MTV. His family didn't have TV in the country.

Alex was the first kid to talk to him. It was the first week in the second semester of seventh grade. They were sitting in class, and Alex removed a small device from his bag, turned to Eddie and said, "Have you played the new Donkey Kong game? This thing is super cool."

"No," Eddie didn't even know what the device was. So he asked, "What is that thing?"

"It's the newest Gameboy. Follow me after class, I'll let you try it."

So he did. After class they went outside and sat on the swings playing Donkey Kong for the entire recess hour. Eddie thought Alex must be the richest kid he ever met, having a Gameboy at school. It was several weeks later that he learned Alex had been living with a foster family, but now he had to move to a new family. The Gameboy wasn't even his, it belonged to his foster brother. Alex had stolen it, and when they found out, the parents sided with their birth son and turned Alex in to social services for theft.

Eddie remembered how Alex changed each time he moved in with a new family. For most of Eddie's life up to that point he had lived in the country. The only big change in his life had been moving to the city, but at least he was with the same family. Thinking back on it, he realized the only constant thing that Alex ever knew was change.

Bonnell caught Eddie's eyes, followed them down to the picture of Alex, and picked up the paper.

"It's a shame. Did you know him?"

"Yes. I think I did."

"That's the thing about this city. There's always some murder or drug bust on the front page. It's sad. This kid was smart. He was a good poet, too. Not sure if he even realized that. But he had layers that hadn't even been opened yet. That's my only goal with my students, is to help you open the layers." He picked up the paper and leaned back in his chair. "My advice, never read the front page news. The front page is a scheme to keep people defensive and depressed." He flipped the paper a couple pages in. "Now this story, this is something." He turned it towards Eddie.

There, taking up half of page 3, was the picture of a white mountain lion splayed out on a stainless-steel table. Standing behind the lion were two people in white lab coats, and another who was dressed like a park ranger.

"What happened?" Eddie's mind was spinning and he couldn't think of anything else to say.

"This mountain lion wandered into the city. It was seen in someone's backyard. When they called it in, nobody believed them. Then somebody else called it in, said the same thing, that there was a white mountain lion in their yard. Animal control was called, so they went searching around, and when they saw the animal, they knew it was a rare breed. They didn't know what to do. Most of their job was spent catching stray dogs. So they called the game warden, who showed up with a team of three. By this time the lion had kept moving. But it hadn't gone far. They found it in a tree outside someone's home. It wasn't that high up, and when they approached it, the thing snarled at them, so they suppressed the animal with bear spray, and then used a tranquilizer dart. I guess the dart took a while to kick in, so the lion started running. They had to track it through an alley before it finally collapsed. After that they brought it to a government lab where a team of scientists euthanized the animal so they could run some tests. It's the only time an albino mountain lion has ever been confirmed on this continent. That's a huge story, and it happened here."

Eddie shifted in his seat and looked at the picture again. "You mean, they killed it?"

"Yes, I agree. It's a bit sad they had to kill the thing, but probably good, since wild animals are unpredictable and this one came all the way into the city. If it would've stayed in the mountains where it belongs, this never would have happened."

"Man, that is…" Eddie thought about those red eyes in the dark, and the way it had moved gracefully down the trail when he saw it in daylight. He felt something swelling inside, but pushed it down, "You're right. That's an unbelievable story."

"Yes, well," Bonnell folded up the paper and looked at Eddie. "Life gets complex sometimes."

Eddie turned his head and looked out the window. In the distance, tall mountain peaks, blue and grey with striations of white and green, etched in sharp lines on the horizon beneath the pale sky. He could hear the wind rustling pine needles, felt the steady pulse of a cold flowing river on his fingertips, and saw those red eyes staring at him in the darkness. A silence filled in around him, this time stronger than before. It was impermeable, silence as strong as the mountain itself. He turned his eyes towards Bonnell, knowing it would be the final time he ever talked with this man. He thought about how much he had said in his voice journal, how much he could never say, and how much more there was to explain. Then a faint smile cracked briefly across his face. He looked Bonnell in the eyes and replied, "Yep."

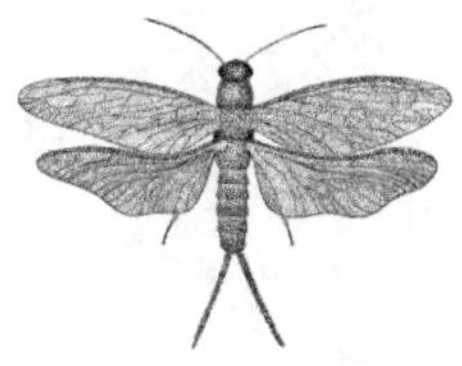

ACKNOWLEDGMENTS

I began writing this book in the winter of 2010 while staying in a cabin at Ruttger's Birchmont Lodge along the shores of Lake Bemidji in northern Minnesota. I owe much gratitude to the folks who worked there for providing a quiet setting, plus the winter birds, squirrels, and the snowy landscape. Many nights I stepped outside after dark, paced around the cabin in knee deep snow, walked out onto the frozen lake, and paused to listen to an owl from a nearby tree.

This story had been in my head for several years, so the first draft came quick. That spring of 2011 I moved into a tent deep in the forest where I lived alone for four months along a river and wrote the books *This Side of a Wilderness* and *The Unpeopled Season.* This manuscript for *Young but Free* remained stashed away on a flashdrive and ignored for the next couple years. In 2013 I opened an ice cream shop, Big River Scoop, in Bemidji, MN, and during the down time I began rereading this rough manuscript. The young people who worked in our shop inspired me to remember the people I knew when I was their age, and the inherent challenges and confusion that come with being young in America.

Several more years passed, and I moved to Montana. I spent the first few weeks living out of a tent in the Beartooth Mountains where my time was divided between getting fooled by the local trout, and working through this manuscript once again. Those fish and the wildlife I encountered were perhaps some of the most influential contributors to my writing process, and if I ever learn their language, I will thank them properly.

I then opened a camping store, Jumping Off Point: Adventure Provisions, in downtown Livingston, MT. Over the next several years, I would periodically work through sections of this manuscript in short bursts, typically while seated in a camp chair beside a mountainous trout stream. Around this time I attended the Beargrass Writer's Retreat at the E Bar L Ranch in western Montana along the famed Blackfoot River. I had never associated myself with other writers because I had always believed that the creative arts were something to be done alone. However, the people I met there inspired me in many ways, and helped me to be a part of a community of writers.

I had been publishing the work of other writers under the banner of Riverfeet Press, and this introduced me to an underground network of authors writing about wildlife, wilderness and the environment. I owe each of them much gratitude for trusting me with their work. Being part of their books kept me woven to the writing process and each of them inspired me with their experiences and voices. I've been fortunate to publish the work of nearly 200 authors, who each deserve a tip of the hat, but I can only list a few here, so I would like to thank Barry Babcock, Tyler Dunning, Tim Goodwin, Chris La Try, Erika Bailey-Johnson, Tom Harpole, David Stuver, Kevin Alltucker, Susan Sampson, Brendan McCarthy, Marc Beaudin, Mike McTee, Scott Hibbard, Cate Belleveau, Michael Meuers, and J.C. Bonnell.

While the characters in this book are all fictional, it is indubitably a semi-autobiographical work. As such, each of these fictional characters on the page have a factual representative who lives symbiotically in my mind. I could not have written this story or imagined the characters without the real people who passed through my life. To them I am indebted, not only for this story, but for the carving of my life. Any shortcomings in the developing of their persona that exist in this book are entirely my fault, because they each lived meaningful human lives that were full of unknown layers.

It's been fifteen years since I wrote the first sentence in the manuscript that would become this novel. During that time I've lived in five states, founded five small businesses, and have known many people, rivers and landscapes. The one constant has been family. Having people in my life who love me is the greatest gift, and I am thankful for my mother, sister and brother.

None of this writing nor these adventures in the past fifteen years would have happened without the support and partnership of my wonderful wife, and I don't mean that in a generic sense, because she pushes me to new experiences and inspires me to be better. There's a previous version of this manuscript covered with her red ink if you require evidence. My life was made complete by my daughter, who fills me with happiness, and as I think about the events in this book, and her approaching the formidable teenage years, I hope she experiences all the joys of mystery and that there are people beside her with good hearts to share in the confusion.

photo by John LaTourelle

Daniel J. Rice was born in Wiesbaden, Germany, in 1979 while his father was stationed in Turkey with the U.S. Air Force, where he moved shortly after birth for the first several years of his life. He grew up mostly in Minnesota where he spent his time playing ice hockey and fishing. He strayed from that path during his later teenage years when he joined a street gang and spent many nights in a holding cell. In his early twenties he returned to the hobbies of his youth, and has been known to say that fly fishing, classic literature, and wild wolves saved his life. He has lived in big cities, small rural towns, and remote wilderness. As an entrepreneur he is the founder of: D&C Drywall, Big River Scoop, Jumping Off Point, Farmgirl Pizzeria & Bakery, Riverfeet Press and Riverfeet Fly Fishing. He has edited and published the work of over 200 writers, and is the author of *This Side of a Wilderness, The Unpeopled Season,* and *Young but Free.* He is also a contributing writer to the Big Sky Journal annual fly fishing issue, and has been featured in American Fly Fishing Magazine. Currently he is the captain of the Woodboogers recreational hockey team, and lead guide at Riverfeet Fly Fishing. He lives on a secluded river in the Blue Ridge Mountains with his wife and daughter.

FURTHER READING

During his four months living alone in a tent deep in the forests of northern Minnesota, Rice wrote the novel *This Side of a Wilderness*, and also kept a daily journal, which would become *The Unpeopled Season*. The novel was a semi-autobiographical version of the events surrounding his time alone in the woods. The journal was the true life account of what happened. While writing his daily journal, he had no intention of ever publishing it; this was simply a personal account for his own edification, something to look back on later in life and remember. After the novel was published, people instantly recognized the protagonist, Eli Sylvan, as having similarities to Rice, so they asked him what the true story was. Rice then decided to publish the journal as a companion to the novel. This is the only instance in the history of literature that an author has published their fictional work along with the factual account of events that inspired that fiction; both written during the same four month period of living alone in a wilderness.

Available from Riverfeet Press

THIS SIDE OF A WILDERNESS: A Novel — Daniel J. Rice

ECOLOGICAL IDENTITY: Finding Your Place in a Biological World — Timothy Goodwin

ROAD TO PONEMAH: The Teachings of Larry Stillday — Michael Meuers

A FIELD GUIDE TO LOSING YOUR FRIENDS — Tyler Dunning

AWAKE IN THE WORLD: A Riverfeet Press Periodical Anthology

ONE-SENTENCE JOURNAL: Short Poems & Essays from the World at Large — Chris La Tray

WILDLAND WILDFIRES: and where the wildlife go — Randie Adams

LOOK AT ME — Stephany Jenkins

AWAKE IN THE WORLD V.2: A Riverfeet Press Anthology

FAMILIAR WATERS: A Lifetime of Fly Fishing Montana — David Stuver

BURNT TREE FORK: A Novel — J.C. Bonnell

REGARDING WILLINGNESS: Chronicles from a Fraught Life — Tom Harpole

LIFE LIST: POEMS — Marc Beaudin

I SENSE MANY THINGS: Ninisidawenemaag series of children's books — Erika Bailey-Johnson

KAYAK CATE — Cate Belleveau

PAWS AND HIS BEAUTIFUL DAY — Stephany Jenkins

THE UNPEOPLED SEASON: A Journal of Solitude and Wilderness — Daniel J. Rice

WITHIN THESE WOODS — Timothy Goodwin

TEACHERS IN THE FOREST — Barry Babcock

BEYOND THE RIO GILA — Scott G. Hibbard

WILTED WINGS — Mike McTee

BETWEEN ROCK AND A HARD PLACE — Maggie Anderson

IT ALSO TAKES THE RAIN — J.C. Bonnell

ARC OF THE RIVER — Brendan McCarthy

THE MULES OF MINERAL KING —Kevin Alltucker

THREE GRAVES TO EDEN — J.C. Bonnell

YOUNG BUT FREE: A Novel — Daniel J. Rice

printed in the USA
www.riverfeetpress.com

www.ingramcontent.com/pod-product-compliance
Lightning Source LLC
Chambersburg PA
CBHW070249130726
48054CB00022B/158

* 9 7 9 8 9 9 2 0 0 7 7 2 5 *